A SCREAM GROWS
IN BROOKLYN

I don't scream, okay? That cliché of a thousand suspense films, the unspellable, unpronounceable, generic falsetto female scream, is just not natural to me. Believe me, the life I've had, if it was going to happen it would have by now.

I didn't scream this time, as he changed. But I tried.

If you go to the movies much, you've probably seen a physical transformation very like it. That was my first thought: state of the art special effects. Skin stretched or shrank, changed color, changed texture, sprouted hair. Bones shifted, melted, extruded. The overall effect was a shrinking, a compacting. There was a constant muffled sound, like someone tearing up a whole chicken wrapped in a towel. I remembered that the moon was full tonight.

Maureen, I thought, you are watching a werewolf change shape in an alley in Brooklyn.

Of course, I was wrong. . . .

BAEN BOOKS by SPIDER ROBINSON

CALLAHAN'S LADY

SPIDER ROBINSON

CALLAHAN'S LADY

A Baen Book

Baen Publishing Enterprises
P.O. Box 1403
Riverdale, NY 10471
www.baen.com

ISBN: 0-671-31831-4

Cover art by Bob Eggleton

First Baen printing, September 2001

Library of Congress Cataloging-in-Publication Number: 88-26299

Distributed by Simon & Schuster
1230 Avenue of the Americas
New York, NY 10020

Production by Windhaven Press, Auburn, NH
Printed in the United States of America

Like all of them,
this book is for

Robert Anson Heinlein
and
Virginia Gerstenfeld Heinlein

with gratitude,
respect, and love

but it is also dedicated to
all the artists, male and female,
who deserve a place like Lady Sally's House
in which to practice their fine art—
or at the very least,
relief from slavery,
extortion, violence
and contempt.

ACKNOWLEDGMENTS

The author would like to thank Jeanne Robinson and Mary Mason for their invaluable assistance in the creation of this book.

DISCLAIMER

Callahan's Lady is a work of fiction; any resemblance to real persons (living, just existing, or dead), place or events is unintended and purely coincidental.

The author, who has heard from dozens of readers who combed Suffolk Country looking for a bar called Callahan's Place, does not wish to be responsible for people wandering around the seamier parts of Brooklyn looking for a bordello. Anyway, it's closed now.

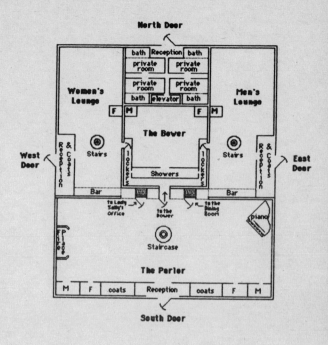

Lady Sally's House
First Floor Layout
(no pun intended)

created by Spider Robinson
with a 512K Macintosh
and an Imagewriter I

(note: scanned for this edition)

BOOK ONE

A VERY VERY VERY FINE HOUSE

CHAPTER 1
THE LADY

It's a good idea to stake out a spot near an alley, if you can manage it without a fight. Occasionally you get a john who's in a big hurry, or who enjoys the thought of making out in almost-public. Either kind can be dealt with in a quarter of the usual time, with minimal effort, and neither kind is liable to insist on a discount. Besides, if you think about it, they are getting a discount since they don't have to pay for a room.

You have to look them over carefully before going up that alley with them. Even the cheapest, sleaziest hotel room has an inhibiting effect on a rapist or mugger or nutcase. Whereas an alley is a place from which he can escape in two directions in a hurry.

But it had been my experience that, while perhaps a quarter of all johns were weird in one way or another, less than one in a hundred was dangerously weird. And I had never met one of those that I couldn't cope with. I used to quote those statistics about how the vast majority of murder and rape victims were assaulted by someone they knew. So when I hit the set that night, the first thing I did was to grab a spot near a good alley. One with no overlooking windows or fire escapes, or intrusive lights. I got there just ahead of Suzy Q, and he glared at me, but surrendered the spot. (Suzy was a pre-op transsexual, who billed himself as the One-Stop-Shop, and he and I had an understanding. He didn't mess with me, and I let him stay a *pre*-op transsexual.)

The moon was just coming up over the pool hall across the street when a well-dressed couple walked past me: a short, sad-looking man and somebody's maiden auntie, talking in low voices.

I only noticed them because of the glance the auntie gave me. Lots of well-dressed aunties looked at me with a mixture of pity and condescension and revulsion. This one's eyes held only pity. Somehow that was even more irritating.

So I half watched them as they walked by me and neared the mouth of the alley. I noticed vaguely that he had awfully big ears, and that she had a pretty fair little shape for an auntie. And then his worried sounding

murmur rose in volume, so that I caught the
last two words "—right *now!*" He thrust something into her hands, and she took it at once,
began doing something to his neck with it. The
gestures she made were oddly familiar, but I
couldn't place them. She stood back, and I got
it. He now wore a dog collar around his neck,
and the end of the leash was in her hand.

And they ducked into the alley.

I broke up. They were just the most unlikely
couple I could imagine to grab an alley quickie—
much less to be into B&D.

I stopped laughing almost at once. When I
was her age, came the thought, I'd probably have
to take the weird johns too.

Or maybe their relationship was personal
rather than professional. In any case, they were
consummating it in *my* goddam alley. I followed
them into the alley on cat feet.

A shaft of moonlight on the alley wall provided dim illumination. I saw them about twenty
yards away, their backs to me. I moved so that
I was no longer silhouetted against the mouth
of the alley for them, and settled into voyeur
mode.

The show was already in progress: he was
removing his clothes with considerable haste.
All of them, which I thought was strange and
rather rash considering the exposed location.
As he removed each garment he handed it to
the auntie. In a surprisingly short time he was
stark naked. Not even socks; not a wristwatch

or a ring. Just the collar. He looked . . . like they all look.

"You'll forgive me if I don't watch," I heard her say, and she turned away from him. She was British, and unquestionably she was someone's maiden aunt. I had heard that some Brits were into this sort of thing. The question was, did I let them proceed with whatever the hell it was they were doing, or chase them off my turf?

While I was deciding, he changed. . . .

I don't scream, okay? I never have, not once in my life. Oh, I've yelled at the top of my voice a few times, hollered "Ouch!" or "Stop!" or "You *bastard!*" or whatever. But that cliché of a thousand suspense films, the unspellable, unpronounceable, generic falsetto female scream, is just not natural to me. Believe me, the life I've had, if it was going to happen it would have by now.

I didn't scream this time, as he changed. But I tried.

If you go to the movies much, you've probably seen a physical transformation very like it. That was my first thought: state of the art special effects. Skin stretched or shrank, changed color, changed texture, sprouted hair. Bones shifted, melted, extruded. The overall effect was a shrinking, a compacting. There was a constant muffled sound, like someone tearing up a whole chicken wrapped in a towel. I remembered that the moon was full tonight.

Maureen, I thought, you are watching a

werewolf change shape in an alley in Brooklyn, while his auntie discreetly turns her back.

Of course I was wrong. Even in the lousy light, I could see the moment the transformation was finished that he was not a werewolf. If he had been, I think I would have refused to believe my eyes. But what they told me was so silly I simply could not disbelieve it.

He was a werebeagle.

There was no mistaking that shape, those ears. I had been in love with a beagle from ages five to seven, and had never really gotten over his loss. I recognized the new smell which was making the alley even riper than it had been a moment ago. Well, of course, I thought dizzily, it stands to reason that a beagle's bowels must be smaller. . . .

Perhaps that small, homely detail made it plausible to me. They'd certainly never mentioned such a side effect of lycanthropy in any of the movies, and I knew I would never have thought of it myself—but it made sense. I didn't stop to work this out consciously at the time; I simply believed what I was seeing.

And did what seemed an intelligent thing: I turned very quietly on my heels and began tiptoeing out of there. This wasn't my alley (although I had thought so until twenty seconds earlier); if people wanted to walk their werebeagles here it was none of my affair.

How could I have guessed that I was walking in the wrong direction?

I'd have sworn my heart was already beating at maximum speed, but it revved up sharply as a large male figure appeared just before me in the mouth of the alley, silhouetted against the lesser darkness of the street. Then I recognized him, and felt a wave of relief. All *right*, I thought. If the gods had allowed me to summon any one I chose to assist me in that moment . . . well, he would have been somewhere above fifth on the list. It was Big Travis, my pimp.

"Hey, Baby Love," he said lazily.

I had always hated that stupid name: now it sounded sweet in my ears. Bad weirdness was behind me, but my protector was here. "Travis! Jesus, I'm glad you came along—you won't believe what I just saw—"

"You won't believe what I just heard."

"—later, honey; first come see this, honest to God you'll—"

I was shocked when he hit me.

I had actually thought I could control Big Travis—that I was controlling him. It was a powerful and necessary illusion for a girl in my position, I guess. I took a great deal of secret pride in being able to control so strong and wild an animal. Perhaps Travis was aware of the illusion, and had allowed it to persist as his means of controlling *me*. If so, the illusion backfired on us both, for it had given me the idea that I could get away with skimming from him. It kept me from noticing a smouldering glow in his eyes that night, and it persisted right up to the moment his big fist smashed into my left side, just below the ribs, and its loss caused me several kinds of pain.

Least of which—at first—was the physical pain. Travis had hit me much harder than that once, back when we'd been defining our relationship. I was convinced that I had *allowed* him to do so then, deliberately given him the illusion that he was the one in control, as a means of establishing my control over him.

But this was different. The last time had been the kind of male violence I was familiar with: he'd picked the quarrel, spent a few minutes shouting and working himself up to it, built his anger to the proper dramatic peak, and let fly. I had had plenty of time to decide how I wanted to react. This sudden explosion of cold violence was shocking, dismaying, disappointing . . . and above all infuriating. I might have accepted a slap in the face; but an unexpected punch in the side seemed . . . disdainful, rude.

"You son of a bitch," I gasped, backing away against the wall. I wanted to rub where it hurt, but I was so mad I wouldn't. "What the hell was—"

"You been holdin' out on me, girl," he said. His voice unnerved me as much as the punch had. Travis *knew*.

I felt faintly dizzy.

I tried anyway. "Bullshit! You know how many guys I do a night, you know what I charge, you get a dollar for every dollar I make, even the tips." Believe it or not, most street girls give all their earnings to their man, in exchange for room, board, protection, and all the luxuries they can wheedle. Since I'd learned where Big Travis hid his cash (pimps don't use banks), I didn't mind that so much—my money was mine on twenty-four hours' notice, anytime I decided to leave—but a girl likes some folding green in her pocket, so . . .

"Been talkin' to your johns. You raised your prices. And still gettin' tips on top of that."

Shit. "Then I must be worth it! If I can get more than the going rate out of those bozos, it's my business."

He shook his head. "No. It's *my* business. And I'm teachin' you what happens when you screw around with my business." He shook his head again and stared closer. "Bitch, what you smilin' for?"

"Because I know something you don't know."

"What that be?"

I felt very tired all of a sudden. "I grew up on Army bases. My father started me on hand to hand combat when I was six. I took a punch from you once because I figured that a bodyguard is more use with his precious male ego intact. But I would say that this relationship has come to an end. You take all my money, and then the first time I actually need you, you punch me. I know half a dozen guys I can replace you with, Travis. Thanks for everything, and you were a fair lay, but I am now going to beat the living shit out of you." I squinted through the darkness. "What are *you* grinning for?"

He laughed aloud. " 'Cause I know somethin' *you* don't know."

"What's that?"

"Look down."

I shook my head. "Nice try, Travis."

He was nearly hysterical now. "No, no," he said, backing away. "I'll stand right here. Just take a peek."

I glanced down and back up before he could have moved. Nothing there. I took two steps forward to attack him before it registered.

If I hadn't been wearing a white blouse I'd have missed it altogether in the dim light. A large spreading dark stain . . .

Suddenly the pain in my side went from dull ache to lancing agony, and I was so scared I seemed to become hollow. He was still laughing at me, rocking slightly back and forth.

"Oh yeah? Well I can *handle* a knife, jerk, that's first year stuff, what do you think of that?" I screamed.

—and fell hard onto my knees—

His laughter tapered off. "I think you in your *last* year," he murmured, and moved toward me.

I saw his knife now. The blade was long and

wet, and I knew I'd taken it all; I was cut *bad*.
Most murder victims, I remembered thinking,
are killed by someone they know. . . .

I swayed on my knees. My arms were too
heavy to lift. So were my eyes. I have seen a
man turn into a beagle, I thought, and now I
am going to die, and my last sight on earth will
be Big Travis's crotch there, coming closer to my
face. No fair. I wasn't ready. Start again—

"Told you once before, be no second
chances, sweet thing. Whore cross me once,
she'll do it again, an' I can't be bothered
spendin' energy keepin' you scared." He took
me by the hair, yanked my head back so that
I was looking up at him, throat exposed. I was
grateful, thinking that I preferred to die seeing
his face. Then I saw his face. "My other
bitches already scared good—but when they
read tomorrow in the *News* what Baby Love
looked like when she was found, the gon' get
in*dus*trious. I don't plan to let you die fo'
'nother hour or so . . . so the first thing we got
to take is your voice . . ."

"You must stop this at once. At once, do you
hear?" someone's British maiden aunt said.

I was not scared. I had passed way beyond
scared, seconds ago. I knew scared would return
as soon as I felt the knife again, but now I was
conscious only of a vast sadness, sadness and the
bitter taste of defeat. It seemed unfair, and anti-
climactic, of the universe to torment me further

by adding dollops of guilt and shame to my sorrow. I had been stupid: the message did not need underlining. So why did I also have to bear the guilt for the death of an innocent bystander, somebody's harmless, brainless auntie? Not to mention the beagle, which Travis was probably going to stomp to death and sell to a Korean restaurant.

"Go 'way," I croaked. "It's a game we play—"

"That's right, Auntie," Travis said, grinning. "We playin' a game. Like foreplay, you dig? Better beat it on home, we jus' gettin' to the good part." He unzipped his fly partway with his knife hand, still holding me by the hair.

"If it is a game, dear boy, then I should very much like to play too, if I may. And in my judgment it is your turn to be It."

Big Travis frowned, confused. I closed my eyes and groaned, because I knew how he always reacted to confusion. Sure enough, he let go of my hair, and as I slumped back onto my heels I heard his snakeskin boots stride slowly away.

"Old woman," he said, "I think it be *your* turn to be *shit*—"

I knelt there marinating in sorrow for a thousand years. I could feel things rearranging themselves inside me where he had stabbed me, cut edges rubbing past each other, but the pain could not distract me from my sadness and guilt. Something exploded in my head, and I knew I had to open my eyes and look at her, had to see her sweet, well-intentioned, stupid face once, so that I could take the sight of it to Hell with me. I deserved to; I had gotten her killed. I turned my head in her direction with a massive effort and forced my eyes open.

There was something wrong with what I was seeing. The point of view was too high. I was on my feet! How had I gotten to my feet?

At once came the thought, Maureen, if you are strong enough to get up on your hind legs, you are strong enough to turn around and run.

I calculated my chances of escape at one in a hundred. But even that one chance made it more imperative than ever that I see the old lady's face before she died. I focused on it, squinting because she was silhouetted against the mouth of the alley.

Then she took a step *forward*, toward Travis. She entered a zone of weak light reflected from something shiny in the trash around us, and I saw her fairly clearly.

She could have been a duchess. Her bearing was as aristocratic as her accent. She was smaller and slighter than me. She was dressed very expensively and very elegantly and very tastefully. She carried no purse. I guessed her an expensively preserved fifty. She carried herself like someone used to respect. She looked like a nice old lady, and my heart sank.

She was still holding that leash in her hand. On the other end of it was the beagle. He looked as sad as I felt.

Getting enough air to shout hurt dreadfully, but I did it anyway. "Lady, run!" I called. "He's got a knife."

She stood her ground. "I know, dear. Don't be afraid." Her voice was deep and throaty, and she sounded just slightly tipsy, as though she'd been nipping at the port. A British Tallulah Bankhead.

"That dog come at me," Travis said, "an' I'll take it away from you, put it someplace you might not like."

"Oh, I've always been one for a fair fight," she said cheerily, and let go of the leash. "I'll take him alone, Charles," she told it. It looked up at her and panted mournfully.

Travis stood still for a moment. Then he shook his head. "Sure is a night for dumb bitches," he said, and moved toward her.

Then something happened and he fell down.

I was looking right at them and that is what I saw. Doubtless it surprised him even more than it did me. It didn't seem to surprise the duchess at all. I swear I never saw her move a muscle.

He got his hands under him, and then his feet, stayed in a crouch and felt his face. He glanced down at his hand, flung something from it that made a splatting sound on trash cardboard. "Jesus, *Christ*," he said softly, "you broke my damn *nose!*"

"It protrudes," she said. "Or did."

Travis's nose was inordinately important to

him. I should know; I'd worked hard keeping it fed. He made an animal sound.

She sighed. "I shall only give you one more lesson, dear boy," she said. "Then if you absolutely insist I shall kill you."

He sprang upward toward her, screamed, and did a back flip. At least it looked as if he tried to. But although he tucked well, he just didn't rotate fast enough, and landed hard on his back. He stayed tucked. After a moment, he began making an odd, whistling sound.

"I, for one, certainly hope we're done now," she said, and waited.

It took him long seconds to straighten out, and more to let go of his crotch and get his breathing back to normal. He got to his feet slowly and with extreme care. He looked down stupidly at the knife he still held in his hand. Then he looked back up to her. Travis's crotch was inordinately important to him, too, and I had no idea what on earth was going on but I, for one, was sure we were not done now. He began to growl—

And she took a step toward him, eyes flashing, and the growl turned into a yelp, and he fled.

He ran so fast he lost his footing, fell head-long, did a tuck and roll and came up running even faster; so fast that when he burst out of the alley he had to run a few thundering steps along the side of a parked Buick to make his turn.

The duchess did not relax. She was already relaxed. She sniffed. "What an asshole," she said delicately.

The beagle, panting happily, seemed to nod.

I was still on my feet, but the alley wall was against my back now. I decided I was hallucinating, that I must have gone mad, like people did in the movies. I thought of a movie they showed us once in one of my dozens of schools, "An Occurrence at Owl Creek Bridge." Was this my dying fantasy? Was Big Travis even now slicing me open, humming thoughtfully and artistically? I *did* feel my feeble reserves of strength draining, and I did hear a humming sound.

I shoved myself away from the wall, tottered forward four steps on my stilts, stared at the calm, unruffled auntie. She separated into two identical copies of herself, like an amoeba reproducing. So did the beagle and everything else. I made an immense effort and resolved the double vision.

"Thank you for not dying," I said. My voice sounded distant. "It was kind of you." Manners. Duchesses placed high value on manners. "But I'm afraid I'll have to now. Terribly sorry. Will you excuse me—?"

Falling to my knees hurt worse the second time. The light at the end of the alley began receding rapidly, taking the deadly duchess and her dog with it.

My last thought was that I'd have to hurry if

I wanted to get to Hell before the evening rush—

But I woke in another place.

Or so it seemed when consciousness first returned. I was lying on my back on a very comfortable bed, under soft warm covers. I had only the vaguest recollection of the fight, something unimportant that had happened a long time ago. Nothing hurt, not even my side. I did not try moving to see if that would make it hurt. I was too weak to move.

Wherever I was, it was quiet and peaceful here. The room was not dark; a soft feeble light source of some kind lay to my right. The air was full of pleasant girl-scents. This was not a hospital room or an emergency ward or a police infirmary. And it certainly didn't seem to be Hell.

With great effort I rolled my head to the right, toward the light, and became much less certain.

My vision was watery at first. But even in the first glance there was no mistaking what I saw. A small naked man.

No, not naked, wearing some sort of odd, leather harness, and slippers, and a short apron-like affair tied around his waist that left his buttocks bare. His back was to me. He seemed to be making an effort to move quietly. He was standing before a large beautiful old dresser, and from its second drawer he was just removing a red satin corset, taking care not to let it rustle.

Jesus God, I thought, while I was hallucinating

killer aunties Big Travis killed me and now he's
rented me to a necrophiliac. A necrophiliac
fetishist. Doesn't anybody just want to get naked
with a nice cool corpse and make love normally
any more?

No, I decided, this will not do. I picked my
johns while I was alive and I'll pick them now,
and *this* guy is entirely too scary! Even for a
corpse. Oh God, I think I'm naked under this
blanket—

I summoned up all the energy I had for a
roof-raising shriek of terror and rage and outrage. What came out was a squeak, such as you
might hear from a sleeping baby mouse having
a bad dream, and almost at once I stopped being
afraid. Because the squeak caused him to leap
a few inches in the air like a startled burglar,
and when he spun around and gasped at me his
face held such a comic mixture of dismay and
confusion and fear and anger with himself that
if I'd had the strength, I might have giggled. He
looked so silly in that apron and straps. Jiminy
Cricket in bondage. Balding slightly, with the
beginnings of a pot belly. He gestured vaguely
with the red corset and began speaking in a high
rapid voice. "Oh God, I was *sure* I could do it
without waking you I'm so *terribly* sorry I'm such
a *fool* oh I beg you *please* don't tell Mistress
Cynthia *please* don't or she won't *punish* me
tonight!" He waited expectantly. Garters dangled
agitatedly from the corset.

"Nng," I whispered.

He slapped himself in the face. "Oh, I'm *such* a fool please forgive me of course I'll go at *once* pretend I was never here just go back to sleep I promise everything is *all right* you're in good hands the best hands the *very* best hands and there's nothing to be afraid of Doctor Kate fixed *every*thing someone will be here soon to look after you if you want anything I'm *really* sorry *please* don't tell Mistress Cynthia *thank* you!"

He sprang for a door I had not yet seen and was gone before I could say "Nng" again.

Then he sprang back into the room, scurried to the dresser, snatched up some nylons to go with the corset and was gone again.

It never occurred to me to doubt that he was real. I know the limitations of my imagination. But those same limits left me unable to guess how I ought to react.

I decided I did not need to. I went to sleep. My first intelligent decision for a long time.

I should have stuck with it. When I woke again I felt just awful, stiff and sore and queasy and sour and sweaty. My mouth was dry and tasted foul. My cheek hurt. My knees ached. My head throbbed. There was more light than last time, and it hurt my eyes even through the lids. But the worst was my side. It felt as if someone had had carnal knowledge of the knife wound. That much pain was scary.

I whimpered, and tried to curl up around my left side. Gentle firm hands touched my shoulders, pressed me back. Woman hands. One of them brushed my hair back, stroked my forehead. The hand was cool, its skin soft. The fingers wandered at first, then seemed to sense little currents of pain beneath the skin and targeted them. I gave up the struggle to remain tense, let myself go as limp as the pain in my side would let me. I kept my eyes closed, because as long as I didn't open them, nobody could scare me or make me think or ask me questions. Not even me. Blindness wasn't a lot of comfort, but it was all I had.

When people rub your head for you they never quite get the right spots. She never missed. Her fingers traced veins of suffering, soothed knots of muscle, stimulated circulation, adjusted their pressure and direction with uncanny precision. As my headache washed away, the pain in my side began to diminish slightly. Which made the fear begin to ease, which caused the faint nausea to wane, which helped the headache . . .

"That's better," she said. "Everything's going to be all right."

Her voice was as gentle and firm as her hands. I remembered it very well. Those compassionate fingers trolling for pain across my forehead were the ones that had wiped up the alley with Big Travis.

I opened one eye part way. The duchess, all right, resplendent now in evening dress. The sad-faced man with the big ears, the one who turned into a beagle when the moon came out, stood silently behind her. No sign of the little man in the apron. Her eyes were kind. She smiled faintly.

"Sleep some more," she suggested.

Splendid idea.

The third time I awoke I did not feel as good as the first time or as bad as the second time. My side hurt as much, and there were aches at my knees and the right side of my face, but I felt stronger. I was alert, and terribly thirsty.

"Water," I croaked.

The light was dim again. Someone got up from a chair in response to my plea, but from the sound and silhouette I could tell it was not the duchess, nor the sad-faced man, nor the cricket in the apron. Someone bigger, heavier than any of them. Another woman, in a robe. She crossed the room, then came back again, stood just outside my peripheral vision.

My head was lifted from a pillow. Wetness occurred at my lips. I drank eagerly.

"Easy now," she said. "Not too fast." Her voice was deep and slightly husky.

Finally I lay back and sighed. "Where am I?"

"That'll have to wait," she said. "I've got more important questions."

"What could be more important than 'where am I?'?"

"Your answers will tell me how much pain-killer I can give you."

"Go!"

"I need to know what drugs you've taken in the last forty-eight hours—scrip, street or even booze. Also, what do you take regularly, and when did you last eat?"

"I don't do drugs."

She said nothing at all.

"Oh, coffee and cigarettes, and some juice with the johns when I'm working, half a pint of tequila, maybe that much vodka. But not, you know, *drugs*. Are you some kind of cop or what?"

She sighed. "In the absence of reliable data, I must reduce your dosage to zero, to be safe." She made as if to get up.

"All right! Forty-eight hours? Five or six joints . . ." She waited, " . . . and three or four lines. No, all right, let me count them up . . . eight total, no more, *really*. Terrible shit; they couldn't get Third World mothers to feed it to their babies any more so they sold it to Big Travis. So hardly any coke, but a lot of that other kind of 'caine that makes your nose numb. Oh, and one of the johns, I think his pot was dusted, but I didn't have much of it." She still waited. "And half a 'lude with a little wine to get to sleep last night."

"But no *drugs*."

"I don't have anything to do with needles!" I snapped, and regretted it. Just talking hurt my side plenty. Emphasis was too costly.

"I know; I looked for tracks. Even the sneaky places. Speed?"

"Not for months. I stopped doing it. I never did really like it."

She put her face in front of mine, close. I saw only the eyes. "Snort smack?"

"Never."

"Your pimp made you stop."

Her eyes were huge. "What have you, been reading my mail? I just let *him* think that! I'd already decided it was dumb."

"And when did you eat?"

"Pizza for breakfast at ten, a bowl of chili after the lunchtime rush, six hours later I got stabbed, *when the hell do I get the god damned painkiller?*"

Her face backed away. "I'm sorry. Right now." She took a black doctor-type bag from the floor beside the bed, got out a hypo and a small stoppered vial, busied herself loading the needle.

"That doesn't look like much," I complained. "What are you giving me?"

"Well," she said, squinting judiciously at the needle as she purged it of air, "with your history I figure you've built up a heavy tolerance, so it's safe to smack you pretty hard. I wouldn't give this stuff to a civilian. You'll like it." She circled my arm with her big hand, squeezed until a vein came up.

"A-a-l-l *right!*" I said feebly, looking away. I hate needles. "Thanks. What is it?"

She slid the point home, thumbed the plunger slowly and steadily. "Fifty milligrams of laboratory-pure Placebo in a potassium chloride/

dihydroxide solution." She took out the spike and rubbed the spot with a piece of cotton.

"Wow. Sounds good." The name rang a bell. "Isn't Placebo the Russian word for 'thank you'?" My father spoke Russian.

She coughed loudly into her hand, and bent to put away her gear. "Yeah, it's Russian-made. Experimental. It'll come on like gangbusters in about four heartbeats."

"I can feel it." The pain, and the body in which it resided, moved about two feet to the left of me and stayed there. I could see it pulsing vaguely in the gloom out of the corner of my eye. "Thanks a lot. What's your name?"

"Mary."

"Hi, Mary, I'm Maureen." I realized I'd given her my real name, and wondered why.

"Hello, Maureen."

She sat at my bedside while I enjoyed the feeling of being distant from the pain. I noticed vaguely that she was holding my hand, though I could not feel it.

"I had morphine once," I said after a while, "in a hospital, and this is better, you know?"

"Yes. It is."

I rolled my head over and looked at her, focusing with some difficulty. She must have been close to two hundred pounds, and she did not look at all like a jolly fat lady, but I got the idea she could be merry when it suited her. "Hey, Mary, where the hell am I, anyway?"

"Lady Sally's house."

"Is that the duchess?"

"Huh?"

"The killer auntie."

"Oh. I think so, yes. Her Ladyship brought you here."

"That's the one. She's got one wild maid, I'll tell you."

"More than one."

"The one I mean was half bald, with his tush sticking out of a cute little apron."

She laughed. She tried to keep it down to sickroom volume, but it was a pretty substantial laugh. "That's Robin. He belongs to Cynthia, not Lady Sally. Don't worry, he's harmless."

"Tell me about it! The shape I'm in, I chased him out with his tongue between his legs. I mean his tail between his teeth. Boy, this Russian shit is terrific. I always knew rich people had secret dope that was dynamite. You a doctor or a nurse?"

"Neither."

"Somebody fixed me up pretty good. This Lady Sally actually got a doctor to make a house call?"

"Kate's on staff. She said it was nice to do some real medicine again, sew something besides costumes for a change. You'll meet her later."

"Fine by me." Everything was fine by me. I made a mental note to tell Travis about this Placebo stuff. Then I remembered that Travis had gone away somewhere and wouldn't be back for a long time. Then I remembered that I didn't like him anymore anyway, for some reason. Then I discovered that while I'd been pursuing this train of thought, I'd mislaid the room in which I'd left my body and its pain. It was around here *some*place. . . .

I went looking for it, and got distracted by other rooms, with funny things in them. Daddy was in some of them, and Mommy wasn't in any of them. It was fun.

CHAPTER 2
THE HOUSE

When I'd got back to the room I'd started from, sunlight was streaming in the window. Lady Sally was there, in a feathered wrapper, with her hair in curlers and her face scrubbed of all traces of makeup. She still looked regal. Since Daddy was with her, I knew I was still dreaming. He was in bathrobe and slippers, chewing on his pipe. I waved, ignoring the tugging sensation at my side. "Hi, Daddy." I was so glad he had remarried again. And to a duchess!

"Good morning," he said.

His voice was all wrong. I tried to get up on one elbow to look closer, and my side shouted at me. I wasn't dreaming after all. This hurt too much not to be real. I was awake now.

He was not my father, of course. Now that I looked, he didn't even resemble him a great deal. What he looked like was the Hollywood stereotype of the Kindly Older Man, the avuncular figure who would need only five or ten years to become the Lovable Grandfather. I must have frowned at him.

"Good morning, Maureen," Lady Sally said. "This is my very dear friend Phillip. He will not bite you, unless you specifically request it." She still sounded just the least bit tipsy, in that cheery-glow phase.

He kept . . . not staring. Just looking at me pleasantly. Enjoying my company, in no hurry to get the conversation rolling. His grey eyes twinkled. If you had a bad acid trip in Grand Central Station you would thread your way through all the leering gibbering zombies until you found this man, and then you would be all right.

"Sorry," I said. "I was dreaming; thought you were someone I knew. Hello, Phillip. Good morning, Lady Sally. Where's the werebeagle?"

She looked politely puzzled. "I beg your pardon?"

"The one you went up that alley with. I saw him change."

"Ah." She took a closer look at me. "Charles is not here at present. He's gone home. You . . . er . . . did not find his metamorphosis upsetting?"

"To be perfectly honest, I found it terrifying. But any friend of yours is a friend of mine."

"Broad-minded of you, child. Good for you."

I realized for the first time that her British accent was bogus, an affectation. She did it well, but if you listened long enough, you could tell. "Thank you for saving my life."

"Think nothing of it, my dear girl. One cannot of course spend one's life hunting pimps; the supply is inexhaustible; but if Fate offers me a chance to assault one without going out of my way, I can only be grateful." We were going to drop the subject of Charles.

I sighed. "Well, I can't say I'll miss Travis, but he did have his uses."

"A tiger in the kitchen will keep the cockroaches away," Phillip said. His voice was soft and deep and furry.

Oh yeah? I wanted to say. I've got that tiger trained as docile as a pussy cat—

—but apparently that was not correct.

In truth, I was shocked at the extent of my misjudgment. It was more than the disappointment felt by an owner whose pet tiger has gone savage and had to be destroyed. Damn it, I had *liked* Big Travis. I had, in a way, cared about him. I had thought that beneath his necessary macho armor he cared about me. I was his special girl. The one he almost didn't want to make whore for him. All the while, deep down, he had thought me such a trivial possession that it had been simpler to kill me than to bother disciplining me. The knowledge put a deeper, sharper hole in me than the knife had.

"I'm in a lot of pain," I said. "I need another shot."

"Shot?" Lady Sally said.

"That stuff Mary gave me, Placebo."

She blinked. "I'm not sure I approve of her giving you that. Oh well, the damage is done. Let me summon your physician. Phillip?"

He rose, went to a phone on the dresser, punched a three-digit number and asked for Doctor Kate to be sent to Mary's room. I gritted my teeth for a wait. Doctors never come promptly.

She arrived almost at once, carrying a black bag. Reading from the top, she wore a doctor's reflector headband, square severe glasses, unbuttoned white doctor's jacket, stethoscope, white lace garter belt, white cobweb stockings, and white high heels. Oh yes, and a wedding ring. She was a natural redhead.

Where the hell *was* I?

"Patty's keeping his vital signs stable," she said to Lady Sally, and to me, "Hello, dear, how are we feeling today? You're looking much better. You had a close call, but you were lucky." She reached the bedside, took my pulse. High and strong and steady. "Are you in a lot of pain?"

Her question took precedence over her costume. "Yes. Lady Sally says I have to see you to get some more of that painkiller Mary gave me last night."

"Placebo," Lady Sally enunciated.

Doctor Kate looked thoughtful. It was weird to see that judicious doctor-look above a pair of large seminaked breasts. Disorienting. "Yes," she decided, "I can let you have some more of that. Mary's judgment is usually sound. Did she say what dosage?"

I thought hard. "Fifty milligrams. In some solution with a long name."

She frowned. "That's a lot. You'll have to take it orally from now on. Here." She took a jar of pills from her bag, gave me one.

Damn. It wouldn't hit as fast, or as hard. Oh well, it would probably last longer. "Looks just like aspirin," I said as she fetched cold water from a bathroom to my right.

"Trust me," she said, returning. "It isn't aspirin."

I gulped it down, lay back to wait for it to work.

"It isn't addicting or habituating either," she said. "In case you were wondering."

"I'd have gotten around to it," I muttered wearily.

"I've got to change your dressing now," she said. "I call your attention to the fascinating ceiling."

I snuck a peek and it was pretty bad, but the medicine was beginning to come on and it helped. When it was over I found that Phillip had come to sit beside me and hold my hand. I half expected him to tell me a bedtime story.

"Phillip . . . ," I asked him quietly, while Doctor Kate was off washing her hands in the john. "Look, where the hell am I? I mean what kind of place *is* this?"

One corner of his mouth crinkled up. "I'm not sure that could be put into words. In fact, I'm not sure I'm wise enough to know."

There was nothing wrong with Lady Sally's hearing. "This is my House," she said clearly, "and you are safe here. You may stay as long as you like, or until I take a notion to throw you the hell out, whichever comes first."

A chilly sensation began just below where my ribs met. I think I kept my face straight, but my hands closed into fists under the sheet. I was a long time answering her.

Oh my *God*, I kept thinking, How could I have been so dumb?

"Thank you, Lady Sally," I said finally. "That's a very generous offer. I already owe you more than I could ever repay."

"Nonsense, dear child," she said. "On the day I leave a stranger to bleed to death in an alley, there'll be a brisk trade in ice skates in Hell. As the old joke goes, it has been the equivalent of a formal introduction."

Doctor Kate came back from the jake. "Will you excuse me, Maureen? Your Ladyship? I have a patient waiting."

"Thank you, too, doctor," I told her. "I peeked while you were fixing my bandage, and you did a good job."

"Wait'll you see the size of my bill," she grinned, and was gone.

I thought: I'll bet you think *I* think you're kidding.

"I'll bet you think she's kidding," Lady Sally said.

I smiled. "I'm grateful that you didn't bring the cops into this. Like, report it or anything. Thank you." I already knew why she hadn't, but I was mildly curious to see what lie she'd use.

"I detest official formalities. Unofficial ones, though, are a different matter: you are welcome, girl. All puns intended."

I made a small sick-patient sound. Phillip frowned in concern. "What's the matter, Maureen?"

"Nothing. This painkiller is making me sleepy." I yawned.

"That's common," he agreed. "Get some rest; you need it. I have an appointment coming up, but I'll look in on you later." He and Lady Sally got up and left.

As soon as the door clicked shut behind them, I closed my eyes tight and groaned.

Now it all made sense. All of it. Oh, I should have guessed! Aw, *Jesus*.

Lucky Maureen. Saved from death and a fate worse than death by a kindly old auntie, a wealthy Good Samaritan who leads werebeagles around on leashes and just happens to be a trained streetfighter. I'd always said if I ever met one real Samaritan in my life, one person who gave without taking, I'd kiss my own ass—and for a minute there, I'd almost been ready to bend over. I'd almost forgotten what the Professor used to tell me, over and over: Always look for the other guy's angle. If it seems too good to be true, it is. What a chump. . . .

She'd said it with a capital H.

"This is my House," she'd said.

A goddam madam!

Of *course* she'd stopped Big Travis from wasting me. Simple conservation. Waste not, want not. Some people can't stand to see a good horse mistreated.

I was in a goddam whorehouse, and from the looks of Doctor Kate and Robin, a very kinky whorehouse, and unless I played my cards *just* right, I was never going to get out of it.

There are basically three kinds of prostitute: street hooker, call girl, and house whore. Each kind is convinced that the other two are the lowest of the low. I was a little more sophisticated: I had started as an independent call girl, then shifted tracks after a few unpleasant incidents persuaded me that it was good to have a protector. But I still had nothing but contempt for house girls.

For one thing, I knew who ran the whorehouses in New York. Better to work the streets! I knew a girl named Marcie who'd been in a House in L.A., once, and she said it combined the worst features of a girls' reform school and a gang rape. You had to work sixteen hours a day and take on any john who wanted you, and do a lot of the perverted kinky stuff. She showed me the scars. You weren't allowed to ask them to use a condom because you were so expensive, yet you got less of the money you made than many street hookers did. Marcie had managed to escape and come East—she'd even managed to kick the drugs they'd hooked her on—but she always used to say that one day they would find her. One day I stopped seeing her around.

My side was giving me hell, but I embraced the pain. I was going to have to get used to it. I was *not* going to let them give me any more of that Placebo shit.

Phillip did come by to check on me later, but I pretended to be asleep so I wouldn't have to talk to him. Then awhile after that, Doctor Kate came back. Her I did want to talk to.

"Look, Doctor Kate—"

"Just 'Kate,' dear. We're going to be friends, I hope."

"Kate, I'm not exactly a blushing virgin—"

"I've treated very few debutantes for stab wounds."

"—I've figured out that this place isn't a Bible Society, okay? So tell me, what's it like? How's Sally to work for?"

"This is the best place I've ever worked," she said happily. "Including some fancy-schmancy hospitals, back when medicine was my main career. And Lady Sally is a total dear."

Uh huh. I wondered whether she was brainwashed, or a tool of management, or just too scared to tell the truth. I decided it didn't much matter which: for my purposes she was useless. I'd already figured out that all the rooms would be bugged—but I'd been hoping for a wink or a grimace or some other sign.

"Really," she was saying, "this is a House of *healthy* repute—no sleaze, fleas or social disease. You have no idea how lucky you are."

"I'm learning. Are we in the city?"

"Brooklyn," she said. "Not far from where you were injured."

"Huh," I said. "Funny. Somehow it doesn't *feel* like Brooklyn."

That made her smile. "No, it doesn't, much."

I wanted to ask for a more precise location, but did not dare. I took another tack. "Kate? I don't mean to be a bother, but . . . would you bring that phone on the dresser over here by the bedside? And tell me what number to dial to reach you? I yelled for help a little while ago, and nobody heard me."

She frowned slightly. "Oh, you must have dreamed it, Maureen. These rooms are very well soundproofed, it's true. But Mary monitors every room in the House during working hours, and even a squeak for help would have brought her on the run."

Maybe that was the cue I'd been hoping for:

an open admission that the rooms were bugged here.

"But we *are* between shifts, now, and Mary's off duty. Besides, you might have people on the outside you want to contact, let them know you're okay. Here you go—"

She brought me the phone!

"What was the matter anyway?" she asked, setting it down on the bedside table. "Are you all right now?"

"Oh yeah," I said absently, dizzy with hope. "Just a twinge."

"That's good," she said. She jotted some three-digit numbers down on a pad. "If I'm not at this first number, I'll usually be at the second . . . and this third number is Main Reception downstairs. Oh, and dial six if you want an outside line, then the area code if it's outside the 212 area. Got it?"

I studied her face carefully. It was open, sincere, friendly. Could there be a hidden camera somewhere? "Got it. Thanks, Kate."

"My pleasure, Maureen. Can I do anything else for you?"

I wondered how often she said those words here. "No, I'm fine."

"I'll run along, then." She grinned suddenly. "Got to wipe down O.R. for the next shift. If you get bored, there's a few magazines in the drawer beside you."

She left, and I held a brief but intense debate with myself.

Was it or wasn't it safe to call for help? Maybe it was smarter to play dumb. This might be a test. Even if Mary really *was* off duty, there could be a tape rolling. Then again, if I could get off a quick enough S.O.S., maybe help would arrive before they got around to playing back the tape. . . .

Which led me right up against the brick wall. Who was there to call? The cops? My *mother*?

Most other working girls either bored the stockings off me, or gave me the willies. I had maybe four sort-of friends among the sisterhood, and none I would trust to take a splinter out of my butt. But who did I know in town besides hookers? I could not recall a single john giving out his phone number—nor one I would call on even if I could. Big Travis's number was permanently out of service. The cops would take their orders from the same people Lady Sally did. And I would not have called my mother if I were being roasted and tortured in Hell.

I thought of someone I could call. It galled me to have to ask him for help. There was no question that he *could* help me, and I had absolutely no other choice: those were the two most galling things. But this chance, if it was one, might never come again; I was dialing his private number even as I cursed.

I had worked with him once. And been his lover, in a friendly sort of way. And I'd been a fool to quit him for whoring.

"I wasn't anywhere *near* there nine months ago," he answered on the third ring.

"Professor—" I began, and shut up. I was furious with myself for the relief I felt at the sound of his voice.

"What's wrong, Maureen?" he asked at once.

I began to cry softly. "Prof, it's a clem. I'm in big trouble—you gotta get me out of here!"

"I will. Tell me about it."

"It's all so crazy! This guy turned into a dog, and my old man cut me, and then I got shanghaied into a House. I don't know whether they're listening now or not, how long I can talk—*please*, Professor, come get me the hell out of here!"

"Where are you? Address and specific location inside, if you can."

"I don't *know*, exactly! In Brooklyn somewhere, a place run by an old auntie named Lady Sally, but I don't even know what floor I'm on—"

He burst out laughing.

I held the phone away as if it had bitten me. It chirped with distant laughter.

"What the hell is so goddam funny?" I shouted into it finally.

"I'm sorry, Mo," he said, still chuckling. "I'm not laughing at you; I'm laughing at the universe. Far be it from me to spoil a joke as good as this. Just listen to me, and believe this: God has sent you what you deserve." He hung up.

I stared at the phone. I was shattered. And totally confused. And almost angry enough to

scream. To be forced to yell "Hey, Rube"—to
him of all people!—and then to have him laugh
at my tears of fright and hang up on me . . .

I was going to get out of this place if I had
to chew my way out. And then hunt him down
and neuter him.

Getting out of bed didn't kill me. The carpet
was soft, and I only fell twice. I couldn't find
my bloody clothes, but the closet was full of all
sorts of outfits and one of them fit well enough.
Four or five pounds of costume jewelry twisted
up in a stocking made a serviceable blackjack.
When Lady Sally came in fifteen minutes later
I was behind the door, ready.

I remembered the sound of Big Travis hitting
cement, and swung harder than my side wanted
me to.

"Wake up, Maureen dear," she said. "You came
all over queer for a moment."

I tried to sit up in bed, but my side hurt
too much. I lay back and glared at her. "Listen to me," I said weakly. "You can kill me, but
you can't break me. Big Travis couldn't make
me work if I didn't want to, and you can't
either!" I was bluffing, of course. Right then
Robin the male maid could have broken me.
"I'm an independent, you got that, Your Ladyship? and if you can't deal with that, then you
might as well finish me right now." I tried to
look tough as nails, and looked to see if I had
pushed it too far.

A smile and a frown were wrestling on her face. The frown won.

"You think that you have been shanghaied into my House," she stated. "That I've appointed myself your new owner. Now I begin to understand that goat dance we just did by the door."

"Did you think I was too dumb to figure it out?" I snapped.

Her face became expressionless. "Maureen, there's probably no point in my telling you this— you won't believe me, and soon enough you'll find out for yourself. But I'll say it just the same. You are free to stay here for a week or two while you recuperate . . . or you may get up and leave now if you feel up to it. I do not recall offering you a position as one of my artists. And I do not plan to."

I said nothing.

"Please do not interpret this as criticism. I'm sure you are talented and skilled. But this is not an ordinary House, and you do not meet my standards. I'll send Kate up, in case our little gavotte has undone her good work." And she left before I could say a word.

I could not decide whether to be relieved, or suspicious . . . or insulted.

I settled on suspicious. She was trying reverse psychology—and it was not going to work.

I refused my next dose of painkiller, told Kate I wouldn't be needing it anymore. Just

after noon the next day a delegation consist-
ing of Phillip and Robin (in mufti, this time)
came to tell me I was well enough to get up
and walk around a little, and to offer me a
Grand Tour. A robe and some very comfortable
slippers were found for me, and we set off at
a pace suitable for a convalescent. I concen-
trated on mapping the place in my head. Out
my door, turn right, a short stretch of hallway
leads to a corridor. Look right: an elevator.
Look left: a doorway marked "Exit"! Look
away . . .

"We're in the Discreet Wing," Phillip said,
steering us toward the elevator. "It's just barely
connected to the rest of the House, and not at
all on this floor. There are doors to the Women's
and Men's Lounges, but except for emergencies
they stay locked during working hours."

"Separate lounges for men and women? *And*
a 'Discreet Wing'?"

The elevator door slid shut and we rose gently. "Well, actually there are *three* Lounges. You
see, some people who come to a bordello feel
easier in their minds if they know that the only
people of the opposite sex they're going to see
are employees. So there are segregated Lounges.
But sooner or later most people figure out that
the best party is in the Parlor. The Parlor is
co-educational—in several senses. And the Discreet Wing is for those few of either gender
who must have absolute discretion and privacy.
Public officials, celebrities, evangelists, and so

forth. If you come on anyone wearing a mask in this section, pay no attention. And if you see anyone you recognize, try to hide it."

This place must be *huge*. And I'd never heard of a house that catered to as many women as men—I'd never heard of one that catered to women at all. Lady Sally was no ordinary madam.

The elevator door slid open and we exited into another hallway, wide and well carpeted. The paintings I saw on the wall were realistic and quite explicitly erotic. Also quite beautiful. "Function rooms straight ahead," Phillip said, "women's wing to the right, men's to the left. Any of the three will lead to the coed wing."

"Let's see the function rooms," I said.

Through a doorway, down a corridor. Doors on either side, impressively far apart. Big rooms, lavish operation. Some of the doors had small red lights glowing. Phillip opened one which did not. "I don't know if you'll remember," he said, "but this is where Kate fixed you up."

It looked and smelled like a doctor's consulting room . . . except that the stirrups on an examination table do not customarily include ankle restraints. It was sparkling clean and seemed well-equipped. I opened a closet. It contained some of those open-backed gowns for patients, some surgeon's gowns and masks, and assorted medical apparatus. Plus a collection of "marital aids" . . .

The next function room we inspected was a

Teenager's Bedroom. Football pennants and pictures of pop stars and horses on the walls, white comforter with embroidered kittens on the bed, cheap desk stacked with school books, letter-sweater draped over the chair, dresser-top piled a foot deep with makeup and perfume and stuffed animals. The closet bulged with clothes; a cheerleader's outfit hung from a hook on the door.

"There's a boy's version across the hall," Phillip said.

Next in line was an Executive's Office, suitable for a captain of industry, authentic in every detail. Phillip, grinning, activated the intercom and said, in a fake Dutch accent, "Missus-a Wiggins, hold-a alla my calls, yew got-a dat?"

I recognized Mary, even though she was using a flat, nasal joke voice. "Yes, Mr. Tudball."

I noted that there was a great deal of room in the well under the desk; that everything on the desk could be swept off onto the floor hastily without breaking or damaging the carpet; that the carpet was extremely soft and washable; and that the couch across the room was designed as a multipurpose utensil.

"Your function rooms are very . . . functional," I said. Privately I was astonished at their quality. My mental estimate of the sheer financial scope of this operation rose sharply with every passing minute. I was no longer surprised that women patronized this brothel. There was nothing remotely sleazy about it. I had fallen into something truly extraordinary. This had to be where the very very rich came.

The prospect of working here began, for the first time, to seem a little less like a fate worse than death.

Suppose you only got to keep . . . say, ten percent of what you made. That could still amount to a tidy sum. And the kind of people you'd meet . . .

But what did the very very rich *want*?

Straight hooking was such a simple, trivial skill: any fool could learn to do it. Hell, it had taken Big Travis about a day and a half to teach me the ropes, back when I got started. Whenever I'd heard or read of those five-hundred-dollar-a-night girls, I always used to wonder what could possibly make it worth that much. I didn't know, and my guesses unnerved me.

"You're looking very pale, Miss Maureen, I'm sorry but you are, are you sure you're up to this?" Robin asked solicitously. I had not been able to get him to call me "Maureen," but I drew the line at "Mistress Maureen."

"I'm fine, Robin. Let's go on."

As we approached the next room, the discreet ruby light beside its door went off. I hesitated, curious to see one of the fabulously wealthy johns that frequented this place. This wasn't the Discreet Wing; it should be all right. I wished I had fixed my face before starting this tour. At least my hair was brushed.

The door opened, and a short slender man emerged. He had a face like a hundred-year-old monkey which had been shaved the previous week. He wore a cabbie's cap, a disreputable denim jacket, black corduroys, and the kind of high-heeled pointy-toed boots which in New York are called P.F.C.'s. Big Travis wore the same kind.

He paused in the doorway, through which I could see that this room was a Victorian Boudoir. "Hi dere," he said to us. Then he turned and called back to the room's occupant, "So long Rachel—yer de greatest!"

"So are you, Eddie," a soft voice replied. "How you got your nickname I'll never know. Say hello to the gang for me."

He grinned, an astonishing sight. "Sure ting." He closed the door, nodded pleasantly to me, said, "Miss. Gents," and walked off down the hall.

"Uh . . . ," I said to Phillip.

"Is there anything wrong?" he asked.

"I guess I don't understand the . . . uh . . . the fee structure around here."

"Neither do we. Fortunately it's not our concern."

"Huh?"

"That's Lady Sally's worry. All we have to do is concentrate on our performance. An artist really needs a manager, don't you think?"

Performance? Artist? "Phillip . . . do you work here? I mean, *work here*?"

He smiled. "I have that honor."

He was certainly the most mature and pleasant male hooker I had ever met. "And you don't collect the money yourself? How do you know Sally's honest on the split?"

He smiled again. "Even assuming I didn't know her, the issue doesn't arise. We're all on straight salary. Plus tips . . . which, to anticipate your next question, we keep."

I blinked. "Do you mind if I ask . . ."

"Not at all." He named a figure. "That's after withholding. And room and board and medical care are thrown in.""

I managed to unpop my eyes. "You can't be serious." As a colonel in the Army, my father had made less than half as much. "She must whack the johns for a *fortune*."

"Each time somebody new comes here, Lady Sally sees him or her in private first. She looks them over, talks with them a little, and then quotes them two prices: one for by-the-evening, and the other for full-time membership. Logic tells me that she must peg the prices to what the individual can afford—you saw the fellow who just left; he's an old regular. But we don't ask, and clients don't talk about it among themselves. All I know is, you don't have to be rich to come here—but if you are, no one will hold it against you."

"How many johns do you have to see a day? Or is it 'janes'?" My subtle way of learning his sexual orientation. And his professional prowess—

No dice. "There's no quota. It varies."

"*Huh?* You're telling me Lady Sally's whores *have no quota?*"

"We don't call ourselves whores. And we don't call them 'johns' or 'janes.' They're clients, and we're artists."

"Mere semantics."

He frowned. "Maureen, every time I hear someone put the word 'mere' in front of the word 'semantics,' I bite my tongue hard and remind myself that I too am greatly ignorant. If you were Jewish would you call yourself a 'kike'?"

"Black people call each other 'nigger,'" I argued.

"Not the ones in this House," he said firmly. "Lady Sally does not permit any kind of contempt here. Not even self-contempt. Maybe especially not self-contempt. Art with contempt in it is always sour. To answer your question, no, there's no quota system. There've been days I didn't see a single client. And days when I took my pants off at noon and didn't put them back on until closing. Art happens when it happens."

"No time limit or anything? You could take a whole shift with one . . . uh, client?"

"Art takes as long as it takes. But that doesn't happen often."

"You can pick and choose your clients?"

"Of course. And vice versa. As a rule, I'll gamble an hour on anyone Lady Sally has admitted to the Parlor, and I've had very few bad experiences. I have some regulars, of course. We all do."

I said nothing.

He grinned. "There just is no polite way to ask what you want to ask, and it's killing you. So I'll take you off the hook. I see both men and women. My clientele happens to break down to about eighty percent female, lately, and that suits me okay. But bisexuality isn't required. Lady Sally tolerates monosexuals; she just doesn't understand them."

I was probably as confused and disoriented as I'd been in that alley a few nights ago. And I was blushing! "Let's resume the tour."

He agreed at once. We left the function room area, passed through a swinging door and down a hallway lined with doorways.

"These are the personal studios," Phillip said. "One per artist. Here, I'll show you my own—"

It looked like a small studio apartment with bath. Thick carpet. Burgundy walls. King-size bed, neatly made up and very comfortable-looking; many pillows. Stereo and a small TV. Beer fridge in the corner. Large closet. Armchair. Hassock. Mahogany dresser with huge mirror which could be pivoted strategically. The only thing that surprised me a little was the bookcase. It was full of books. Real books: I saw old friends. *Stuart Little*. *The Princess Bride*. It looked like a very pleasant room in which to make love. I spotted the bug, but most people wouldn't have.

"Funny," Phillip was saying. "New clients usually want to come here the first time . . . but they ask a lot of casual questions about the various function rooms. Then the second through seventh visits, they either try half a dozen different rooms, or one of them half a dozen times. And from then on, they'll want a plain studio session nine times out of ten. Oh, everybody's different—but you'd be surprised how often it works out that way. You can't eat spicy food *all* the time."

"So this is where you live."

"No, no! This is where I *work*, most of the time. My studio. My *apartment* is up on the third floor with everybody else's."

Jesus Christ. "Along with a twenty-four-hour kitchen, no doubt."

"No, that's in the basement. Clients are permitted there during working hours as long as they behave themselves. Generally that means letting us win the food fights. Are you feeling strong enough to continue?"

As we left I noticed that the door would not lock in either direction. He led me back out into the hall, and through a series of carpeted, softly lit corridors. He did not chat—even Robin was silent—and I was grateful. I was distracted by my own thoughts.

What the hell did she mean, I didn't meet her goddam standards?

We came to the upper terminus of a spiral staircase so grand and beautiful that it jolted me out of my self-absorption. It was iron and might have been the lifework of a whole family of artisans. I could not guess its age.

I realized that I had been hearing music for the last while without noticing: this was the source. Solo piano downstairs. Excellent piano. Honky-tonk, barrelhouse piano, exactly the sort I'd always imagined they must play in whore-houses. You know how you listen to Tatum or Peterson and think, this guy can play any damn thing he can imagine, and he's got a better imagi-nation than me? That good. Listeners were laughing and clapping along. That had to be the Parlor down there—and the afternoon shift was in progress.

"Terrific," Phillip said. "Somebody talked Eddie into sticking around for a while. Let's go."

"Phillip!"

"Yes?"

"There is a damn *party* going on down there. And I am in a bathrobe and slippers with no makeup."

He looked thoughtful. "Oh. There *is* a dress code in the Parlor. But it only applies to employees. I'm sure no one will mind."

I'll never understand men. "It's not *their* feel-ings I'm worried about!"

Robin understood at least. "You look lovely, Miss Maureen," he said, so earnestly I almost smiled. "And you haven't really seen Lady Sally's House until you've seen the Parlor. Why, some of the clients spend all their time there, never come upstairs at all. Just a few minutes?"

You could not descend that splendid staircase without feeling that you were making a grand entrance into the Imperial Ballroom. Doing so in a bathrobe and mules made me feel unutterably silly. Halfway down I relaxed. As advertised, no one was looking at me—and what I was looking at was more interesting than my own embarrassment.

Have you ever seen, in the movies maybe, one of those very elegant and exclusive men's clubs in London, where the rich and powerful hang out? They have them in New York, too, but it couldn't be the same. Picture one of those, three hundred years old, richly furnished and decorated with exquisite taste. Islands of furniture groupings afloat in lots of open carpet. Chandeliers equal to the staircase in magnificence. *Two* bars.

Now I understood how I fell short of Lady Sally's standards. It wasn't any of the things I'd been thinking. I didn't have enough class.

Then I took a closer look at the couple of dozen *people* in that splendid Parlor, and was confused again. The membership committee of the exclusive men's club had apparently been infiltrated by proletarian radicals. Or perhaps just galloping eccentrics.

Roughly half the people were women, of course, and they were dressed more conservatively than I had expected. No lingerie, no negligees. Some dressed elegant, some casual. Most of them looked like they were going to a reception at an upscale art gallery.

But there was a girl in genuine hippie drag, long dress and gypsy scarf and all, and a redhead in Navy uniform, and what appeared to be an authentic bag lady. And a *nun*—

And the men were a much more mixed group.

Oh, there were banker types and diplomat types and lawyer types. I recognized the Police Commissioner from his pictures. But there was also a guy in a bus driver's uniform, some Japanese in Bermuda shorts and flowered shirts, two honest to God native Indians with braided hair and patched jeans, a big balding redhead who looked like a bartender, three coal-black Africans in robes, and a lighter-skinned black man who sat legless on a small wheeled platform. And there was a priest sitting with the nun.

The only other place I'd ever seen this broad a spectrum of people together was the lobby of a modern dance concert the Professor took me to once.

It didn't seem to make sense. Most of this crowd just could not afford the kind of rates that must be necessary to maintain an operation this lavish. Maybe the evening trade was more upscale.

Everybody gave me a glance and a nod; nobody gave me more. Their attention was on the piano playing of the partly shaved monkey

I had seen upstairs. I couldn't blame them; he was really good. Eddie, that was the name. Weird to hear barrelhouse coming from a concert grand . . .

I looked more closely at the women, looked beyond their dress and hairstyles. From what I'd learned of Lady Sally's House, I expected them all to be stunning, in face and body. And some were . . . and some were merely pretty . . . and some were homely even by street standards. I decided those must be clients—for what other kind of woman would need to come to a brothel? (God, I had a lot to unlearn!) Some looked sophisticated, some funky. Some looked bright and educated; at least one looked dumb as a bag of hammers. I saw a saintly grandmother, and a 400-pound native Indian woman who looked mean as a snake.

What the hell standards did I fall short of?

The piano wizard got himself into trouble, noodled his way out onto the end of a long fragile limb—then recovered so adroitly that you realized he'd been teasing you, and thundered his way to a conclusion. Loud applause, in which I joined; shouts and whistles. "Hey, Silas," one of the Indians yelled, "let's kidnap this white man and take him back to Hobbema with us!"

Eddie got up, wrinkled his face up into a remarkable imitation of a dried apricot, took a quick bow, and left with the big redheaded guy. They made an odd pair. The party became general again. Earnest conversation here, raucous laughter there; some drifted to the bars. Over by the fireplace, the bag lady lectured to a small circle of attentive listeners. The police chief and the big Indian began playing chess. A sound system began playing upbeat bebop sax, Dexter Gordon or someone who loved him, in the background.

It came to me that this was the party I had always wanted to be invited to. I began to cry, almost noiselessly. Phillip stared at me, thunderstruck, and Robin began to panic, but I couldn't help it.

Lady Sally was suddenly there beside me, although I hadn't seen her come in. (I was to learn that this was typical.) "Are you all right, Maureen? Do you want Kate?"

I shook my head no, and somehow she knew I was answering both questions. "Thank you, boys," she said cheerfully, "I'll take over now."

She led me out of the parlor; I followed blindly. We ended up at what had to be her office, and sat down together on a sofa. She held me while I cried it out, and after I was through.

When I moved away she let go at once. We sat side by side in silence for a time.

"What it is," I said finally, looking at the floor, "I never had a *home*. Just places to live for a while. I was an Army brat until my Dad died. I've wanted a home so bad for such a long time. Out there: those folks are home.

Maybe some of them have other homes outside of here, maybe not, but this is *a* home for
them. Right?"

"Yes."

"Could you maybe just skip being polite for
a minute, and tell me what standard it is I don't
meet? Is it anything I could fix?"

She sighed and turned away. "I'll give you a
straight answer. There are three basic problems.
First, your age. I do not employ artists under
eighteen. You are sixteen at most, and doubtless
can pass for twelve. That is not an asset in this
House.

"Second your training. I've had very bad
luck with street girls. Most of what you think
you know about The Art is wrong, and
unlearning takes more discipline than I think
you've got.

"Third and most important, your attitude. You
don't much like yourself, and you don't much like
your clients, and you don't much like what you
and they do together. That, more than anything,
makes you no use to me."

I remembered Phillip saying, "Art with contempt in it is always sour." I could understand
that. The difficult part was to grasp the concept
that inducing a genital sneeze could qualify as
art. . . .

She frowned. "The first problem is self-
correcting; the second is correctable with a lot
of hard work. I don't know whether there's anything you could do about the third. I place a high

value on acceptance and tolerance. I'm inclined to give you points for the way you accept and tolerate my friend Charles, and his . . . peculiarity. But not enough points. I'm sorry."

I closed my eyes. After a long silence, I opened them and said, "Thank you for your honesty."

She frowned again. "You're right to thank me; honesty is hard work." She turned back to look at me, and started. "Dear God, child, you're exhausted. You look, in the words of a horseman of my acquaintance, like you've been rode hard and put away wet. Sit there and I'll fetch a wheelchair to take you back to your room—"

I started to protest, and realized that I really was wiped out. My side hurt. My pride hurt. "All right."

CHAPTER 3
FINAL EXAM

If you've lived a bad life, they send you to Hell. But if you've been truly *wicked*, they give you a tour of Heaven first. . . .

I didn't cry until I got back to my room and chased out Phillip and Robin. Then I didn't stop for hours.

Nice going, Mo! Sweet sixteen, and already beyond hope. Anyone else might have been satisfied to be a whore by now—but *you've* managed to become too clumsy and jaded to *be* a whore. A decent one anyway.

Hours went by that way. My pain became so large I could not bear it alone; some of it turned into anger, and spilled over onto Lady Sally.

Says I don't have the skills. The bitch. How the hell does she know? And where was I

supposed to learn? Says I have no discipline.
Let her try living with Big Travis, see how long
she can keep a straight face. Says I don't like
the clients. Christ, almost two years I've been
tricking, and all I've ever had were creeps and
jerks. Says I don't like screwing. Well, I used
to, once. Maybe I could learn to like it again,
if I had someone who wasn't a creep or a jerk,
in a place that wasn't sleazy, and I didn't have
to hurry. Maybe I could even learn to believe
that it could be some kind of art. . . .

Says I don't like myself—

How the hell am I supposed to like myself?
She doesn't want me. Big Travis doesn't want me.
Even the Professor's turned his back on me. The
only people that have ever wanted me have been
creeps and jerks and . . . and . . . and . . . and . . .

I became aware of intense pain in my knuckles. I had been rhythmically banging my fists
together, hard. I shook my fingers violently as
if I were shaking off boiling water and got up
from my bed to pace the room.

My side hurt, like a toothache. So did my
head. My eyes were red and my nose plugged
from crying. My belly was full of rocks. I cata-
logued all the physical discomforts, cherished
them. They were perfectly satisfactory hurts.
Sooner or later every one of them was going to
go away. It was only a matter of waiting.

But the emotional hurts were not going to go
away, no matter how long I waited. The loop
began again:

Lady Sally doesn't want me. Big Travis doesn't want me. Even the Professor has turned his back on me. The only ones who've ever wanted me have been creeps and jerks and . . .

I still could not make myself complete the thought. The loop went into rewind:

. . . dna skrej dna speerc neeb evah em detnaw reve ev'ohw seno ylno ehT .em no kcab sih denrut sah rosseforP eht nevEven the Professor has turned his back on me—

I stopped pacing.

After a while I took a deep breath. Then another, and another. I went to the bathroom, washed my face, brushed my hair. I came out, tried the closet. The only outfit in a one-size-fits-all was a kimono and sandals. Not great, but you work with what you've got. I returned to the john and applied makeup with extreme care. When I was done I looked twenty-two years old and wealthy enough to carry off Eastern affectations. With the right resumé I could have applied for a job in a Tokyo bank. A vice cop or a hotel dick would have looked right past me.

I didn't really think this would work. But it was worth a try.

If it didn't work, *then* I would cut my throat.

As I stepped out into the hallway I saw the Mayor coming into the building through the Discreet Entrance; at least, it looked like him under that silly mask. It was dark outside; I had cried for a long time. I ignored him politely and went to the elevator, retraced the maze that led to Lady Sally's Parlor. I met no one along the way, and heard nothing; either the night was young or the soundproofing was excellent. When I reached the spiral staircase I heard party sounds from downstairs. I paused, listening for Lady Sally's distinctive deep voice, but I didn't hear it. I was nervous as hell. Suddenly I remembered the Mayor. If that was really him . . . did he, while he was at it, ask his famous trademark question? "How'm I doin'?" The giggle helped. Not enough, but some.

I squared my shoulders and descended the staircase.

There were three or four different parties going on simultaneously in the Parlor. No one paid any attention to me, so I scanned the room. One group of fifteen or so was watching two Chinese, a Marine and a transvestite play cards; they appeared to be wagering Peek Frean cookies. A slightly smaller group at one of the Parlor's two bars was having a liar's contest; the big Indian I'd seen earlier held the floor and his audience was loud and appreciative. A dozen people were singing "Baby, It's Cold Outside" a capella by the fireplace, the men taking the Ray Charles part and the women giving the Betty Carter responses. On the other side of the room a man and a woman sat on the piano bench, facing a hushed crowd, and took turns blowing smoke figures. She took a deep drag on a cigar and blew a dragon; it had scales, and emitted a plume of smoke from its nostrils as it rose. He watched it until it dissolved, nodded admiringly, and blew an angel. With a halo and a harp. It hung motionless in the air for a moment, spread its wings, flapped them majestically, and ascended, shimmering into nothingness. They smiled at each other. In another corner of the Parlor, a stunning redhead and a priest shared a computer, gesticulating excitedly, typing simultaneously, watching the screen together, then gesticulating again. A couple with matching wedding rings sat on a couch nearby, holding hands and looking intently into each other's eyes, oblivious to the universe.

I wanted to belong here so bad my teeth hurt.

Between that and the ache in my side, I yearned to go to one of the two bars and order something with authority. Or slide back to my room for some of that Russian dope. The girl I had been, way back when I had first gone up that alley, would probably have done one of those things. Instead I looked for familiar faces. No sign of Lady Sally, my first choice; she'd have stood out even in this crowd. No Doctor Kate. Nor Phillip, nor Mary, nor Robin. Stranger at the feast. Oh wait, there was someone I knew—

Charles.

There was no mistaking those ears on that

bald head. He was standing by the bar, watching the two smoke artists. I wondered what he was doing in human form; surely the Moon was up by now? I realized for the first time that there were no windows in the Parlor. That's something I usually notice right away about a room. Perhaps Charles had to be physically touched by moonlight to go into his act. I started toward him, and saw that a *real* dog sat by his feet. I grinned, some of my tension going out of me. Maybe she was his artist.

You had to wonder what he'd be like . . .

He recognized me as I approached, and his face took on an odd, guarded expression. The phrase that popped into my mind was, like a dog wondering if he's about to be kicked. He knew I had seen him change, and we had not exchanged a word since. Awkward—

The girl I had been when I went up the alley would probably have said something like, "Hi, snoopy," or if I'd been really clever, "Give me your paw and you can have my maw, arf arf." Instead I said, "Hello, Charles. We haven't been properly introduced; I'm Maureen."

Can a face relax into a smile? His did. "Hello, Maureen. It's good to see you up and around. Uh . . . may I present my good friend, the celebrated author, Ralph Von Wau Wau?"

I followed his gesture, didn't see anybody.

"Down here, *fräulein*," came a voice from below.

I gaped.

"You got something against short people?" the German shepherd asked.

"Oh, stop it, Ralph," Charles said. "Maureen is new here, and you know you take a bit of getting used to."

The dog hung his head. "Aw, Curly, I vas chust teasing her a little." Now he mentioned it, Charles did look like an underweight Third Stooge.

"Ralph is a mutant, Maureen. A psych experiment with serendipitous results. High IQ and a surgically modified larynx."

Ralph barked with laughter. *"Mein Gott!* De t'ree uff us are Mo, Larynx, unt Curly!"

I took a deep breath, and then another. Then I squatted and held out my hand. "No offense, Ralph; it was rude of me to stare. Pleased to meet you."

He extended his paw and we shook. "Zat wass a fast recovery, Maureen."

"I'm learning about this place. Will you excuse me, Ralph, Charles? I'm eager to get to know you both, but right now I need to find Lady Sally; it's important that I talk with her. Do either of you know where she might be?"

"Priscilla will know," Charles said. "Oh, Priscilla! Here she comes—"

I gave Ralph a friendly scratch behind the ears, straightened up and turned to see Priscilla approaching. She wore sweatpants and a skintight muscle shirt. She was entitled. I would not have believed a woman could have so much

sculptured muscle mass and still look totally
feminine. She was astonishingly light on her feet.
She had to be the bouncer.

And was. Charles introduced us—her grip was
firm but not aggressive—and stated my problem.
She nodded, murmured into her wristwatch,
waited, then smiled at me. "Come on, hon."

She led me to a door directly opposite the
main entrance, between the two bars. We went
down a short flight of stairs, through a fire
door, went right along a short corridor and
stopped at another door. Priscilla knocked a
complex pattern.

"Come in," came that distinctive voice.

Lady Sally sat behind an antique desk, on
which were a computer, a printer and a Lava
Lamp. The air smelled faintly of fine coffee, and
a good stereo was playing good music at background volume. Books lined the walls. She nodded to a chair. "Sit down, dear. Thank you,
Priscilla."

"Sure, Boss." Priscilla closed the door behind
her.

Lady Sally held up one finger, typed a few
keys with her other hand, shut down the computer and put away the startup disk. "Now then,
darling, what can I do for you?"

It was hard to get enough air. I had rehearsed
this a dozen times, and couldn't remember my
lines. "You've already done a lot for me, Lady."

"No, dear," she said. "I did that for myself.
I hate a knife."

Maureen, quit waiting for a better argument to occur to you and say what you came here to say—

"Do you know a man called the Professor?" I blurted.

She looked surprised. "I am acquainted with a gentleman of that name. Is yours a swindler?"

"The best in the world," I agreed.

"Well, on the East Coast, at any rate. Yes, I know the Professor. Why do you ask?"

I hesitated, then went for broke. "If I dial his private number, will you speak with him for me?"

"You know him that well?"

"I lived with him for almost a year. And worked with him."

I had succeeded in surprising, if not impressing her. "And you left *that* to work the streets for that Travis creature?"

I shrugged and sat back in my chair. "I've kicked myself a few times."

"But *why*?"

I sighed deeply. "The best I can say it is that I started feeling sorry for the marks. It wasn't easy: you know the Professor's maniac thing about only conning creeps. But it got to me. Look: the Professor and I both screw people for a living—but the ones I screw are grateful afterwards. We both sell illusion; I just work cheaper. I know it doesn't make much sense."

"On the contrary, child," she said slowly, "it makes a certain sense to me. Why do you wish me to speak with him now?"

I sat forward and met her eyes. "You said I don't much like myself. I do and I don't. If I try to give you a big sales pitch for me I'll have trouble passing a lie-detector test; the best I can tell you is I'm not as bad as I could have been. But right after I first got here, I called up the Professor and told him where I was, and he laughed and said I'd finally gotten exactly what I deserved and then hung up, and I want you to call him up now and ask him why he said that—" I was crying now. "—because if he was right and this place is what I deserve, then dammit *you gotta take me and teach me!*"

She blinked at me.

I had shot my bolt. I met her gaze and waited for her reply.

And a speaker crackled into life somewhere on her desk. "Boss!" Mary's voice rapped, "Trouble in the Parlor! Sounds like one hostile. Pris is down; I'm on my way!"

Lady Sally was already loping up the stairs. I scrambled after her, hampered by a costume designed to keep the women from being able to run fast enough—

Richard Fariña once said, "There is a tide in the affairs of men, which taken at the flood, you're liable to fucking drown." As I burst into the Parlor, cursing at the pain in my side, the first thing I saw was the man who had put it there.

"God damn, Baby Love," Big Travis called

happily, "you lookin' *bad*. You lookin' like some solid citizen bitch, like a growed-up lady been around the world. That ain't a bad look, that Jap shit; we'll make us some money with that." He gestured with his Saturday Night Special. "Bring it on over here."

He was crazy-eye high on crank. The room was full of quiet still people. Priscilla lay face down at this feet, also quiet and still; I saw blood on the back of her neck, trickling along her splendid trapezius. He had to have sucker-punched her; he could never have taken her in a fair fight.

I hesitated a second, then smiled joyously.

The hesitation was fake. My brain was already up to speed from making my pitch to Lady Sally, I was full of adrenaline from running, and I'd just been thinking about the Professor, who can invent a new identity in the time it takes to shake hands. Shifting mental gears took no time at all: Travis would think the hesitation in getting my smile on was because I knew I was in for a rough time when he got me home.

"Travis! Thank God you found me—they've been keeping me prisoner! Get me out of here, baby!"

It must be gratifying to see a girl you recently planned to torture to death light up with joy at the sight of you. He grinned so big I could see the insides of his ears. "I can do that," he said, nodding. "I don't see a problem in the world with that. Everybody here be nice people, we just motor out of here and," in mid-sentence his face changed instantly to total rage and he was bellowing *"nobody be gettin' crazy!"*

It got even quieter in the Parlor. I could see one uniform cop (female), a couple of Marines, and three or four football players, all of whom looked dangerously close to having had enough of *this* shit. I remembered the moment in the alley, when I had been afraid that Travis was going to kill Lady Sally. I was tired of nice people being in danger because of me.

"Oh, I don't t'ink anyvun here iss crazy," Ralph Von Wau Wau said slowly and distinctly.

It should have worked. When you are addressed by an attack dog with bared teeth and flattened ears, you generally lose your train of thought. But Travis must have been flying—he took it in stride, and there was never a second when he could have been jumped. All he did was grin again. "Tell you one thing, Rin Tin Tin: you crazy enough to come at me, you one dead son of a bitch." They stared hard at each other, baring their teeth.

Ralph dropped his eyes—

"Hostage," Travis said. "We need a hostage and then noobody'll bother us."

Inspiration came from Heaven. "Get that bald guy with the ears, Trav honey; they all like him."

He nodded approval and aimed his gun at Charles. "Head for the door, Curly," he said. "Don't fret: once we get a few blocks with nobody following, we turn you loose. Come on, Baby Love, we gone."

I moved to join him.

"*Konban mangetsu ga mirareru-hazu-da,*" Lady Sally called out.

"Say *what*?" Travis said.

I pointed at her, then rotated my finger against my forehead. "High," I explained.

"*Bikkuri-suru-na,*" she said softly. "*Keihô ga hasse-rareta.*"

"Hey, burn that pig-Latin shit," Travis ordered suspiciously.

She shut up. "High," I said again, hoping she got the pun. I hate puns. "The hell with her, lover, let's *go!*"

He nodded again and grabbed my wrist firmly. We followed Charles through swinging doors into a reception area. Travis paused in the doorway, thrust me through ahead of him. "Almost forgot," he muttered. "I owe that bitch for bustin' my damn nose." He turned and took a dead bead on Lady Sally's impassive face, steadying his wrist with his left hand.

I was caught leaning the wrong way. I wound up to punch him above the elbow, knowing I was going to be too late—

—and a dozen men and women stepped calmly and instantly into the line of fire.

Others joined them within seconds. They all stared fearlessly at Big Travis. He held his stance for several long seconds . . . then pointed the muzzle at the ceiling. "Fuck it," he said, and backed through the doors. As they swung shut he reclaimed my right wrist with his left hand and waved to Charles to open the outer door.

Then it closed behind us, and suddenly we were back in Brooklyn. It was a warm night. I smelled the streets for the first time in days, heard city-sound whispering in the distance, and over it the pounding of my pulse. I mustn't get caught leaning again. If I was lucky, I'd get a single, split-second opportunity . . .

Six feet from the door, Charles stopped and began undressing.

Travis made no comment until his sportscoat and tie were on the sidewalk and he was half-way through unbuttoning his shirt. "What is wrong with you, fool?" he said then. "You want to die?"

Charles took the undershirt off with his shirt, dropped them both. "Not in these trousers," he said, and unzipped them.

Travis giggled, moved so that he could keep an eye on the door, and watched as Charles dropped pants and shorts, and managed to step out of them and his shoes and socks without using his hands. A milkman couldn't have done it faster.

"What you figure to do?" Travis asked, smiling broadly now. "Sneak up on me while I'm tryin' to find your pecker?"

For reply, Charles changed.

And for the second damn time, it didn't work. Oh, it affected Travis, all right. A man can

be so stoned that he doesn't find a talking dog
disturbing—but a werewolf transformation at
arm's length is a different proposition. He gasped
loudly, gaped satisfactorily, and turned to stone
while Charles's body rippled and contorted. He
would have been a perfect sitting duck target,
except for one thing: among the muscles which
turned to stone were the ones in his left hand.
The one which held my right wrist.

If I tried to free my hand, or reach across
his body and get to his gun with my left hand,
I would break the spell. If I hit him, he'd probably pull the trigger. I didn't know if werebeagles were vulnerable only to silver bullets
like werewolves were supposed to be—and once
the change was complete, and Travis realized
he was facing not a wolf but a beagle, he would
start shooting. I decided my move, pitiful as it
was, was to go for the gun: it would give
Charles a chance to attack while Travis was
shooting me. I tensed—

Then I remembered Lady Sally's last words—
don't worry; the alarm has been given—and
made the instant, intuitive decision to believe
that she knew what she was talking about. I
relaxed, waited to see what would happen.

And close to two hundred pounds of fighting
female landed on Big Travis's shoulders with both
feet.

Of course—Mary, who eavesdropped on
everything in Lady Sally's House, had said, "I'm
on my way," and then never showed up. Instead

she had positioned herself at a window overlooking the front door. Any move I'd made
would have screwed her up.

The gun went flying and he let go of my wrist
as he went down. The shattered collarbone made
him scream, but it cut off short as his face
smacked the pavement. When the dust settled,
Mary was seated on his shoulder blades, facing
forward. Blood oozed from his nose and mouth
and one eye; as I watched, it stopped. Mary put
two fingers to the side of his neck, being careful to avoid the blood. "Doornail," she said with
satisfaction. She got up nimbly and checked her
jeans for stains. "Nice set-up, Mo. You played
it just right."

It took me a few seconds to get my voice
working. "My pleasure. I always thought Mary
rose *up* into Heaven."

"An ungrounded Assumption," she said.

Charles, change complete, waddled forward on
his four stubby legs, lifted one, and expressed
an opinion—whether of Travis or Mary's pun I
couldn't say. The former, probably, judging by
his aim.

The front door banged open and Lady Sally
came out the door fast and low with a shotgun
in her hands, closely followed by Phillip, Doctor
Kate, Robin, and others. The cop and Marines
were among them, also displaying firearms now;
there must be a gun-check in the reception area.
"Film at eleven," Mary called to them, and they
slowed and lowered their weapons.

Lady Sally approached me slowly, putting the safety back on her scattergun. She looked me in the eye. "Are you all right?"

I looked down at the fresh warm corpse of what had, until some forty-eight hours ago, been my favorite pet tiger. My lover. My owner. I had been smarter . . . and he more cunning. I was horrified to discover how much I would miss him.

"Yes," I said, "but oh, I have been so stupid," and on "oh" the tears spilled over and ran down my face. So many tears tonight . . .

She embraced me, and I felt Mary's big strong hand on my shoulder. "Step into my office," Lady Sally said, and led me past the crowd at the door and back into her House with her arm around me.

Back in her office she offered me a drink. I didn't turn it down to win points; I already felt smashed. "How did you know I spoke Japanese?" I asked.

"You said you were an Army brat. And your obi is tied correctly. I took a chance."

"Oh. Yeah. I spent the last half of junior high in Tokyo."

"Is that where the bad thing happened?"

I looked up at her. "You know about that?"

She shook her head. "Only that it happened. Not what it is. I'm not a mind-reader, child."

I snorted. "So you say."

She said nothing.

"Yeah, it was in Tokyo. My real mother died

when I was born. When I was nine, Daddy married again. Captain Phyllis Langerhut. She was clever, very smart. I adored her from nine to twelve. I called her Mom. And I had a terrific crush on her best friend, Sergeant Alice. They were both terrific female role models. Strong, tough, independent. Dashing, you know? On my twelfth birthday, while Daddy was off in the States, they made their move. You know what they say about women in the Army? Well, once in a while it's true. And once in a *very* long while, they're aggressive pedophiles, too. Alice had talked Mom . . . Phyllis into marrying Daddy so they could have access to me.

Like I say, they were clever. They knew about power. I hated it and enjoyed it. So I belonged to them from twelve to about thirteen and a half. Then I told Daddy. And pretty soon Sergeant Alice was dead and Daddy was dead and Phyllis was dishonorably discharged and I was in an institution. After a month I cut a new door in it, and I met the Professor on the Greyhound platform at Port Authority. I started out roping for him, and by the time I quit him I was telling the tale and even running the store sometimes. He was the first man I ever . . ." I broke off. "You don't care about all this soap opera."

Lady Sally was looking at me strangely. "On the contrary," she said. "I am interested in everything about my employees."

✧   ✧   ✧

I spent the next couple of years learning Lady Sally's House from top to bottom. Or rather the other way around. I spent the first year working in the kitchen, the laundry, maintenance, housekeeping, and Lady Sally's office, all of which are located in the basement. Then I moved upstairs and worked reception at each of the four entrances, and toward the end of the year I put in some time spelling Mary in the Snoop Room on the top floor. During all this time I was completing high school; the dean of the night school program gave me credit for a completely mythical freshman and sophomore year, on the basis of my test scores and because I had been doing very well in the genius program when I'd left junior high school; the fact that he was a regular client at Lady Sally's House was irrelevant. Meanwhile I was taking daily classes in The Art between shifts, from Phillip and Mary and others, and for the last six months I was allowed to sit in on Lady Sally's weekend master classes.

And on my eighteenth birthday, six years to the day since I had decided once and for all that I was utterly worthless, I became an Artist.

Just lucky, I guess.

BOOK TWO

REVOLVER

CHAPTER 4
REPEAT BUSINESS

Have you ever been to a party that was so much fun, you didn't particularly care if you found a lover there or not? And still had the warm feeling that you probably *would*, a skilled and gentle guy, without fuss or anxiety before the night was through? And that meanwhile there were ideas to be stalked, songs to be sung, belly-laughs to be shared? Have you been so blessed?

That's how much fun it is in Lady Sally's Parlor most nights of the week.

Skillful interior decoration permits half a dozen *different* parties to be going on simultaneously, in separate "interactional nodes" shaped largely by furniture arrangement. But the parlor is, in the end, one large open room, so if merriment insists on being contagious, an epidemic can flare up at any time. The two major focuses of infection generally seem to be the piano in the northeast corner, and the fireplace across the room in the west wall. (Hardly anyone stays at the bar longer than it takes to get served: turning your back to a room like that just doesn't seem to make sense.)

One rainy night in late summer I was sitting with a group of about twenty, watching Marie dance in the cleared space near the piano, when I became aware that a word-game was spreading rapidly from the fireplace area and threatening the rest of the Parlor.

It takes a lot to divert my attention from Marie when she's dancing. She doesn't do it often. She is a client in her late thirties, and if she were eight inches shorter she could dance anywhere on Earth that she wanted. As things are, she's unemployable except as a choreographer. (The growth spurt came *after* she had studied dance from six to sixteen.) I would leave a very warm bed at the rumor that Marie was thinking of dancing a few steps, and wouldn't be surprised if my bedmate beat me downstairs. She was moving lazily, hypnotically, to a solo sax that came from concealed speakers, and I was paying full attention.

But I was also a sucker for word-games, even ones that incorporate punning. This one seemed to consist of finding variants on, "If a lawyer gets disbarred, then—"

"—then a female-to-male transsexual is

disbra'd," I heard Sleepy Jim say. Jim was a paperback editor; he was always good with words. It was partly his strong voice that drew my attention. Funny guys are my favorite clients. "And dismayed," he added.

"—and dismissed and dispersed," his wife Joanie riposted quickly. "And a male-to-female transsexual fish gets deboned." She got a smattering of applause.

"—and they both get dismounted and delayed for a while!" he volleyed, drawing cheers and laughter. "A traveling salesman is decommissioned—"

"And a hairstylist is distressed and departed," Marie said without appearing to leave her dance trance.

That made it okay for me to share my attention too. "A preacher could get deflocked," I offered, but it turned out that someone had used that one already. "Uh—let's see . . . I suppose a person that had to give up eating chili would be deflated? And disgusted? And distinct?" That brought a chorus of protests ("Distinctly disgusting!"), but was deemed acceptable.

Father Newman jumped in. He never goes upstairs or into the Bower, of course, but he's been a regular in the Parlor for over a decade. When asked why, he always says, "I came to Lady Sally's House out of curiosity, looking for sin. I haven't found any yet, but I'm a patient man." He's officiated at a couple of weddings in that parlor. "Not many people know," he boomed in that hearty pulpit voice "that, when-ever a national embassy is torn down—"

"—it becomes disconsolate!" four or five people finished, Lady Sally herself among them. "All right, darlings," she went on in her delightful bogus Oxonian accent, "let's make this interesting. Form a circle and pass it round, elimina-tion style, and the last one standing gets an hour upstairs with me."

There was a general intake of breath. Male and female. Then a vague circle began forming, artists and clients alike. Twice a month Lady Sally gives well-attended master classes in The Art, for both men and women, and we compete to be chosen for demonstrators—despite the fact that only three of us are within twenty years of her apparent age (which may or may not be within twenty years of her calendar age). Happy is the rare client who is invited upstairs by the mistress of the House; few ever give up hope.

"Father, if you win, we'll pray together," she added demurely. "Lord Highpockets, perhaps you would care to serve?"

Lady Sally always called anyone who's name she couldn't come up with Lord This or Lady That: the client addressed was a stringbean guitar player named Jake, another of my favorite cli-ents. "Well," he drawled, "I spent most of my school years wishing I could be detested and degraded—"

And we were off and running.

I knew I had no chance—no one did, with

Jake and Sleepy Jim in the room—but I tried anyway. Oh, I could have had half an hour of Lady Sally's time, in or out of bed, just by going to her and telling her I needed it. But when you win her in a contest, she makes you feel . . . well, rewarded, somehow. But as I expected, on my third turn I came up empty.

When it's your turn in one of these Parlor games, you have an unspecified time in which to take your shot. Then, after an interval inversely proportional to your skill, someone will say, "Five!" If enough others join in on "Four," the countdown proceeds to zero. If not, there's another pause until someone says, "Four," and waits for corroboration on "Three." The system allows the crowd to give weaker players a break, and I usually got all the time I needed— but that night I knew the extra time wouldn't help; I started to resign.

And noticed a guy in my field of vision furtively gesturing. He kept discreetly making the classic sign of the female shape with his hands, and then grimacing ferociously. Finally I got it. "A model gets disfigured," I blurted, and the deal passed on.

He sat beside me. I recognized him vaguely; he'd never been a client of mine, but I'd seen him around. Slender, forties, well-dressed and nondescript. One of those shy-looking guys. I couldn't recall his House name. "Thanks," I said in a prison-yard whisper.

"Maybe I shouldn't have helped," he murmured

back. "Now you'll want to stay—and I'd really like to go upstairs with you. Like, right away." So much for my judgment of character—

I looked around and mentally shrugged. Honor was satisfied, and he looked acceptable. "I'm flattered. I guess I'd always rather be a prize than win one. What's your name, stranger?"

"Colt."

No House name sounds weird to you after a while. We once had a Cherokee client named He Wears Funny Hats, called Hats for short. (Never wore a hat, oddly enough.)

After considerable thought and consultation with my brother and sister artists, I had selected "Sherry" as my own House name (firmly resisting the suggestion that I spell it with a terminal *i*; I was vaguely afraid that some drunken night I would dot the *i* with a little heart). I had always liked my milk name—Maureen—but I had to admit it was not a great name for a courtesan. Besides, everyone at Lady Sally's House gets a House name, artists and clients alike: only Sally knows everyone's real moniker, an eccentricity that many clients appreciate. I picked "Sherry" because Juicy Lucy said the word meant "a little tart, a little sweet, intended to be delicately sipped." (And managed to make me blush for the first time in ages.)

But Colt didn't ask *my* name. He stood at once and headed for the spiral staircase in the center of the Parlor. He did look over his shoulder halfway there to make sure I was coming, but it seemed less like politeness than impatience.

I let it pass, and followed him. It's not that the poor dears don't know any better, I thought indulgently: sometimes they just can't help themselves. I made myself a promise that his descent back *down* those same stairs would be considerably more leisurely.

He went up that staircase like a snake disappearing up a trouser leg, hanging onto the centerpost and swinging himself around the curves. I decided that a better House name for him might be Lickety Split. Doubly appropriate if his tastes coincided with my own—oh damn, the place was getting to me. I was punning.

He was waiting when I reached the top of the stairs, uncertain which way to go, shifting his weight from one leg to the other like a kid who has to pee. I pointed the way, and he scampered down the corridor ahead of me. He waited at each door to see if I would stop at it, then scurried ahead to the next one. By the time I opened the door to my studio, I could no longer hide my grin.

He didn't seem offended; he didn't appear to notice. He didn't look around the room. He didn't make small talk. He didn't even stop to undress. Either of us. Fortunately, I was dressed for work.

I might almost have thought that somehow a horny teenage virgin had been made up to look like a man in his forties—but apart from that odd, barely controlled urgency to be about it, the event itself was totally unremarkable for a client of his age and condition. He made love like a man in middle years. He caught cues. He was careful with his weight. He rationed his energy. He had an adult's "three o'clock" erection rather than a boy's "half past noon," and he lasted as long as I would have expected. He was aware of my existence throughout, and knew that my own climax was not faked.

And then, just when I'd decided he wasn't at all like a teenager, I noticed that . . . how shall I put this? . . . the swelling had not subsided.

It *is* possible for a man to fake a climax, but I knew he had not done so. Still, it isn't totally unheard of for a man of any age to find himself ready for a second helping right away. I decided again to be flattered, and offered him a rematch, no tip necessary. (One of the best things about Lady Sally's House is that there is never a clock ticking; Her Ladyship believes that art takes as long as it takes.) And he accepted on terms so favorable that before long I had given him that new private nickname, having been most delicately sipped.

This time I not only fired the weapon, I succeeded in lowering the barrel. But not for long: in the few minutes it took him to get his breath back and collect his clothes, it started to rise again.

But my offer of a third round seemed to almost panic him. He concealed his weapon, dressing quickly, and thanked me kindly and tipped me generously but not extravagantly and left. By the time I had washed and repaired my makeup, buzzed Robin to come clean up the studio, and gone back down to the Parlor, he was gone—and the word-game was just being won by Father Newman, with something horrid about a priest who had broken his vow of chastity on a subway getting disPennStation. He and Lady Sally went upstairs together, to pray, to thunderous applause (I couldn't repress a flicker of curiosity as to whether Father Newman used the same method of prayer that I did), and I was approached by a couple I knew for a session in the Bower, and the evening went on.

The business with Colt was just odd enough to stick in my mind, not odd enough to be worth gossiping about.

He returned the next night, gave me a warm greeting and a kiss on the cheek, but did not invite me upstairs; I got the message and drifted politely away. He chose Bingo Katy within five minutes, and was back downstairs and out the door within half an hour, nodding pleasantly to me as he left. The next night I happened to see him go upstairs with Cynthia; he took an hour that time, but then Mistress Cynthia's art involves more elaborate theater. The next night, Juicy Lucy; twenty minutes. At that time, Lady Sally's roster included (biologically speaking, at least) twenty-three females and twenty-one males; it became apparent that I would be entertaining Colt again in about twenty days; I put him out of my mind.

And he kept popping back in.

Why? It was atypical for a client to show up every night, but not unheard of: Lady Sally's flat-rate membership policy encouraged frequent visits. His name never came up in aftershift gossip sessions, by whorehouse standards his rather . . . straightforward approach just wasn't that odd. He was like a guy who orders his drinks from a different bottle every night, methodically working his way through the shelves, and God knows we get a few of them. It seemed like a rather dull hobby to me, but that was his business. What was it that kept me vaguely aware of him in the crowd? Why did I feel vaguely sad whenever I noticed him?

"It's like it was a sentence," I found myself saying to Phillip finally, as we were winding down over Irish coffees in the dining room one night. "There just doesn't seem to be any *joy* in it for him."

Phillip smiled. "Why does that bother you?"

"It's as though he typified what's wrong with men."

He arched an eyebrow, and licked sugar from the rim of his coffee glass.

"All right, some men. Maybe even most of them, though."

"Now there's a rewarding topic for a

symposium," Lady Sally said, joining us with
a coffee of her own. " 'What's wrong with
men.' Might be worth discussing at some
length."

"Yeah, but who's got a spare week?" Mary
asked, sitting beside her and lighting a
cigarette.

"Let's take a month," Phillip suggested mildly.
"Then we could cover what's wrong with women
too."

"*Whoa!*" Mary and I chorused ominously, and
Lady Sally raised a hand.

"Darlings!" she said with her usual slightly
tiddly good humor (I have never seen Lady
Sally take a drink), "the ancient ritual combat
is over for the night, both sides retired victo-
rious: why reopen old grudges? Let's keep this
on a friendly plane and perhaps we can learn
something. Sherry, dear, can you state your
objection to men? To some men, I hasten to
amend."

I was hesitant now. I'd been living in Lady
Sally's House long enough to know that if you
didn't like your clients, she believed you
belonged in some other line of work—and I *did*
like men, as a species, a lot. But this thought
had been in the back of my mind for a good part
of my life; I pressed on stubbornly.

"Well, Your Ladyship, the client I was talking
about is only a slightly exaggerated version of
something I've seen a million times. He . . . how
shall I put this? . . . he doesn't do it for pleasure,

so much, as for relief. You know what I mean, don't you?"

"Mmm," she said, sipping coffee thoughtfully. "I believe I do."

"I sure do," Mary said. "We spend hours here learning how to be the erotic equivalent of a gourmet treat—and then half the time the darlings fall on us like we were fast-food burgers, never mind the garnishes, just keep it coming, chomp chomp."

"Take your complaints to God," Phillip said. "God knows we have. I know it's unflattering when someone figuratively wolfs down the meal you slaved over, but it's a simple matter of hydraulic pressure. We've been cursed with a more desperate hunger than you ladies: give us not scorn but sympathy. For our part, we find it maddening the way you can take it or leave it alone: it gives you an advantage we can barely tolerate. We envy your lesser itch."

"Whereas we," Mary said, "find it maddening the way *your* itch can get so decisively and conclusively scratched. Once you get us going, it's hard to stop us again; no gal is ever quite as eager to as when she just has—and just about then, you poop out on us, every damn one of you. Well, except the teenagers, sometimes."

"Not us," Phillip said, "just our erections. That doesn't necessarily end the party."

"Eight times out of ten it damned well does! Oh, you're a professional, Phillip, and you'd be a nice guy even if you weren't—but with most men, once they can't cut the mustard, they lose interest in even licking the jar. Tell me I'm wrong."

"I recline to answer, on the ground," he said. "Shall we discuss the way women—other than those in this company, of course—make a habit of waving food under the noses of starving men, just to see how high they can drive the price? Or shall we just agree that human behavior varies: that cruel fate gave the lesser need to those with the greater capacity to enjoy, and we all simply have to live with it? Some men are cursed or blessed with such a huge hunger that they will always be gourmands rather than gourmets, and some women are blessed and cursed with such a mild one that they can nibble haute cuisine all day. It makes it a bit difficult for us to get along, but it is possible—and if it can't be done in this House, I for one am going to enter a monastery."

"Can I be the proverbial Nun of Your Lip?" Mary asked.

"I'll have a stable of 'em," he said. "It's habit-farming."

She tried to put her cigarette out in his Irish coffee, but he had laced it so liberally with 12-year-old Jameson's that she almost burned her knuckles. Me, I figure she had it coming.

"I'm not sure I know the difference between a gourmet and that other you mentioned," I said while they glared affectionately at one another.

"A gourmand," Phillip said, pointedly not taking his eyes from Mary's, "doesn't care so much what's on the plate as long as there's plenty of it."

Mary is probably the only 195-pound woman I've ever met who is not even remotely self-conscious about it. Perhaps with good reason—she currently works the Security Room, monitoring the countless studio bugs for sounds of trouble, but before my time she was one of Lady Sally's most popular and sought-after artists. "Yeah," she said, meeting Phillip's gaze tranquilly, "you know: a healthy, vital person. Someone who takes life in big bites. Whereas your gourmet is frequently something of an effete wimp." He grinned at her, they're good friends, licensed to insult each other.

"Maybe so," I said. "But I still think that guy I was talking about is sad. Maybe he was taking big bites—but he didn't seem to *enjoy* them that much. He went twice in no time, like it was a chore to be finished—and then insisted on leaving as soon as the edge was off, even though he clearly still had rounds in the chamber! And he hasn't spent more than half an hour total with anyone he's picked so far. I can't shake the feeling that if somebody could just get him to stick around for a third or fourth time some night, and do it for fun instead of for relief from need, they'd both have a wonderful time. Why do men want to leave right afterward so often? When they could be cuddling, and being held?"

"Sometimes because the intensity of the relief, the depth of their gratitude, makes them feel small or out of control," Phillip said. "Sometimes because in their secret miseducated hearts they believe they've done something disgusting to you, and are glad of it, and so are ashamed. And sometimes just because they were *doing* something when the dread compulsion came over them, and now they want to get back to whatever it was."

I stared at him, surprised and oddly touched. One of the best things about my profession is that occasionally I get to hear men speak with total honesty; it is always fascinating and disturbing.

"And sometimes," Lady Sally said, "because the darlings can find us and our appetites just a little intimidating. There they are, out of gas, and we're just starting to reach operating temperature. They fear cuddling might restart something they can't finish. In all such cases," she added pointedly, "it implies that one hasn't done one's job as well as one should have."

I felt myself flush.

She went on, carefully not to me. "If a male client does not want to cuddle after, that does not mean that there is a 'problem with men.' It does suggest that there is some deficiency in his artist's technique, that *he or she* has a problem with men. Any time a client achieves release but not joy, he's been shortchanged. Even if he leaves my House content. The proper spirit is not to resent his nature but to come to terms with it, learn how to make him *want* to stick around for a more leisurely loving—and if you fail, resolve to do better next time." Now she did speak to me: "Please don't interpret this as criticism, Sherry dear; I've had them tuck it away and bolt for the exit on me once or twice myself. But don't waste time blaming the bull if you can't make it moo: try and puzzle out what it wants. Much more productive approach."

I sighed. "You're right, Your Ladyship. But I can't help feeling it'd be much less trouble to fix men than fix me. And I really did try and persuade Colt to stay. Oh well, I've got over two weeks before he gets back to me to figure something out. An artistic challenge."

"Why wait?" Mary asked.

"He seems to like variety."

"One of those, is he?" Lady Sally asked. "Sampling all the bottles?" I nodded.

"So offer him variety," Mary said practically. "Grab him firmly by the handle and lead him off to the Bower."

"Huh. Do you think he'd go for it?"

"How many of the men who've been taken to the Bower ever left unhappy?"

She had a point.

"That is, in large part," Lady Sally pointed out, "because we do not bring them in there unless we're fairly sure they'll like it, Mary."

She had a point too.

Lady Sally's House is designed to accommodate

a broad range of tastes, some of them mutually incompatible. The majority of clients are happy in the Parlor, which is essentially an ongoing, formal-but-relaxed party for men and women, artists and clients. Within certain broad limits, decorum is required there: dress is formal for artists, optional for clients; no skin is bared or fondled, and although the conversation sometimes passes beyond "risqué" to "raunchy," only Lady Sally can use four-letter words.

But some clients, as I said earlier, prefer that all the members of the opposite sex they will see tonight will be artists. And others do not care to see members of the opposite sex at all. For them there are men-only and women-only Lounges, like smaller versions of the Parlor, each with its own private entrance and spiral staircase. (Gay or Lesbian clients are expected to use discretion in cruising other clients, and virtually always do.)

And I've spoken of clients who for one reason or another require utter discretion: public figures, preachers, and so on. For them there is a whole section of the building, the Discreet Wing, so laid out that they can enter, be entertained, and leave without ever seeing more than a single, professional human being.

But at the opposite end of the spectrum, for those who can handle it, is the Bower.

It is located in the heart of the first floor, can be entered from any of the Lounges. All three entrances lead to lockers and a warm clean unisex shower with plenty of fluffy towels (one year Lady Sally's clean-towel bill reached five figures), from which you enter the Bower proper.

It appears to be a fairly large rock grotto, a natural cavern with a hot spring chuckling in one corner—but the "rock" beneath your feet and that of the walls is actually some marvelous stuff that is soft and yielding and resilient and warm to the bare skin. I don't know what it's made of, but if you pour a cup of water on it, the spot will be dry within a minute, and a cigarette won't burn it. The floor is contoured, providing an abundance of nooks and supports and cuddling-places. The cavern is softly and indirectly lit, with small pools of shadow here and there, but none big enough for two people. There is a dance-studio-sized mirror near the pool. Elsewhere a versatile sling dangles from stalactites, and assorted small appliances lie about the room. The air is pleasantly warm and fresh, and there is a very slight echo.

In the Bower, anything consensual and sanitary goes.

A married couple may go in there together, make love all night in the presence of dozens of strangers, and go home without ever having physically touched or been touched by any of them. Or a husband may watch while his wife takes on a hockey team. (As frequently, a wife will watch while her husband valiantly and foolishly tries to take on several women. But it's over sooner.) Or a mother and daughter may share the same artist as a graduation present. (That happened once, but it was Mom's graduation. Darling daughter!) Or a dozen or so enterprising souls may collaborate to try and invent a new geometrical shape. One is equally welcome to simply watch all night, masturbating or not as suits one—but one will have to be prepared to politely decline a lot of offers.

The rules are:

1) Take "No" for an answer; take "Stop" for an order.
2) Don't pee in the pool.
3) If what you're doing is making someone else unhappy, you must both leave, and come back when you've worked it out. And:
4) Never discuss or describe anything that takes place in the Bower outside the Bower. (Except with other participants, when you're sure you won't be overheard.)

I find the Bower exhausting as a steady diet, myself—too distracting—but it has its charm, and many clients and artists swear by it.

It sounded like it might just be the ticket for Colt, now that Mary suggested it. If you've got a guy who treats sex like fast-food, take him back into McDonald's kitchen, and maybe by the third helping or so he'll be ready to appreciate a delicate curry.

But did he, like so many men, suffer from modesty? Would he be comfortable naked with strangers, of both sexes, in a sexual context? He hadn't been naked with *me*, in private, that first time. Too busy. But he *had* undressed us both for the rematch, and he had not seemed body-shy, and thinking back on it, I was sure he had no reason to be. If anything, he'd been built a little thicker than average. (Okay, there are other parts of their bodies that men can be self-conscious about—but that's the one that counts.) He certainly didn't seem the kind of man who would have any problem with stage fright—that night in my studio, I didn't think he'd have much cared if there'd been a herd of cops present, or troop of Girl Scouts, or a Martian.

"It might do the trick, Mary," I said. "Thanks."

"Don't be disappointed if it doesn't work out, darling," Lady Sally said. "All I've seen of this Colt chap was the usual preliminary interview when he became a member, and he did seem rather an urgent sort. Some men are simply not epicures by nature. As the poet tells us: once a king, always a king—but once a night is often sufficient. Still, it can't hurt to try the experiment. Good luck." And she emptied her mug and went off to bed, humming to herself.

I fell asleep planning my good deed.

But I didn't get to do it the next night. He had

not yet arrived by late evening, when a new client took on about three more drinks than was good for her, and I was deputized to go along in the cab and make sure she got up to her apartment all right. (All part of the service—as long as you don't let it happen too often. In this case, the lady had reason.) I didn't bother to phone for a cab, there are always a few trolling round outside the door, and sure enough, one pulled up just as I got the semiconscious client outside.

Colt got out of it, nodded hello. I started to ask him would he mind waiting until I got back, I had a surprise for him—but he tipped his hat and was past me and in the House before I could get word out.

I shrugged, promised myself that I was going to take the edge off that appetite the very next night, and got the client into the cab.

"Hi, Sherry," the driver said. "You're looking great tonight."

"Thanks, Ben." I've known Ben since my street days, before I came to Lady Sally's House. "We're going to Prospect Park South, okay? How're you making it?"

"Not as well as you are. Gee, I'm glad you got in with the Lady. I used to worry about you." He pulled away from the curb.

"You're sweet. Yeah, I got lucky."

"Damn right. Hey. Tell me something?"

My charge was snoring blissfully. "If I can."

"Well . . . uh . . . you know that guy I just dropped off?"

"Yes."

"Well, does he . . . I mean . . . what I'm gettin' at—aw, hell, you know what I mean."

"No, I don't."

"Well, look, does he actually *do* . . . anything?"

I giggled. "I don't think it would be violating Lady Sally's rules to say that he . . . does pretty much what most clients do. Males, anyway. Why?"

He shook his head in wonder. "The guy ain't human."

Again I giggled. "Oh, I guarantee he's human."

"No, you don't understand: this mook is a legend! All the hacks in Brooklyn are startin' to talk about him, he's like a force o' nature."

"What are you talking about?"

"You know where I picked him up tonight? Madame Sasha's."

"Huh!" Sasha's is about as good a brothel as you're going to find in Brooklyn, outside of Lady Sally's House. I wouldn't work there.

"Wait, I ain't started yet: Short Black took him there, not an hour ago, and where did Short pick him up? The Harem." A distinct cut below Sasha's dump. "And Laughing John took him to the Harem from Olga's crib."

"Good God—" I wouldn't steer an enemy to Olga's.

"Now, Aunt Betty drove him to Olga's: would you like to know where he called Betty from? The lobby of The Hard Corps."

By now we were down to a massage parlor

so sleazy that most junkies wouldn't go there to cop. "Jesus Christ, he must have got his tax return or something! Flattering that he saved us for last, at least. Oh, this is great—I've got to hurry and get back, this is *just* the mood I've been wanting to catch him in—"

"You still don't get it," Ben said. "There's no hurry at all. This mood is not going to pass."

"Huh?"

"He does this every night. He's been doing this every night for goin' on two weeks."

"Come *on!* Get serious."

"My right hand to God. And he don't save you guys for last, either. He does go home, after your place . . . but he usually has a couple o' outcall girls sent over. They stay an hour or two."

"And after that?"

"As far as we can figure out, from three A.M. to a little after suppertime the guy is totally celibate."

There was a short silence.

"Of course, he may spend the whole time jerking off, what the hell do I know?"

I stared at the back of his head. "You're not kidding."

"Look, I know about the Lady's rules, but you and I go back a long way. Would you talk to the guy for me? If it's like, a pill, I'd go as high as a grand or two for a weekend's worth."

I frowned. "Can this thing go any faster?"

"No."

It had been a foolish question; Ben never

drove slower than was humanly possible. But Colt would be done and gone in another twenty minutes. Or less . . .

"Look, Ben: do me this and I'll talk to the guy for you, and tell you whatever he says I can, okay? Get on the horn, get the nearest hack to meet us and take me back to Sally's—then you get this lady home for me, see her upstairs? She got some bad news today."

"For you, no problem. I owe you." He made the call, connected with someone I didn't know named Angel.

"Thanks, Ben!"

"Look . . . uh . . . if it *ain't* a pill . . . I mean, if it ain't like something he could share . . . would you ask him—" He hesitated, looking for the right words. What do you ask a legend? "Would you . . . well, would you just ask him what's it's like?" His voice was wistful.

"I promise."

CHAPTER 5

REVOLVER

I spent the ride back to the House in Angel's battered cab trying to rearrange my perceptions of Colt. And trying not to feel like a jerk. How could I have read the signs so wrong? What fantastic irony, that I had been in the presence of legend, and had thought he needed loosening up. Mary was going to howl when I told her. . . .

I *was* going to tell her, wasn't I?

I was *not* particularly worried that Colt might be bringing unwanted microbes into Lady Sally's ecosystem, despite the fact that he had been spending time in some very unsavory places— for two reasons. First, even the sleaziest House is much more concerned with hygiene than the general public imagines, for reasons which ought to be perfectly obvious. Second, Lady Sally is even more fanatic about prophylaxis than most madams. This was before AIDS, but the lady had *coined* the term "safe sex," years, maybe even decades, before the general public knew herpes or chlamydia existed: it was one of the cornerstones of her reputation. (As an aside, the safest commercial sex you'll find outside of Lady Sally's House is escort services: being semilegitimate, above-ground businesses, they're concerned with things like lawsuits. It's independent, street girls and boys you have to watch out for—though even they are statistically not much riskier than, say, the customers at singles bars.) Clients could either conform to simple House guidelines regarding inspection, cleaning and bagging of firearms, or leave a small blood sample on every single visit with the House physician, Doctor Kate—or take their business elsewhere. Colt had borne upon him—at least at the start of our first session—the little saline-soluble rubber stamp that said, in an imitation of Bogart's handwriting in *Casablanca,* "OK Prick." (Kate has one for female clients that reads "OK Trick"; and, of course, she gets blood samples from each of us artists—including herself—every working day.) We've rarely had a problem; never a serious one.

No, it was not Colt's physical health that worried me. Well, yes it was, in a sense: it seemed to me there was a distinct chance that he might kill himself if he kept up the pace he had set. But I was equally concerned with his mental health.

Forget for the moment about the kind of compulsion it must take to make a man seek out half a dozen women a night, night after night. Forget about the psychic conflict it must take to power that kind of relentless engine. The more pressing psychological question was, *what kind of a moron would go to all those different places for so long?*

At Lady Sally's House, he could have *had* six women a night, for the same flat-rate membership fee that Lady Sally had assigned him—by a formula known only to her—on his preliminary interview.

I had never heard of Sally raising anyone's dues, only lowering them in rare hardship cases (although not infrequently a client would voluntarily raise them, as his or her income improved). At worst, perhaps, she might have doubled Colt's fee. Instead, he had opted for a system which required enormous exertion and time, increased his risk of infection, hemorrhaged money needlessly . . . and provided him with one or at most two quality experiences a night. Which he treated like fast food.

Sad? This guy was *tragic*.

If there is anything a woman will find more sexually attractive than a tragic figure, it is a man on the verge of becoming a legend. If what the tragic man is legendary *for* is his virility, and he seems to have money to burn . . .

Did I *have* to tell anybody back at the House? Right away?

❖   ❖   ❖

Oh, hell, of course I did.

I was not particularly in the market for a man. God knew my sexual needs were well taken care of, and at Lady Sally's House you could always find someone to sleep with or hug or cry to or argue with or get your back scratched: we all took care of each other's emotional needs pretty well. I was better off financially than many of my clients, with free rent and board, modest straight salary, and frequent tips—and *most* uncharacteristically for my profession, I got to keep every dime I earned, banking it for college. (I planned to be a Psych major. But I found later that I could get at what interested me better if I switched to History.) Aside from sexual, emotional, and financial needs, the only other reason you need a man around is to put out the garbage and keep the TV working right, and I had Robin the houseboy for that. There was no reason to get possessive with this sad little superman.

Of course, just because I didn't especially want to own him didn't mean I couldn't drive him around the block a few times before returning him to the motorpool. I would share this stunning secret with my sister artists . . . just as soon as I had deployed myself at the head of the line.

"You're back quick," the receptionist said. "Say, what's with this fella Colt?"

For once a pun made me giggle. The significance of the House name he'd chosen had just struck me. Not the horse. The revolver. The six-shooter . . .

"I'm not exactly sure yet—" No lie! "—why?"

"Big Mary actually came down from the Snoop Room. In a housecoat with stockings and heels underneath. She said to tell you she'd be waiting for you with him in the Bower. She said not to hurry, she'd handle the preliminaries, and you'd know what that meant. She dragged him off like a lamb to the slaughter. He kept blinking. Should I have a stretcher waiting, or what?"

I was giggling even harder now. Like a lamb to the slaughter! Mary was the little lamb. No good deed goes unpunished, indeed. "Yes, but there's some question who'll be on it." I gave her my cab vouchers and went on in through the Parlor to the lockers. I eeled out of my clothes, pranced under the shower spray, and entered the Bower. You wait in the doorway, for your eyes to adjust to the soft light, and for people to get a good look at you. I didn't bother.

I saw almost at once that I was far from the head of the line.

And Mary wasn't on it anymore. She was asleep or unconscious over by the pool, head pillowed on her bunched up housecoat, a broad smile on her lips. She looked like something Rubens might have done for a wealthy private collector.

Colt had the total attention of the room.

Currently at bat was a client I knew socially, an accountant named Donna. An artist named

Rose was hovering nearby, sort of assisting in a supervisory capacity; she was clearly on deck. Two other clients, a sweet old gay named Uncle Joanie and a diplomat named Svetlana, were trying to jockey for position without being crude about it. Donna's husband Keith, a school teacher if I remembered right, was staring from the sidelines with an expression of awe and wonder. He was being absently worked on by Mei-Ling, but neither of them was putting a lot of attention on it. She usually avoids the ones that are built thick, but she looked like she was talking herself into it.

"Gum, gum, gum, gum," Donna kept saying loudly.

I caught Mei-Ling's eyes and mouthed, "Gum, gum?"

"Well," she whispered back, "she kept saying 'No, no,' but you know Bower rules. There was some question of whether she meant it or not, so Keith asked her to say something else and that's what she came up with."

"Oh."

The most fascinating thing—I think any of us in the room would have agreed—was the expression on Colt's face. Assuming that anyone else in the room was paying attention to his face.

Once I was in a position to observe a man suffering from poison ivy of the penis. If you think that's a funny affliction, may you get it someday. When he first realized and diagnosed his problem, he acquired a look of horror, then disbelief, and while he struggled with it, his face changed to profound dismay. Followed by dogged, hopeless determination *not to scratch*. A fascinating series of expressions, and perhaps one could be forgiven for finding them comic. I hope so, for I did. But soon he yielded to relentless compulsion and scratched *once*—and within moments, a new expression washed over his face. The one that made it stop being funny, the one that Colt wore now.

The mindless, despairing animal awareness that, now that he had started, he was inexorably committed to keep doing this thing that brought him no relief until his heart exploded.

Which looked like it might take months. If he hadn't been in especially good shape a month ago he certainly was now, after weeks of training: wind good, color good, rhythm steady, eyes clear, an athlete in the peak of condition.

He just wasn't having any fun. There was nothing behind those clear eyes, nothing human, only the glowing embers of the primeval fire that powered those remorseless hips. The sound effects were like that scene in *Rocky* where Stallone is breaking ribs on sides of beef; they rang like pistol shots in the echo of the Bower.

Donna appeared to have been climaxing steadily for some time, but as it became clear that he was climaxing himself, she tucked her head and clutched like a drowner and joined him with a long high deafening final "G—U—M!" There was mild applause. Nearly at once he pulled

away, raised up on his knees—flag still flying—
and reached for Rose.

"Next," he said dully.

"Jesus," Mei-Ling breathed.

Donna was apparently comatose, like Mary,
but I noticed that unlike Mary she was not
smiling in her sleep. And Rose, although she
did not move away, was clearly going through
with this not so much because she was attracted
anymore, as because she knew she was in the
presence of history.

So many men seem to have the idea that what
women secretly want most of all (no matter what
we say or even believe ourselves) is a powerful
and remorseless engine of flesh impersonally
hammering away at us without pause for hours
at a time. They become upset with themselves
if they cannot deliver this silly commodity. I don't
mean that, on the one occasion in my life when
it actually happened to me, it was an *unpleasant* experience, exactly. (Until I tried to get up
and walk the next day.) It's just that maybe once
in a lifetime is plenty. And I've never seen that
guy since, don't much care if I do.

I mean, you could buy a machine to do that.
They exist. And women don't buy them. Neither
do gay men.

Still, it was an impressive spectacle to witness.
Mary had clearly enjoyed herself.

"Maybe I should—" Keith murmured hesitantly.

"Donna looks comfortable," Mei-Ling pointed
out.

"Yes, she does," he agreed, and stayed where he was.

Rose had, with a professional's pride, positioned herself a little more effectively for the audience. She made a small sound of disbelief as the hammer struck for the first time, then settled down to the challenge. The dance resumed—

I reached a decision.

I touched Mei-Ling's shoulder. "Go get the Lady," I whispered. "Tell her I need her."

She looked stubborn. "Why don't you get her?" she whispered back.

"Because there's a client in pain here, and he's my responsibility, damn it! It's a long story, Mei, will you do it for me?"

She stared at me. "He's in pain?"

"Look at his face."

She leaned slightly so that she could. "But they always look like they're in pain."

"Trust me, okay? I know about this guy."

Mei-Ling's a decent sort. "Okay, Sherry."

"Thanks, munchkin," I took over Keith from her without missing a beat; he failed to notice. "Tell the Lady to hurry."

"Okay . . . but it doesn't look to me like there's any hurry."

"And Mei—don't tell anybody out there about this, okay?"

Now she looked offended. "When have I ever discussed the Bower outside the Bower? Or gossiped to a client about a client?"

"I know, I know . . . but don't even hint, okay?"

❖　　❖　　❖

But Lady Sally came in the entrance before Mei-Ling had straightened up.

(Mary was, for once, not upstairs in the Snoop Room monitoring the House for trouble, and though she had doubtless arranged a relief before abandoning her post, the Bower was the only part of Lady Sally's House that was not bugged. You tell *me* how the Lady knew she was needed.)

I handed Keith back to Mei-Ling and went to her; by the time I reached her she seemed to have taken in the situation. "You seem to have created a monster, dear girl."

"Not *me*, Milady! I just got here. I was coming to get you."

"Two down, four to go, eh? Keith will have to carry Donna home. Not the first time, but there's usually a dozen men involved. Gad, I haven't seen that expression on Mary's face since . . . well, perhaps she'll tell you about it sometime. The man must be a phenomenon." Just then Rose hit E^b above high C.

"You don't know the half of it." I hastily explained what I had learned from Ben. "Mary brought him up here while I was away, to prime him for me, and . . . well, you see what happened."

"Good Christ," she exploded, "do you mean to tell me that we took an addict, desperately struggling to control a massive habit, and—"

Rose reached F, a clear tone with a perfect vibrato.

"—and dropped him into a large bag of the stuff, yes, Lady."

"Saints add preservatives to us! We must fix this at once, Sherry—he could bloody kill himself. Look at his face!"

The friend I spoke of with poison ivy: some of us who loved him held him down and tied his hands behind him for a day. He told us afterward that if we had not, he might have ripped it out by the root. He said the only other thing restraining him had been the conviction that if he did, it would *keep on itching*, and there would be nowhere to scratch. . . .

Lady Sally nudged me. "Let's clear the room as quietly and discreetly as we can, shall we? If anyone gives you an argument, tell them it is my order. I'll not have a man's affliction gawked at in my House. Even one as spectacular as that."

We both went about the Bower, whispering in people's ears. Mei-Ling already had Keith ready to travel. In a short time the grotto held only the two of us, Rose, Colt, and the sleeping Mary, whose weight could not be shifted without summoning extra help anyway, and the doors were locked.

Rose was just reaching her third crescendo. Colt, it seemed, had beaten her to it by a full minute, but had not let it slow him down. When she finally went limp, he paused for a moment, his weight suspended on his arms, his breathing fast but steady, eyes shut. Then he sighed slightly and disengaged, looked vaguely around.

"Get her to the other side of the room, Sherry," Lady Sally rapped out.

I obeyed, taking Rose by both ankles; she made no protest, and stayed where I left her, blinking at the ceiling.

Colt focussed on Lady Sally's voice, got to his feet and approached her. His stride was catlike and bouncy. He glistened with sweat and other things. His chest rose and fell in great surges. He seemed to sense that there would be some preliminary difficulty in target-acquisition: he growled deep in his throat, and his fingers flexed menacingly. He was a stud bull in heat, out of control, and Lady Sally was an old woman, smaller and lighter than Mei-Ling, unarmed—

—who stood up on tiptoe and smacked him right across the chops.

It was a ladylike slap, not a punch, but it spun his head around like a roundhouse right. He stood for a moment, blinking, as the report echoed in the Bower.

"Don't point that thing at *me*, young man," she said clearly.

He burst into tears.

And wilted, in all senses of the word. Lady Sally moved in and held him while he cried, the way a compassionate teacher might hug a crying child, making consoling sounds. As she was patting the back of his head, she waved me over and into the hug. Between us we got him seated, and rocked and stroked and soothed him. And when his breathing had returned to normal, and we had let him go, and there had been silence for long enough that he was sure no one else was going to break it, he sighed and explained.

He used a lot of words I don't know. And he rambled quite a bit; he was not a socially sophisticated man, he didn't know how to talk about himself very well. This is the gist:

He was a neurophysiologist with a background in genetics. His research specialty was nerve regeneration, and why human nerves almost never regenerate. There are many different highly specialized kinds of nerve tissue. Male sexual nerve tissue is one of the most distinctly different kinds, useful to study. (This much is obvious even to a layman like me: how many other human nerves are designed to fire so emphatically and then become useless for an extended period? Or, for that matter, to lie dormant for the first dozen years of life? And because a local hospital had recently found it profitable to cut a big slice of . . . that is, to aggressively enter the sex-change market, Colt found himself with access to great quantities of the stuff, as fresh as he wanted it, at reasonable cost.

Still, his field was arcane, his overhead high and his grant proposals distasteful to most funding agencies; he might never have gotten anywhere at all if he had not hit the lottery for half a million tax-free dollars.

The resulting fateful combination of quirky field of study and unreasonably high funding produced a breakthrough.

"In every cell," he told us, "there is a set of programming instructions that says, in effect, 'make copies of yourself, until the following environmental conditions are achieved, and then stop.' If something deletes or modifies that last clause, 'and then stop,' you get a cancer. If something modifies the second clause, the conditions under which to stop growing . . . well, you might get a giant, or a dwarf, or an Elephant Man.

"Or, if you did it under controlled conditions, and got your reprogramming instructions just right, you might, you just might . . . be able to regenerate a severed spinal column. Or give sight to a blind person. Well, I found a way to modify that clause. But of course, it wasn't those kinds of tissue I was working with."

He was a shy bachelor, the kind whose low sexual self-esteem had become self-reinforcing. Even as a teenager in the throes of first passion, he had never been capable of a second engagement until at least the next morning, and several lovers had taken the trouble to tell him how unusual this supposedly was. (It is not.)

So when he stood in his laboratory one day and gazed upon enough male orgasmic nerve matter for six men, which he had coaxed to grow from the abandoned luggage of a single former gentleman, "—the first thing that occurred to me

was how little of it there was, how little such
stuff masses in relation to its importance. It came
to me that this represented the equipment of a
superman, and that it was small enough to tuck
away even in . . . well, it just seemed like the
natural next step to see if my gene-altering agent
worked on tissue *in situ* as well as it did in the
Petri dish, so to speak. By injecting a compar-
able dosage into myself. There being no likeli-
hood of other volunteers. To calibrate the effect,
I cut the strength by half, figuring I'd settle for
the strength of three."

But it turned out the stuff worked twice as
well on fresh tissue, living naturally in a live body
rather than a culture medium, more receptive
to the molecular command, "Copy yourself." His
thick organ was now snugly packed with the
freshly grown penile nerve bundles of an entire
basketball team plus their coach.

For all his talent (or luck), Colt was a rather
unimaginative man; it took him a surprising
length of time to get it through his head that
this represented a disaster.

"Why, you perfect chump!" Lady Sally said.

"I can't argue," he said miserably. "Horniness,
you see, is in large part a function of those
nerves wanting to fire. Some of that is in
response to hydraulic pressure in the seminal
vesicles, and some to simple intellectual yearning, but an equally large part is the fact that each
of those nerve clusters just wants to fire at regular intervals. So now I have to go through at least

half a dozen women a night just so I won't be too horny to keep my mind on my work next day. And I *still* have to do a lot of labwork one-handed. Thank God I work alone."

I noticed for the first time how highly developed his right bicep was, compared to the left. Even more so than all men, I mean.

"Good God," the Lady breathed. "You didn't *solve* the male dilemma: you *sextupled* it."

"Do you want to know the worst?" he cried. "I didn't even solve the problem I originally set out to! I have a chemical compound which will encourage nerve tissue to duplicate itself—but *only male sexual nerve.* It doesn't work on any other type, and I can't seem to learn why not. My lifework is useless. Who but a fool would let me use it on him?"

"Jeez, I don't know," I said. "There are a whole lot of fools."

He nodded. "That's why I can't publish."

"But there are unfortunates for whom your elixir would be a godsend—" Lady Sally began.

"But at what social cost?" He shook his head. "There's always a chance that someday I may succeed in adapting my compound for other kinds of tissue; that's why I haven't cut my throat yet. But until then I dare not publish." He stopped, shook his head again, more violently. "But I'm forgetting. The secret is out now, isn't it?"

There was so much pain on his face that I searched for something to distract him. "Why six

different girls a night?" I asked. "I mean why
six different *places?* Why sextuple the inconvenience and expense?"

He hung his head. "Because I didn't want anyone to know. Because I was afraid if I didn't
keep myself under rigid control, if I let myself
go, I might . . . do what I just did." He swallowed. "Because I was half afraid I might kill
some poor girl. Because I was ashamed. Embarrassed. Didn't want to be gawked at and pointed
to and chuckled over." He swallowed again. "The
way I'm going to be now."

"Not if I can help it," Lady Sally said stoutly.

He stared up at her. "Right. Thanks."

"See here, young man," she said, "are you
enjoying your life?"

He groped for words. "Are you insane? Haven't
you heard me? Not *only* am I infuriated by
a professional challenge that will not yield to
anything in my arsenal, and exhausted from
chasing this damned thing around Brooklyn in
search of ten minutes' peace, and shamed by
my inability to control myself, and tormented
by a chafing problem you wouldn't believe,"
his voice had risen in volume and pitch; he was
roaring now: "on top of everything else I'm
hemorrhaging money so fast the God damned
lottery money is going to be gone soon!"

Try the math yourself. Six women a night,
average expenditure, say, eighty-five dollars a
piece, in Carter-era dollars. (Outcall girls come
high by the hour, bringing up the average.) Plus

cabfare and Intensive Care Lotion: call it fifty
bucks a night additional. Times seven. Times
fifty-two. An annual budget of just over two
hundred and seven grand—just for sex. Assume
he'd spent only half of his winnings on his
research. Even if he held living expenses to a
bare minimum, and spent nothing further on
his work, he was going to be broke in about
a year.

Or dead of heart failure. Of one kind or
another.

"Then it seems to me, dear boy," Lady Sally
said cheerfully, "that it is time for a change,
wouldn't you agree?"

He drew in a deep breath—and I had to
admire him. Instead of biting her head off, he
held that breath a long time, and when it let it
out he said only, "Madam, I am open to suggestions."

She drew herself up formally—difficult to do
while seated, but no challenge for Lady Sally—
and said, "You do well to address me by my title,
sir. For I propose to offer you a shot at a part-
time job."

"But it's not safe, I tell you," he cried. "You
just *saw* that: I nearly assaulted you! I just can't
control this thing!"

"Look at it," she rapped.

He did so. It had gone to about half-mast
when Lady Sally had slapped him, but it was
back to its former glory again now.

"You're in the presence of two highly trained courtesans," she said. "Are you raping either of us at the moment? Have you ever thus far raped *anyone?*"

"No, not yet, but—"

"Did you cripple anyone with that tonight? Darling, popular myth to the contrary, it is not possible to kill a woman with a penis alone. Not even an implacable one. Well, I suppose in theory one could starve, but—"

"Still—" Colt began.

"What you've got there is *not* the gold-mine some teenaged boys would think it was, darling. A piston can do what you do, longer on less fuel. That's not why I'm willing to take you on: I am not running a circus. It is because of the ethical behavior you seem to have exhibited throughout your folly. It suggests to me that you care about people—a quality I find much more impressive in a potential employee than breaking-strength."

He averted his eyes.

She reached out a graceful, lightly wrinkled hand and touched his cheek. "Son, listen to me. *Every* man finds it difficult, often impossible, to control *one* of those things. Ask a prison guard what it's like to try and control half a dozen. I think you've done a remarkable job of controlling yours, all things considered."

He began to cry softly.

"Until we, for the proverbial best of reasons, goaded you into letting go," Lady Sally went on.

"That was my fault," I put in. "I'm sorry, Colt—honest to God, I just thought—"

"It was a joint decision," she corrected, "under my direct supervision." She turned back to Colt. "This leaves me obligated to you, and I would like to make amends, if I can." He dabbed at his eyes, and looked up at her redly. "The choice is entirely yours, but if it influences your decision in any way, I have seen you in action, and I believe you to be trainable: given time, and willingness to study on your part, I think I could make an artist out of you. If we have to use up an artist or two every day making you safe to turn loose on the customers . . . well, we're still ahead of the game mathematically, and I'm sure there'd be no shortage of volunteers."

He studied his hands, I think, and frowned. "But I don't want this secret to become common knowledge—"

"So we simply keep you out of the Bower." He stared at her.

"Listen to me, boy. There are perhaps half a dozen houses in this country that have a performer of your caliber on staff, no puns intended, freaks of nature rather than augmented specimens like yourself, and they are reasonably famous—in a small, discreet circle. If a female client comes here and finds an artist who is still capable after two or three rounds, she's not going to find it all that astonishing—it's more or less what she was expecting from a place with a reputation like mine. She'll be pleased, certainly, she'll tell her best girlfriend ... but she won't drop a line to *Scientific American*, or to whatever professional journal you neuromancers use. And she doesn't have to know that after she goes home, you're going to see two or three more clients. You'd have to get used to popularity— but not, I think, wide notoriety."

"But—"

"All my artists are on straight salary plus tips." She named the apprentice-scale and beginning artist's salaries, and his eyes widened. "Plus room and board on the third floor, plus medical and pension benefits; it's all in the contract."

"Lady Sally actually has us on contract," I agreed. "Perhaps the only actual prostitution contract in the world, quite explicit and of course quite unenforceable in any court. Except the court of opinion of the rest of us artists. There have been remarkably few contract disputes."

"Three shifts a day; you work each one twice a week in any order that you can coordinate with Personnel; two months vacation with pay, to be arranged the same way. If you want or need to work extra shifts, we can discuss it. I think I should have to insist that my resident physician monitor your health carefully on a daily basis. Your free time is your own, barring the occasional refresher course or seminar, and if you want to spend it doing experiments I suppose we could find a corner of this drafty old barn to accommodate you: I'll tolerate anything that doesn't have a tendency to explode. As to the work itself: you will never be required to do anything you find objectionable, and you keep any tips. Have I left anything out? Well, lots of things, but those are the basics. Is the idea worth discussing?"

"Say 'yes'," I suggested. "You're being offered the opportunity of a lifetime."

He hesitated for a long time, studying her face and mine.

"Do you really think I'm trainable?" he asked shyly.

"You can keep on plugging away until you get it," she pointed out, and a shared three-way belly laugh is a very nice way to join any company, isn't it?

BOOK THREE

THE PARANOID

CHAPTER 6
FOR THE ASKING

It's amazing how many of the remarkable stories that could be told about Lady Sally's House have to do with secrets.

Oh, any bordello hears secrets, by definition: if our culture were not so sick that natural healthy urges are deadly secrets, there would be little need for bordellos. Father Newman suggested once, only half kidding, that we artists—that all prostitutes—function rather like priests for people who feel more natural confessing their sins while naked. (He also pointed out the conveniences of doing so while the sins are still fresh in one's mind: one of the several reasons the good Father likes to hang out in Lady Sally's Parlor himself.) Like any brothel, Lady Sally's House has probably triggered more confessions than St. Patrick's Cathedral.

Two things distinguish us from St. Pat's: the different nature of the absolution we offer, and the fact that every single prayer voiced in Lady Sally's House can be *proven* to have been heard on high, by an All-Hearing Ear. The ear, that is, of Mary, who sits in the Snoop Room on the third floor monitoring the dozens of bugs, for the protection of artists and clients alike. (Do you have any idea how much thirty seconds can mean to a paramedic in a heart case?) Her rig has a fast-scan mode that can deliver her a slice of every conversation in the House within five seconds: to me it's just gabble at that speed, but Mary swears she can follow everything at once, and she's never lost a bet.

As is true at St. Pat's—and not, I think, true of any brothel but ours—no secret ever leaves the House. One of the most inflexible House rules is that we may gossip about clients only with fellow artists, privately. Even then we're not supposed to identify them by even House name. Mary talks to the rest of us about what she hears only when she thinks it's needful.

What seems to make Lady Sally's House *unique* is that we get secrets so weird that half the time there's no point in gossiping, because no one would believe you. Like the werebeagle, and the talking dog, and Colt the Six-Shooting Stud, and the woman client who had three . . . well, you get the idea. A place as special as Sally's just naturally tends to draw bizarre and wonderful people. Luckily, the

Lady's magic is white magic: the oddballs she attracts are almost invariably benign. (The rest get what she calls "an invitation to the world.")

Occasionally, though, the secret can be something so downright creepy that you don't *want* to gossip about it.

Hell, I've already told you Lady Sally's deepest darkest secret, something you'd have to be a client to know, something even the cabdrivers don't know:

She permits *puns* in her Parlor.

Well, okay, she hasn't got a lot of choice. Her husband suffers from the filthy habit: she couldn't very well ban it in the Parlor and then let Mike do it. Not that he's ever around before closing, except Sundays, but you see her problem. (Have you ever tried to cure a loved one's addiction? Little joy there.) So any night of the week you're liable to hear things in the Parlor like:

"Hey, did you hear about the vampire typesetter? All his mistakes are Type *O*s."

To which someone is liable to reply, "Then hemostatistically normal than anything else." And people actually applaud.

If a new client turns out to be a carpenter, someone is sure to ask him, "How do you know your wife is true?" just to hear the ritual response, "I check her out with a plumb bob." One carpenter achieved instant Parlor celebrity by suggesting in deadpan return that his questioner "go see Uri Geller and get bent."

All I can tell you is that there's no such thing as a perfect place to work: not even at Lady Sally's House. I suppose all things considered it's not really *that* big a price to pay. But I don't have to like it.

Maybe I'm being illogical. I like word games, anagrams, palindromes, verbal puzzles: why are they okay and straight puns abhorrent? I think because in a straight pun, all the cleverness and wit has been used to poke a hole through the very idea of language, the possibility of communicating unambiguously with words—and that's too dismaying to be funny to me. Puns are my idea of rubber-crutch jokes. I'll concede that there are some excellent and witty rubber-crutch jokes . . . but few I want to hear.

Nonetheless a girl has professional pride. If a client thinks a pun will make him or her look more attractive to me—and I'm constantly stunned at how often they do—I'll try and keep my real opinion my *own* secret. (In some ways, men have it tougher than women in this business.)

One night in late February, two years after I became an artist, I was sitting by the fireplace at the west end of the Parlor, in the opening stages of conversation with a new client. She was a tall stunning statuesque blonde in her mid-thirties, whose house name was Diana. New chums are almost always self-conscious, so you have to play them delicately: you don't want them to feel pressured into selecting you out of politeness rather than desire, but you don't want to give the impression that you couldn't care less, either. I usually just keep the conversation general and watch their eyes, and if I haven't seen what I'm looking for within thirty seconds or so, I sadly remember an obligation on the other side of the Parlor and ask if I may be excused.

Of course, this woman could not be *too* self-conscious, or she would not be here, but in the adjacent Women-Only Lounge, which exists for that very purpose. Still, I was feeling my way carefully with neutral chatter, classic Parlor anecdotes and so forth, and observing attentively: I found her Valkyrie looks quite attractive, and was hoping for her business. She had an intriguing pair of earrings, big dangling milk opals, well domed and full of rolling blue fire; I remember finding it odd that they were clip-ons. There was a matching ring that had never known saw or wheel. I love good opal: these looked Australian. (The world's best, to my mind.) Her teeth were perfect and uncapped. There was an oddly endearing imperfection in one eyebrow, as though there'd been a slight wrinkle in the blueprint.

One of her conversational responses was drowned out by a stentorian suit full of wind on a nearby sofa, one of those City Hall bureaucrats who're always going on about what good shape they're in. "I'm telling you, Phil, right from the factory it had the spokes with that little curve to 'em, like they do, you know? and it kept making this little *whicka whicka* sound." Phillip, who hates being called "Phil," was looking a bit glassy-eyed, but nodded gamely. "So I had my bike man take 'em all out and straighten 'em and put 'em back in, and now it just goes *whirr*, and I put another point zero one five em pee aitch on my top speed. Just like everything else on a bike, it all comes down to wind resistance."

Phillip is a dear. I had halfway decided that it would be my good deed for the night to gracefully abort my present contact and go see if I could rescue him from that bore by sacrificing my fair young body in his place, when Diana made it unnecessary. She held up a hand for the bureaucrat's attention, got it, and said loudly and distinctly, "I'm sure truer spokes were never *whirr*ed."

He frowned, blinked, cleared his throat twice, got up and wandered off to the nearer of the two bars. He looked back over his shoulder on the way, and all three of us were absolutely pokerfaced. When he turned away again, Phillip and I slumped in our seats and let broad grins spread across our faces. Diana too was smiling faintly.

"Perhaps that was a little severe for his offense," I said, "but thank you on behalf of everyone in earshot. Which in his case was the whole Parlor."

"Oh, Sherry," she said, a little disappointed, "you're not one of those people who doesn't like puns, are you?"

"Well . . . honestly?"

"Of course, honey."

"I'd rather have a rash."

"Oh no! Oh, it's so much worse when some-one's clever like you and still dislikes them. Come on, now: won't you please make a pun for me?"

You can probably think of several reasons why I might have decided to accommodate her. So can I. I didn't think of any of them then, I just did it.

"Okay. I finally bought one of those new-fangled gearshift bikes, after my old clunker finally rusted apart. There's a dozen dogs in this neighborhood, and all but two of them claim possession of my new bike; so now it smells so bad I can't ride it. Which proves what I've been saying for years: a tens-peed bicycle really stinks."

Phillip reacted as if a small rat had appeared before him in midair, on fire; he sat up straight and sucked air through his teeth and averted his gaze. But Diana *relaxed* slightly and smiled with pure pleasure. Her eyes glittered oddly.

"Will you come upstairs with me right now and do anything that makes me happy?" she murmured. "Please?"

"Of course." I rose from the couch and smoothed my dress.

"Will you excuse us, Phillip?" she asked.

"Certainly, my dear," he said, raising one eyebrow. "And thanks again. I owe you one."

"They all do," she said mysteriously, "and I intend to collect. Don't worry."

"I won't," he promised, and she took my hand and headed for the spiral staircase in the center of the Parlor.

It's always a pleasure to climb on that grand old staircase, to feel its sturdy risers beneath my feet and run my hand along its graceful iron drolleries. Some master blacksmith who was also a gifted artist made it by hand, and it may have been the work of more than one lifetime for all I know. It would not look out of place in Buckingham Palace.

I paused at the top, and asked the perennial question.

"Would you like to go straight to my own studio, Diana—or would you care to see some of the function rooms first?"

She smiled. "Now what, in a place like this, would constitute a 'function room'?"

A common response from a new client.

"Well," I said, "there's the Executive's Office, and Mistress Cynthia's Dungeon, and the Doctor's Examin—" I don't know what instinct caused me to name those two first.

"Do you take many of your clients to the dungeon?" she interrupted.

"No. One or two, as an occasional thing. Folks that are seriously into that sort of game generally gravitate to someone who really enjoys playing it full time. Mistress Cynthia and Master

Henry are the best in the world at domination—although the name of the studio is a clue as to which one is tougher—and Brandi and Tim are absolutely first-rate submissives. I could introduce you to any of them if you like."

"It's not your cup of tea?"

"Rarely. Unless you know the client very well it can be like juggling nitroglycerine. No matter which end of the leash you're on. I'd just as soon relax, as a rule. Uh . . . I've never taken a new client there, for a first time I mean."

She moved just a little bit closer and bent slightly; the tip of her nose entered my personal space. A pretty nose, I noticed. A good three inches higher from the ground than mine, despite her stoop. I blinked up at incredible turquoise eyes. "If I asked you to come to the dungeon with me and let me put you in chains and do nasty things to you, right now, would you do it?"

"Yes."

"Does the idea excite you, Sherry?"

"No. It might, once I got into it. That would depend on you."

She smiled broadly, approvingly, as if I had said something clever. "Yes, that's right, it would." She bit her tongue and mock-frowned prettily, a practiced expression that must have kickstarted a thousand prostates. "I suppose it won't actually be necessary after all. Why don't you show me your studio, honey?"

"All right, Diana."

It did occur to me as I led her down the

carpeted corridor that I seemed to be in a
remarkably obliging mood. What had possessed
me to agree, even hypothetically, to a B&D
session with a first-timer? I knew what most
often makes me agreeable: apparently I found
this Viking maiden even more attractive than
I realized. Which was certainly odd, despite her
beauty. I like sex with women—I'm not crazy—
but I've always strongly preferred men. And I
had not responded so . . . *docilely* to a woman
since I'd figured out at thirteen that my step-
mother and her friend Sergeant Alice were taking advantage of me. In fact, come to think of
it, I hadn't responded to anyone like this since
the night four years ago when Big Travis stuck
a knife under my ribs, and I was carried bleeding into (Thank you, God, if you're listening)
Lady Sally's House.

As if sensing my unease, she said, "You're not
afraid, are you, Sherry? Please don't be." She was
holding back her stride to let me stay in the lead.
Amazing legs.

"I'm not," I said, and I really wasn't. With
big Mary up in the Snoop Room, and Priscilla
the bouncer and her lethal hands down in the
Parlor, an established maximum of seventeen
seconds away from any studio, what could possibly go wrong?

We reached my studio; I let her in, turned
on the light, closed the door behind us, and
switched on the little red *in service* light out
in the hall. She seated herself with easy grace

on the bed, leaned back against the pillows and surveyed the room like a lazy lioness.

"Before we get started there's a little spiel I—" I began.

"I'll bet you have a very beautiful body, Sherry."

I started to show her, and then caught myself. "Can I *please* just—"

She made another studied gesture, a tucking-one-blonde-wing-of-hair-back-over-the-shoulder, and twiddled her fiery opal earring. "I'd really like to see it," she interrupted softly.

Again it seemed to take an enormous effort to keep from reaching up and behind me for the zipper. But rules are rules, and all Lady Sally's rules make sense: if you strip while you're giving the client the set-speech, you might as well not bother. All right, so I could condense it. "Can I please just—"

Again she didn't have to raise her voice to interrupt. "Please, Sherry? And please don't talk unless it's absolutely necessary?"

The zipper purred.

"Slowly, please. Yes, that's just fine, honey."

I wanted to ask if she wanted music of any kind, but I also didn't want to talk just then. It made a small internal conflict, and that threatened to distract my attention from making Diana happy, so I suppressed it.

"Stop just a minute. Turn around, would you? Lovely. Now back this way. You're very pretty, Sherry."

I suppressed the urge to thank her.

"You aren't afraid, are you, hon?"

"No, you asked me not to be, would you like some music? thank you," I said in one long blurt. There, that was better.

"That's right, I did," she said, ignoring the last two clauses. "But you know what, sweet? I think I'd like it if you sort of *pretended* to be a little bit afraid. And reluctant. Like you were a successful professional woman, and I was some creepy son of a bitch who could wreck your career if you didn't make me happy, could you manage that for me?"

"Sure." I cringed. "All right, you bastard, you win: I'll do what you want. Will that change your mind?"

She twiddled her earring again and smiled faintly. "An attitude problem like yours could take quite some time to correct. I guess we'll have to wait and see, won't we? Continue with what you were doing, bitch."

Warmly confident in my acting skills, I completed undressing. When I was naked, shifting my weight nervously from leg to leg, making small attempts to cover myself with fluttering hands, she had me twirl slowly around again.

Then she asked me to do something I didn't want to do.

No, I'm not going to get more specific than that. Even the most oppressed of street hookers have their own standards, their own unique personal and private set of lines they do not ever plan to cross even if their pimp kills them for it, and if you really want to know what mine are then come to Lady Sally's House and pay your membership and take me upstairs some Spring night and ask me, and if I like the way you ask I might tell you a few of them. What Diana asked me to do was not something I would have rather died than do; more along the lines of a taste I had zero interest in acquiring.

I did it at once.

Then she had me undress her as well, remaining in character, and the moment I had finished carefully folding what were supposed to be her boxer shorts, she asked me sweetly and musically to do something I would have rather died than do.

I never hesitated.

Then she asked for something I would have rather killed a friend than do, and I was genuinely happy to do it for her.

In a very short time, she urgently demanded something I was quite prepared to do at any time, so vanilla that I literally fell all over myself striving to oblige. She had to ask me to stop when I was done. When her breathing had returned to normal, she asked me very politely not to ever tell anyone downstairs what had just happened between us—boy, was that going to be an easy request to honor!— and not to call anyone or go downstairs to the Parlor until tomorrow. I promised. Then she took a silk robe from the closet, tied it around her waist, whistling softly to herself, and left me there in a heap in the middle of the floor.

After a while I got up and blinked at the pile of tangled clothes on the carpet. I had the vague, undifferentiated feeling that something trivial somewhere was wrong, but the warm sense of accomplishment easily overwhelmed it. I found the book I keep around for intervals like that, and stretched out on the bed.

The time passed pleasantly enough. But eventually I looked up from my book, noted that about an hour had passed, and decided it was time to shower. There was a shower in my studio, of course. But Phillip had one upstairs in his personal apartment that was better, with a special pulse-mode, and he let me use it whenever I wanted. Also he had a special shampoo, a new formula that was very good for people who sometimes must wash their hair four or five times in a single night. Diana had only asked me not to go *down*stairs until tomorrow. . . .

I wandered dreamily out into the hall, and headed for the third floor. A client I passed on the way looked at me a little oddly, but I decided he was one of the rare prudes we get and ignored him. Phillip's door was unlocked as always.

The shower was already running. When I entered the bathroom I could make out Phillip's silhouette through the translucent shower curtain. No problem; every shower in the building has room for at least two. I called out a greeting and pulled aside the curtain.

We both cried out.

I had seen a client in that condition, once. But Cynthia and Lady Sally had talked to him for an hour beforehand, and he had to be carried out, and though he sent flowers the next day (the same ones his wife had given him in the hospital) Cynthia said afterward that she did not ever want to take a client that far again, and lady Sally had said good, she didn't much want that sort of trade anyhow. To see Phillip's beautiful body so badly marred was like seeing a beautiful painting covered with graffiti. Drawn in red. I couldn't imagine anyone wanting to do such a thing. Such things . . .

"Oh, my God," I said. "Phillip!"

"I think so."

"I didn't think you went for that sort of thing," I babbled.

"I didn't think *you* went in for *that* sort of thing, either."

Oh, that was right. *He* had cried out when he had seen *me*, too. And that client had given me a double-take. But I wasn't cut up anywhere. What could be that wrong about my appearance? . . .

I stepped back and looked at myself in the mirror.

After a long time I yanked my eyes away and got into the shower with Phillip, and we both burst into tears and sat down together, hugging each other and sobbing under the warm spray.

I washed my hair three times. I had him scrub me, first with soap and then a washcloth and finally with a stiff brush. Then we got out together and I did what I could for his cuts and abrasions. He hissed a few times but did not cry out.

"I'm okay, now," I said, "but you ought to be looked at by Doctor Kate right away. A couple of these need stitches, I think.

"Later, maybe," he said. "First we have to kill Diana."

"I'm sorry, you're right. Priorities."

"All right, let's plan it. It seems to me the first thing we—"

"Phillip, *what is it she did to us*?"

"Isn't it obvious? She made us do anything she asked."

"But *how*?"

"She said please! What difference does it make?"

"Don't we have to know what she's doing to stop her?"

"Not necessarily, if we're smart. Let me check some assumptions. You've been asked not to tell anyone downstairs about what happened to you? And not to call anyone or go downstairs until tomorrow?" I nodded. "Okay, look: if she came back upstairs and we tried to jump her, she'd just ask us to stop. And as long as she's between us and the front door downstairs she can bolt at any time, and once she's out in the world we've lost her. But if we could just find some way to make a disturbance *at* the door, and stampede her back upstairs, where someone was waiting with his trusty softball bat . . ." He paused, looked thoughtful. "Maureen," he said, distracted enough to use my real name, "I'm afraid for once you are going to have to think like a punster."

"Huh?"

"You know the layout at the top of that staircase. Unless she comes up those stairs at a dead run, it's going to be hard to ambush her. That means we need our best hitter at that post. So *you* have to make the disturbance at the door and panic her into running."

"But I *can't*! She asked me not to. She said 'Please.' "

"That's what I mean. What *exactly* did she ask you not to do?"

"The same thing she said to you. 'Please don't go downstairs until tomorrow.' "

"I thought so. But she just asked? I mean, she didn't write it down, or anything, just asked verbally?"

"Yeah."

"All right, now I want you to cast your mind back to one of your first nights in this House. You're outside on the sidewalk, your pimp Big Travis has come to get you and is taking you at gunpoint back off to slavery again. Mary kills him. Now: *how did Mary get there?*"

My eyes opened wide. "Oh, no. Oh, Phillip, no. I don't think I could—"

"—sure you can—"

"—I don't think so—"

"—you're young, athletic—"

"—*that's not what I mean*—"

"—*what then?*—"

"—*SHE ASKED ME NOT TO!*"

We both stopped and let our voices echo.

"Speaking of Mary," I said, much more quietly, "how come she didn't pick up on all this and sound the alarm? She knows what we won't do: remember that time somebody drugged Lucy?"

"Maybe Diana asked her not to. Or maybe she did and Diana asked the Lady not to pay attention. That's why we've got to move fast, love, now listen: you did not see her request on paper. Think like a punster, now, let yourself think literally. If I wrote her words down now, I could legitimately choose to put a space between 'down' and 'stairs,' couldn't I? People who fall one flight by definition do not go down stairs!"

Mary had gone out the second floor window, landed on Travis, all two hundred or so pounds of her, and snapped his neck like a twig. If she could do it, I could do it. In theory.

"Sherry, have you ever heard about the course they make you take at Annapolis, where you are given a theoretical problem and told to cut a set of orders for your classmates, and if any of them can manage to misunderstand your orders enough to screw up the problem, you bilge? Diana is going to bilge that course, tonight. Just start a fire or something to drive her this way at high speed—without letting her see you."

I wanted to go along with Phillip. The notion that *Lady Sally* might even now be dancing to Diana's tune was primevally *wrong*; the simple fact was more wrong, somehow, than the specific outrages that had been done to me. I wanted to drink Diana's blood, and she had never asked me not to. But she *had* asked me not to go downstairs until tomorrow, and in my heart I could not deny that I knew how she would have written it down. I just could not assemble the will to oppose her expressed wishes.

"I'm sorry, Phillip. I don't think I can."

"You've *got* to."

"If you think it's that easy, *you* do it."

"I think I could."

"Fine, good luck—"

"How good are you with a softball bat? Can you be sure of silencing someone with a single blow?"

I waved my hands helplessly, close to tears with rage and frustration.

"Come on, let's give it a try, at least. Please? We can't just sit here: *how do we know what's going on downstairs?*"

He was right; we headed for the door. Maybe I could manage it after all, if I could manage to think like a punster, just kept it fixed in my mind that I wasn't actually going to be going down any stairs. . . .

And it blew up in my face. I found that I could no longer walk back down from the third floor to the second. If "don't go downstairs" meant literally, "don't descend any staircases," then this one qualified too.

"Phillip, I've got a problem."

"Yeah, me too. I never thought of this."

"It looks like I'm a high-living girl from now on."

"Atta girl! You're getting it. Come on."

"Where?"

"Your problem is not changed in kind, but only in degree."

"What are you talking about?"

"It's possible to land safely from a third floor window."

"Are you out of your goddam mind?"

"You're right; let's use your plan instead." He turned angrily and started walking away, swinging his softball bat.

"Oh, shit," I said, and followed. "Wait up." Stop and grab fresh clothes from my own apartment? No, no time, no need, no time!

I thought at first he went to the wrong apartment. "Mary's flat is above the front door," I pointed out.

"Yeah, but this one is above the dumpster. Garbage is a more resilient landing zone than cement, as a rule." He went to the window, did not open it, looked out and down at the drop.

"Sherry, maybe this isn't a good idea after all. If you're really reluctant to do this, you could land wrong; your subconscious could bitch you up to resolve the conflict honorably. Let's switch: I jump, and you beat her brains out."

"No, Phillip. For the reason you've already mentioned, and three more. One: the lighter the body, the easier it lands. Two: my Dad was a paratrooper; maybe I inherited something. Three: you're in no shape for combat. Get out of my way."

Like I said, my father was a paratrooper. He always said the classic error was to pause in the doorway, looking down; most of those who did never jumped. So I was careful not to hesitate for a second, just hopped up on the sill, slipped the hook-and-eye catch, flung the side-hinged window open, put my attention on targeting the dumpster, and stepped out into the night.

Nearly at once, even before I began to be scared, I realized an elementary oversight in my planning. I was naked; it was February. Oh well, it would give me an honorable excuse for shivering.

Then I began to get scared.

But by then it was too late; I had landed.

Take it from your Aunt Maureen: if there is any way you can arrange your affairs so as to avoid dropping into whorehouse garbage from a great height, naked in February, then that is almost certainly the course your life should take.

Still, I reflected as I climbed out of the dumpster, nothing seemed to be broken, and I was much cleaner than I had been when I had gone up to Phillip's place to shower. Most important, I had the use of my brain back.

Or did I? I had had the two seconds' resolution necessary to step off a ledge. But the closer I got to Diana, the closer I was to contravening her implied wishes. Could I go through with this?

So maybe it was a break that it was February midnight and I was naked. My body got me started in the right direction, and my brain got carried along.

We all take turns working reception. Ruth had it that night. She is the oldest working artist I have ever met (pushing sixty then) and one of the most popular in the House. I can give no better explanation than what she did when she saw me. I was expecting to provoke consternation or at least major surprise when I came in the door, but her unhesitating reaction was magnificent.

"Oh my God," she said, "the damn sign fell down again."

Any other time I would have applauded. I was busy confronting the fact that I didn't have a plan. Create a disturbance that would drive Diana upstairs. Simple. I didn't have a match . . . or a place to put one. "G-g-get me a coat, will you, Ruth?" It was cozy in the foyer, I was already warming up—but I couldn't enter

the Parlor naked. As she was getting me one,
I heard a distant shout from the Parlor. "Is anything going on in there?"

She looked torn. "I've been asked not to say."

"I see. Is it bad?"

"Yes." She closed a man's heavy overcoat
around me; it covered me to below the knees.
"What happened to you?"

I too felt strong internal conflict. "I've been
asked not to say."

She nodded. "Then you understand."

"Yeah."

"I sure wish I could worry about it," she said
plaintively.

"Asked you not to, eh?"

"Yes. But for some reason I keep thinking
about it a lot just the same. I guess I'm
just . . . interested. You know. Involved."

"I assume she asked you not to call the
cops."

"Not to call anyone—or let anyone else make
any calls. *Please* don't try, Sherry."

"I can't." What in the hell would I *tell* the
cops? Officer, we've got a woman here at the
brothel, and you have to do anything she asks.
Lady, quit braggin'. "Look, Ruth, is there any
heat in the weapons-check tonight?"

She hesitated. "Well, yes, as a matter of fact
we're heavy on ordnance at the moment. Johnny
Rats is in the House, and you know those two
gorillas with him always pack enough for a small
war. And there's some other stuff too."

"Finally, some good luck. Unlock it for me, will you, Ruth?"

She frowned, clearly torn again. "Well, now, that's kind of a problem, sweetie."

My heart sank. Was I going to have to fight Ruth? Could I? "She asked you not to let anybody in?"

"Oh, she said if any clients came to show them right in. But she said if anyone came who looked like they might disturb her, I should keep them out. You'd probably be thinking of disturbing her, wouldn't you, dear?"

"That depends. Would you say a bullet through the head would disturb her?"

"Now, that's an interesting question, all right. Kind of philosophical, like. Let me give that some thought for a second." Her face went through a fascinating interplay of expressions, ending with sad. "I guess I'd have to say that it definitely would disturb her. Not for very long, mind—but a whole lot. I'm sorry, dear; you know I'd like to help."

"I know that, Aunt Ruth," I said gently. "How about this? Suppose you just get me the guns anyway, and I'll just sit out here with you and fondle them?"

She felt compelled to split hairs. "Well, but you see, that would amount to the same thing. Suppose you changed your mind, after I gave you the guns, how would I keep you out then? You see my problem."

I was running out of ideas and time, and I

didn't much want to fight Ruth. For one thing, she plays a good game of handball for sixty, and knows gutter-fighting. But she seemed to incline toward a strict interpretation of the Talmud, and I knew just how she felt. Thank God Diana hadn't thought to ask *me* not to disturb her. What the hell was I going to do?

And a pun saved me.

"That's okay," I told her. "Kind of ironic, isn't it?"

"How's that?"

"I mean, all those years of effort Lady Sally put into building and maintaining good relations with the cops and City Hall, and here we are now, victims of Please Brutality."

She winced. You cannot wince without shutting your eyes. I didn't much want to hit even a junior senior citizen hard enough to put her lights out, so I used a pressure point Daddy told me about once, and released it the moment her face lost color. She blinked at me and folded slowly.

The damndest thing. Just before her face went slack, she tried to smile.

I made her comfortable. The weapons-check locker key was where it's always kept. Ruth hadn't been kidding about Johnny Rats's goons. I liked the look of the Uzi, but an Uzi does not make a thunderous enough noise to panic someone who is not familiar with firearms: it is a terror weapon only to someone who knows what that asthmatic-sewing-machine sound means.

Instead I selected the over-and-under pump shotgun and the Russian handgun. I'd never seen one
like it before, couldn't read the Cyrillic script
on the barrel, but its design was utterly straightforward and it made a Magnum look like a cap
pistol. My father used to say that you couldn't
trust Soviet technology—unless it was a weapon.
"Paranoids," he said, "can be relied on to make
the best weapons." To complete my disguise as
a large dangerous male, I got a big furry sable
hat that also looked Russian from the cloakroom
and stuffed my hair up under it, found a pair
of boots tall enough to conceal the fact that I
lacked a pair of pants.

My plan was to slip through the door, locate
Diana, shoot her if possible, and if not, quickly
put enough slugs in the ceiling and floor to
create the impression that the revolution had
begun. She had every reason to feel confident;
it would not be easy to stampede her. Perhaps
Phillip's idea of a fire made more sense. But
while I was prepared to risk winging a few
innocent bystanders—friends!—to get Diana, I
could not make myself set fire to Lady Sally's
House. Even shooting it up was going to hurt.

Let's see: shotgun in left hand, sloppiest
weapon where accuracy is least. Check ammo on
both guns. Spin cylinders, pump scattergun.
Safeties off. Pause at door, feeling like something
out of a movie. Review procedure one last time.

Earmuffs!

I grabbed a pair from the cloakroom, put

them on under my furry hat. They weren't very good at muffling sound—why hadn't I thought to fetch my isolation headphones from my room?—but they would help. I decided if I could not get a clear shot at Diana, I would fire off my first rounds near my ears and trust to that to finish deafening me. But hopefully that would not be necessary.

Back to the doorway, feeling like a Viking in all that gear. Appropriate. Set a Viking to catch a Viking. Hurry before resolution leaks—deep breath—

—through the door—

—located Diana at once—

—saw that I had no shot—

—raised both muzzles—

Shit!

There is an easel-like affair near the door, on which Lady Sally is accustomed to post allegedly humorous signs to greet the clients. How many other places have a sign saying, "Come again," on the *way in*, for instance? But tonight's sign was peeled back, and on the next sheet on the pad someone had hastily but legibly scrawled a new message with a black felt-tip marker.

PLEASE DON'T MOVE.

CHAPTER 7
THE PARANOID

In retrospect I'm surprised I didn't freeze instantly, and fall on my face. My brain must have been a strict constitutionalist, and decided that that moves least which comes to a safe smooth stop: I got to complete my stride before turning to stone. I wished I hadn't had that inspiration about firing off both weapons close to my ears: they were going to get mighty heavy by and by.

I was absurdly put out with Diana. What the hell had she put *that* there for? Didn't she trust Ruth, for Christ's sake? But then I stopped thinking even silly thoughts, because by then I was becoming aware of my surroundings.

Lady Sally's wonderful Parlor had become a carnival of horror.

And perhaps the most horrible part was how *funny* all of it might have been under other circumstances. Even as I cursed Diana's sign for preventing me from shooting, I blessed it for preventing me from breaking into an involuntary grin for which I could have never forgiven myself. Whatever else you could fault Diana for, she had a literally diabolical sense of humor. I've already said I don't much care for rubber-crutch jokes—but some of hers were inspired.

Not everyone was naked. Johnny Rats, for instance, was wearing a bra and panties that must have belonged to Big Mary, and Father Newman was wearing a teddy and hose in addition to his scapulars. Juicy Lucy wore most of the whipped cream that was intended for Irish coffee, sculpted into a bikini; two Maraschino cherries had been strategically and whimsically placed. Tim wore a fetching little blue ribbon, whose tails fluttered gaily. A client named Willa, who always overdressed, was wearing nothing except what appeared to be every piece of jewelry in the room. Most upsetting to me, Lady Sally wore a great deal of lipstick, almost none of it on her lips or even her face; several people had apparently been playing tic-tac-toe on her.

As near as I could see, every person in the room except Diana was doing something embarrassing or grotesque, and in several cases she seemed to have tailored her requests to the victim's personality for maximum degradation. Mistress Cynthia was licking Master Henry's

boots, looking as angry as a person can look with
their tongue out. Robin, her pet houseboy, was
using Cynthia's own quirt on her while she
worked, his face flooded with tears. Even Henry
looked unhappy: one of his secret fantasies, no
doubt, yet it was ashes in his mouth because the
commands had not been his. Ralph the talking
dog was trying to extricate himself from some
client's large white Angora (a cat, not a sweater),
swearing in German. Father Newman was pop-
eyed, sweating, monotonously blessing the room
with his rosary over and over again. Brandi, a
good Catholic, was kneeling at his feet, looking
for all the world as if she were praying, and
perhaps she was, too, for all I know. Johnny Rats
was noisily kissing one of his naked bodyguards,
the fat one called Vito; as I watched, the other
one, Tony, tapped his partner on the shoulder
with obvious reluctance and cut in. When they
traded places, I saw that someone had fetched
some blue paint up from stores: Vito and Tony
were a teenage boy's lament come true. I also
saw—anyone could see—that even Mary's capa-
cious panties were close to bursting. I glanced
up to Johnny's face and felt sad for Vito and
Tony; whatever else happened tonight, they were
dead men.

All around the room artists and clients were
humiliating themselves in assorted ways, alone
or in groups of up to six, in an earnest, deadly
silence with one ghastly exception. Not all looked
anguished: some had apparently been asked to

enjoy themselves. Brian, for example seemed to be having the time of his life with Rose—and Brian is strictly gay. And surely Mary did not really find what she was doing exciting.

But the majority clearly showed their revulsion and shame and fury. Lady Sally, twirling in a constant slow circle to witness everything that was taking place in her Parlor, looked as if her eyelashes were about to catch fire. The only completely empty expression in the room belonged to Priscilla the bouncer, the deadliest human being I've ever known: it seemed as though she had been asked to try and knock herself out, and had succeeded after a dismayingly long time. Doctor Kate, the house physician, kept glancing over wistfully at this patient in need, but could not stop what she was doing with her sphygmomanometer to help Priscilla.

I took all this in in the most appalling state of dreamy confusion. I mean, I saw every detail, and will remember them all to my dying day—but meanwhile a good half of my attention was taken up with the serious question: when someone has asked you not to move, does breathing count? Blinking I could handle, blinking was easy, it would be at least thirty seconds more before my eyes began to hurt, but what about breathing? It was a thorny question: if I stopped, shortly I would pass out, and therefore almost certainly move. On the other hand, since I'd be unconscious at the time, would it really be "I" who moved?

And then my eyes focused on Diana, and the fog burned away.

I had been aware of her all this time, while avoiding thinking about her. I knew she had seen me come in, had watched me *most* carefully until she was sure I had seen the sign . . . and then had dismissed me and my useless guns from her mind for the moment and gone back to what she was doing. I saw what she was doing, and who she was doing it to, and became so angry I had to warn myself sternly that, just as you can't wince without closing your eyes, you can't have apoplexy without moving. Now I understood where the damned sign had come from; I even knew what the sheet underneath it would probably say. I could guess how it had been for Judith, guess at how it must be for her now.

Judith is deaf. Somehow everybody seems to think that all deaf people know how to read lips—that they could pick it up in a week, themselves, if the need ever arose. Try it sometime; I have. Judith couldn't do it. God knows what she must have thought when everyone around her started going mad. How long did it take before she managed to identify Diana as the focus of the infection? Once she had, she must have realized she was the only one immune, and done or tried to do something that had frightened Diana.

It hadn't worked, of course, since Diana could get unlimited willing accomplices as fast as she could ask for them. Now she was returning the fright to Judith, with terrible interest. (Oh God, thought a portion of my mind, another pun.) What she had done was simple. I couldn't help but think how eagerly Judith must have watched, struggling in the grip of her dearest friends, as Diana began writing on the signpad, how anxious Judith must have been to find out what was going on. How disappointing it must have been to read only, *PLEASE DON'T MOVE*. Perhaps hope flared again as Diana scratched out a second message, then died as she held it up.

PLEASE KEEP YOUR EYES SHUT, it must have read.

Now Judith was about as helpless as a human can be. More helpless than a deaf person, more helpless than any blind person. I wondered how Diana planned to ever get her eyes open again. Probably she didn't care. She had borrowed someone's belt. . . .

Apparently enough pain could mitigate the compulsion of even one of Diana's requests—or perhaps the limited movements she was making were as involuntary as my own breathing reflex. But an unkind God gave us more tender places than He gave us hands to cover them. The result was a horrid guessing game that Judith always lost. She was the one ghastly exception to the silence in which the others were suffering, emitting a sound so nakedly, indescribably ugly that no hearing person could have made it even in extremis. My earmuffs were no help at all.

I was not in the dreamy, cooperative frame of mind I'd had earlier, upstairs: if enough pain could make Judith writhe and dance like that, in defiance of Diana's wishes, couldn't enough rage allow me to just adjust the angle of one wrist slightly, and twitch one little finger—?

—no.

Damn it. I was completely in thrall. I couldn't even get a good look at Diana: she was at the edge of my peripheral vision, and I couldn't move my eyes.

Either Diana finished, or her arm got tired. She dropped the belt, turned away and, now that she was no longer busy, came to look me over and see what sort of amusement I might afford.

When she got close enough to recognize me, her eyes widened in momentary panic. *"How the hell did you get down here?"* she barked, instinctively raising her hands in self-defense.

Don't move, speak, I wished she'd make up her mind. Well, at least this implied that breathing was allowed. I explained the tortuous and torturous thought process that had gotten me downstairs without going down stairs, wishing she would stand directly in front of me so I could see her better.

She relaxed. "Jesus. Imprecision of speech, is that what it was?" She began to giggle. I could hear her quite well despite the earmuffs. "Serves me right. Damn lucky I thought to put this sign here for insurance—that old bag out there *looked* like she might be worthless. All right, let's see if we can't build a failsafe into this. No matter how I phrase my requests from now on, would you please interpret them so that your actions are not, in your best judgment, liable to make me unhappy in any way?"

"Yes, Diana." Damn. I had to make such a judgment call right away. I had been implicitly given permission to speak. If I used it without orders, would that make her unhappy? Only one way to find out. "May I ask you a question?"

"Sure. One."

I was pretty sure the question wouldn't make her unhappy. "Why are you doing this?"

Across the room I could see Lady Sally, with what must have been titanic effort, nodding at me. The motion was so slight I might have imagined it—but her eyes were glittering as they spun away.

And indeed it was my best and only shot. Villains love to justify themselves to their victims, and by doing so they often give away their weaknesses. Back when I was sixteen, and a chattel of Big Travis, I had thought to ask him once *why* he was beating me, and when I got past the obvious "'cause ya'll won't *mind* me," to the root of why he would want to beat a woman for not obeying him, we had ended up crying in each other's arms together. The bastard.

Diana laughed out loud. (I was, I'm disgusted to say, intensely relieved by this confirmation that she was happy.) "Don't you want to know *how* I'm doing this?"

I wanted to shake my head, but instead had to say, "No. What's the point? I wouldn't understand it anyway. And if I could, I don't want to know, I don't want *anybody* to know." I almost added, *you included,* but that might have made her unhappy.

She kept laughing. "You're not as dumb as you look, honey—and you *do* look dumb in that getup. Just call it magic and let it go. If it matters to you, it was so difficult to stumble across that no one else is going to figure it out any time soon."

"But why? Why *use* it . . . like this?"

"Please shut up and I'll tell you, since you ask."

I was committed now. If I had not managed to ask her the right question, I might never get another.

"Look at me," she said.

Just for the hell of it I tried to flick my eyes *away* from her for a second before training them on her.

No good. I'd been wondering if her commands had to be phrased as questions to be effective. I had noticed that they carried more force when she said, "Please." But no soap. A command is really just a request you don't bother to phrase politely. She usually asked because it amused her to do so. How had I ever managed to resist her will enough to get down here, sophistry or not?

So I looked at her.

Bright. God, she was bright, in so many ways.

Madwoman's eyes, radioactive turquoise, sparkling like the earrings that framed them. Glowing cheeks. Forehead glistening with sweat. Hair so long and straight and shiny it looked almost like a blonde helmet. Face of a model. Body of a Norse goddess, well over six feet of lithe grace, visible beneath my unbelted bathrobe. From the thighs down and the shoulders out she was muscled like a swimmer; in between she was as soft and opulent as Marilyn herself. Her features and her actions so far showed that she was bright in the mental sense as well. She stood straight, and proud, and bright. She had, I realized suddenly, the face and body and hair and carriage I had always yearned for myself; we even had the same taste in jewelry. She was *perfect*. What had made her a monster, when I'd survived a childhood like mine?

She seemed to read my mind. "Do you think I look nice?"

"Yes." Again, by requiring me to speak she broke the ice. God, the two guns were getting heavy! "May I—"

"Hush. Short answers to direct questions only. Would you like to look like me—would you trade bodies with me if you could."

"Probably." Especially now. I was beginning to tremble from the strain of remaining motionless so long.

A face that pretty should never hold a grin that twisted and malevolent. "Honey, you're a jerk." She turned to address the room and raised her voice. "Would everyone please stop what they're doing for the moment and stand still and pay silent attention?"

All the horror came to a halt. Except the sound Judith was still making, less forceful than before but just as awful.

Diana grimaced in annoyance. "Another oversight. Now how the heck can I shut her up?"

I didn't want to tell her, but she'd asked. "Bone conduction."

"Huh? What did you say?"

"Bone conduction."

She waited—then sighed with amused exasperation. "Would you amplify that?"

The pun center of my brain was still operating: I thought briefly of cupping my hands and yelling "bone conduction!" But it might make her unhappy. "If you put your head against hers and talk, she can hear you, like astronauts touching helmets."

"And she understands speech?"

"She wasn't born deaf." Or she'd have learned to read lips by now. For the first twenty-three years of her life, Judith just wasn't paying enough attention to lips. She didn't need to.

"Good." Diana went to her, again moving to the extreme edge of my field of view, touched her head to Judith's in a horrible parody of tenderness. "Would you please try very hard not to make any noise, honeybunch?" she asked loudly, and Judith became silent except for her hoarse breathing. Diana patted her like one gentling a horse, and came back toward where I stood. As she did so I became overwhelmingly glad that I could not move my eyes. They could not give me away.

Someone was creeping down the spiral staircase behind her.

Not Phillip. A client, dressed in jeans and a white shirt, barefoot. I recognized him vaguely, a Russian attached to their U.N. delegation. I was holding his pistol, might have been wearing his hat. He was moving carefully, gracefully, like a trained athlete, and in his hands was not Phillip's softball bat as I had expected, but the most lovely, beautiful fire ax you ever saw.

My pulse rate must have jumped sharply, but you can't see that. I know my face stayed wooden. Others within my range of vision could see him too, but none of us made a sound or a twitch.

Sergei, that was his House name, the trite joke being that he was anything but gay, sir. Come on, Sergei!

Thank God iron stairs don't creak. He reached the bottom safely and then I couldn't see him because Diana was blocking my view. I willed her to talk to me again instead of turning to address the room, and she did.

"So you think if you had my looks and brains, you could do better with them than I have?"

"Yes."

She slapped my face. "Stupid. No imagination.

Look at me again." The slap had spun my face, and I'd been unable to turn it back to her without orders. "You didn't *seem* unimaginative, upstairs. Can't you—"

Some paranoid instinct or barely perceptible sound warned her. She leaped sideways, hit the floor in a tuck and roll as Sergei bisected the signboard in front of me with a hissing grunt. The two syllables she hollered were louder than the sounds Judith had made, and nearly as harsh.

"DON'T MOVE!"

My heart nearly stopped.

It took him a second or so to end up at rest with the ax dangling from one hairy hand, his face frozen in a comic look of disappointment.

She rolled easily to her feet and paced around him a circle three times, breathing hard, murderous rage draining slowly from her bright turquoise eyes. She stopped in front of him. Slowly and carefully, she slapped him six times, much harder than she had slapped me. When the last report had faded, she straightened his face toward hers with a contemptuous hand.

"You jerk," she snarled. "Did you really think you could threaten me?"

"*Da,*" he said.

She brightened. "Russian. What do you know?" She began to giggle. "Oh, my. My, my. This must be your very worst nightmare come true, isn't it?"

"*Da.* May I speak?" He had made the same discovery I had, that an order to speak implied speech was permissible.

"Why?" she asked cautiously.

"So that I may curse you."

"Really?" she said, delighted. "In Russian? I think I'd like to hear that. Go ahead."

He did. It lasted over a minute, and sounded like two large cats in a sack.

"Are you done?" she asked when he wound down.

"Da. Spasebo."

She told him what to do with the ax.

He succeeded. But along the way he must have decided that the command implied a rescinding of the earlier general order not to move. His face distorted, and he fell to the floor on his side.

"Come on, for God's sake," she said, kicking him, "get up! I've had worse than that done to— Jesus Christ!" She broke off short, bent over his rigid form, and whistled. "Well, I'll be damned. They really have those things. I guess this really was his worst nightmare come true."

I could smell it too, now. Bitter almonds, just like in the books.

It shook me. I was as unhappy about all this as I'd ever been about anything—but I didn't want to suicide. I wanted to kill Diana, and then cry for about a year. For the first time I began to wonder how this was going to end. Would she politely ask us to drop dead? Or simply ask us to forget we'd ever met her?

Come to think of it, which *did* I prefer, if I had my druthers?

She straightened and backed away from him, bumped into me, jumped three feet and whirled. *"Jesus, don't do that!"*

I made a mental note never to back into any paralyzed people.

She gave him one last long glance, then dismissed him from her thoughts. "All right," she said, turning back to me, "as I was saying . . ."

She raised her volume so the others could all hear:

"Now I maintain—and you, of all people, ought to agree with me—that anyone born into this son of a bitching world with female genitalia has got it rough. Am I right?"

"Sure," I said.

"Sure, I'm right. Men run everything, and we've got something they need, so we're a threat. What is more threatening than a female?"

"I don't know."

"Quit answering rhetorical questions, you'll screw up my rhythm. What is more threatening than a female? A tall female." True. "And what is more threatening than a tall female? A tall, muscular female, who *hasn't* been trained to be awkward." Also true. "What's more threatening than a tall, muscular female, as tough as a man? What if she were gorgeous?" I was beginning to get what she meant. "I mean, suppose she was this bombshell, like blonde and bosomy? And suppose worst of all, worst of all, her mind was awake? Say she was intelligent and educated and confident and ambitious. Now you've got a tall gorgeous strong smart woman; to any man who sees her, she's a prize he can't have and a threat he can't beat; now you tell me: is there a man alive who wouldn't spend every single minute from the moment he met her until the day she passed out of his life for good *trying to control her, one way or another?* And keep her controlled?"

It was a rhetorical question. But I knew what I would have answered.

"And the only people who've usually treated me even worse than men are most of the *women* I've ever met. I'm an unforgivable threat to them, too—because I'm a superior candidate for enslavement. They actually resent the fact that most men would prefer to rope and break and brand me than them. So I got into bisexuality, thinking that would help me find people who wouldn't want to control me *or* compete with me. Fat chance. Even to hard-core Lesbians I was either a prize or a threat—so they used their own little schemes to try and control me.

"I am a scientist," she went on, anger building in her voice. "I won't tell you what kind, because it would be a clue, and I've learned tonight that I can't be too careful. But I'm a damned good one, and every day of my working career I have had to deal with what I look like! Are you one of those jerks who think scientists must be clear-thinking types with wide-open minds, liberal hearts, enlightened attitudes? Honey, take it from me: the worst, most Stone

Age male chauvinist apes on this planet have multiple doctorates in things you couldn't pronounce." She was yelling by now. "Science is the last great Old Boys' Club in America, and the very worst strike against me was that I had a mind as good as theirs, that I wasn't just an incompetent, clumsy but ornamental lab mascot. God damn it, *of all the people on Earth, they were the ones that should have been my brothers*. They didn't even have *stupidity* for an excuse!"

She broke off, annoyed at herself.

"Shouldn't lose control like that," she muttered. "Control." She giggled suddenly. "Control." She frowned darkly and said it again. "Control. Laboratory controls, you know about those, Sherry-hon? Those bastards invented the *word*. They thought they could control me, control my lab, control my mind, *control me*, because I wasn't born with a piece of gristle hanging off my belly. I might have gotten away with it if I'd had a face like a foot or the body of a bag lady, but anything that came in a package like *this* was meant to be kept out of the lab, with the civilians and pets, lower than a graduate student, preferably in a nice third floor walkup on Gramercy Park with a big mirror on the ceiling and a—"

Again she cut herself off.

For the first time I remembered the scene she and I had acted out upstairs together. That, I realized now, was one scenario this imaginative woman had not invented. That one she had been reliving. From the other end of the leash, so to speak.

"Well, I've got control now," she said softly after a moment. "I played their games for long enough, and managed to sneak what I needed out of them, and found what I was looking for in spite of them and every disgusting thing they could do to me. I used some of the very gifts he thought he bought me with, the bastard. And my beta test has been just a *wonderful* success, everything I hoped it would be. . . ." She glanced down at Sergei's body. "And maybe even a little more. So now I intend to go out and change the face of contemporary American science. And contemporary American malehood. And any damn thing else that annoys me."

My arms ached dully. Damn, I'd picked heavy guns. Should have used Phillip's idea of a fire. What was Phillip doing upstairs? Listening and wishing he'd been able to give Sergei a gun, no doubt. What else could he do? I envied him his place out of the line of fire. I hadn't wanted to start this, hadn't wanted to come downstairs in the first place. . . .

God, I suddenly realized, I really *hadn't* wanted to. It had been Phillip's idea. I had been *terribly* reluctant to even misconstrue Diana's wishes, had been adamantly opposed to Phillip's proposal even before I realized it involved dropping an extra story and freezing my butt off. Since that time I had not succeeded in misconstruing any requests for even a moment.

How had I been able to do so, upstairs?

Phillip had asked me to. He had said please.

My brain went into high gear. She was a scientist. The force she was using on us was not black magic or some kind of ESP power, but a device of some kind, a physical utensil. It worked on anyone within its range, made one amenable to *anyone's* requests.

Except Diana. She was immune somehow.

Where was the thing? Internal, tucked away inside some body cavity? She had left her purse and all her clothes upstairs, was it there, broadcasting through carpeting and oak floors and ceiling? She'd had nothing in her hands when she'd left my room, had been wearing only my own robe and slippers. Had I wandered dreamily away from the very thing that could have saved us all?

No, that couldn't be: the Russian would have been affected upstairs as well.

But wait! Maybe he had been affected. The only request he'd have had time to hear before descending was, "Would you please try very hard not to make any noise, honeybunch?" Which was his earnest intention anyway.

Figure this out, Maureen, there's a clue here somewhere! And time is running out. . . .

It was, as I might have known it would be, Lady Sally who saved us all.

She and the others had been asked to "please

stop what you're doing for the moment and stand still and pay silent attention." She had no choice but to obey. But it is possible to construe "stand still" so as to conclude that it is all right for you to use your arms and hands. She was waving for my attention, and when she decided she had it (there was no way she could have been sure), she made the classic gesture you use to tell someone that the two of you are about to play a game of charades.

There was no need for any additional gestures; I took her meaning at once. Now I had it narrowed down: Diana's control gizmo was in one of three places. But what in the hell could I do about it?

"And for a start," Diana said, "*you* annoy me, Sherry-hon—with your stupid 'why' questions, and your *wicked* attempt to control me with these, after all we meant to each other once—"

She yanked both the weapons from my cramping hands, and I actually might have thanked her if it had been possible—it felt like my arms were falling off! She looked around thoughtfully for a moment, then dropped both guns on the wrecked sign, where anyone trying to pick them up would fail. Every one of us irrevocably rooted where we stood, and she secured the weapons. God, she was paranoid! If only she'd been as paranoid as Sergei, and killed herself the first time control was ever taken from her ...

"—and besides, you're the only one in the

room who's overdressed," she went on, malicious amusement creeping into her voice. "I think that's rude, don't you? Here, let me just . . . well, you're not *too* overdressed now, are you?"

"No." It looked like it was my turn in the barrel again.

"My, you must have been cold, hon," she chatted on. I was getting awfully tired of the sound of her voice. "You can talk if you like, I rather like the way you protest . . . oh, hell." My elbows were locked against my sides to brace the weight of the guns; the coat would not come off. "Okay, would you move just enough to help me?"

I had considerably less than a second to make my decision, so I probably didn't change my mind more than a million times. But in the end I went with the only real shot I had with cramped fingers. Praying I was correct, and taking the most elastic possible interpretation of "help me," I lowered my arms just enough to snatch both her earrings off.

And said, before she had time to react, "Would you *please* SHUT UP?"

An astonishing spectrum of expressions passed like skirmishing armies across her face, but none of them succeeded in opening her lips so much as a fraction of an inch. That may have been her least favorite question in the world, even before she invented her gizmo, and she hated it now. I'd guessed right!

"And *back off*," I added, suddenly revolted beyond all bearing by her beautiful hands on my body.

She took two paces backwards, clutching toward my throat futilely as she went.

"Stand still."

She obeyed.

"This *isn't* going to make you unhappy, you know," I said. "Not in the long run, anyway. I started realizing how many slips you kept making, even with that paranoia of yours. You wanted to be stopped. You're no unhappier now than you were when you came in here tonight."

It shames me a little to recall how long I just stood there, drinking the sight of her struggling face like a fine wine. I don't know whether anyone else would have moved if they'd been able to. Maybe to get a better view.

Eventually I turned my mind to practical matters.

Let's see. The tools at hand included a shotgun and a Russky hand-cannon. But for sentimental reasons, I favored the fire ax Sergei had wanted to use on her. I've never minded getting my hands a little dirty in a good cause. I felt his shade would be grateful. I knew just where I wanted to put my first shot.

And then I would free my friends, one at a time to keep it orderly, and allow them each a shot. And then we would . . .

And then we would . . .

What were we, a totally heterogenous group of

eccentric denizens of the world's best whorehouse, going to do with a couple of fresh corpses and absolute power?

"Lady Sally?" I called. "Would you please get fixed and come over here and help me figure out what the hell to do?"

And burst into tears.

She came at once, already barking orders. "Kate, would you see to Judith at once? And then Priscilla, please, and anyone else who needs you? Would the rest of you—*excepting* Diana—please be calm and untroubled, and get yourselves cleaned up and dressed properly again when you're able? And please talk softly if at all, dears, we need to think."

There was a general sigh of relief, of several kinds of tension. People dressed rapidly. Very few had anything to say.

And then she had reached me.

I swam in Sally's hug. I needed that hug more than I've ever needed anything. "You did *splendidly,* darling," she murmured in my ear as she stroked me. "You were magnificent. You've upheld my highest traditions. A client was in need and you moved enough to help her. It's over now." She did *not* say, "Please don't cry," and I sobbed and sobbed in her arms until I had cried it all out, all the horror and panic and disgust and fear and awful hope and disappointment, and even, toward the end there, a good deal of the rage that had shaken me to my core. Perhaps the very worst of what I had experienced was that I now understood, deep in my heart, the profound sense of violation and outrage that must have driven Diana to invent what she had. I had just walked a mile in her shoes, and could no longer even simply hate her.

"Sherry," Lady Sally said when I had finally cried it out, "would you please consider yourself now and henceforth, and no matter what anyone else ever asks of you, free to do any damned thing you want that doesn't hurt someone unnecessarily?"

It was the most sweeping freedom anyone had ever offered me. Citizenship in the freest nation on Earth doesn't confer that much freedom, even to its richest citizens. Perhaps especially not to them.

But of course she had already offered me— recommended to me!—that same freedom, in almost those exact words, years before. On the night she accepted me into her employment.

"Thank you, Your Ladyship. I believe I will," I said, and stretched until every muscle cracked.

"Then I am well pleased." She scrubbed at the lipstick on her and began to dress herself, ignoring the helplessly glowering Diana.

"And the first thing I'm free to do is thank you about a million times for tugging on your ear like that," I said. "That saved us."

"Well, it had to be either the ring or the earrings; she simply wasn't wearing anything else of her own. And she had to be using something to shield herself from the effects of the damned thing, and it made sense that one would keep the shield nearest the brain. Here, let's try them."

She took the earrings from me, and put one on each of us. "Let's try a test," she said, and characteristically picked the first thing that came into her head. "Please hug me."

Grinning, I hugged her.

We giggled together as we hugged. In a joke voice she said, "*No,* no, no—"

"We're going about this wrong," I said. "Please *stop* hugging me."

She disobeyed me. "Please stop hugging *me,*" she said.

And with exquisite pleasure, as much as that stretch had given me, I ignored her too.

But we cut it short; we were busy. "So they work even one at a time," Lady Sally said, taking mine in her fingers and examining it. "Two earrings for symmetry, surely, but there didn't have to be a shield-generator in each one. Braces *and* belt. God, how paranoid she must be. Afraid of her own magic. How bad could it have been if the shield had failed? She'd still have been the only one who knew what was going on, still in control."

"Lady, what are we going to do?"

She frowned. "Some distasteful things. I've dawdled long enough." She checked on Judith and Priscilla, then approached the silently writhing Diana, who clutched vainly at her as she approached. "Stop that at once," she said, sounding for all the world like a stern aunt taking a rectal temperature, and Diana slumped resignedly. "Please don't struggle, now," Lady Sally admonished her. She took Diana's right hand in hers, and with some effort managed to remove the milk opal ring. "Answer by moving your head: you want this?" She held it up so Diana could see it.

Diana nodded vigorously.

"Answer me by moving your head: you think you need this?"

Again.

"Think about how much you want this. Think about why you think you need it."

Diana's face was suffused with a hopeless naked yearning.

Lady Sally said, looking her square in the eye, "Forget it. Really."

Diana's face smoothed over.

"Please forget all about it," the Lady amplified, "what it is, and what it does, and why you felt it was necessary, and at least the last three crucial insights that allowed you to create it, and above all forget everything—except my orders!—that has transpired from this moment back to the time you walked in my House."

Diana now had the preoccupied expression of someone who is playing a game of chess with herself that is going to take hours.

"Are you mad at anyone anymore?" the Lady asked her softly.

She shook her head no, slowly, wonderingly, and went back to her chess game.

Lady Sally turned back to me. "I must confess that a part of me is tempted to just put this thing back on her finger, ask her to make sure that it never leaves her finger, and turn her loose. She'd never figure out exactly what was wrong, but for the rest of her life, she'd be exactly the sort of agreeable, pliable blonde that some men dream of. She certainly deserves it, for what she has done to my friends this night. But there's too much risk that someone else would figure things out, and take it from her dead hand. And besides, I'd hate to be responsible if someone asked her to drop dead."

I giggled. "Me, I'd kind of want to be around the first time someone asked her to go—"

"Please, dear. Vengeance is counterproductive. Not to mention the fact that it gets your soul all sticky."

Vengeance made me think of something. "Lady, what's going to happen when Sergei's people find out he's dead?"

"Oh, God. Well, there's no publicity problem at least. When a KGB man dies in a—"

"Sergei was KGB?"

"No, dear, he was a private citizen who carted around a poison tooth and a small cannon as eccentricities. As I was saying, when a KGB bites down in a bordello across the river from the United Nations, there is very little difficulty in making it didn't happen. But we must be very careful never to let them suspect for an instant *why* he didn't do it. You and I must give that some thought. But first things first. Wait here patiently, everyone!"

Together we dragged Sergei's body out into Reception, where Ruth still snored. We left him curled up as naturally as we could on a couch, covered him with his coat. I changed to my own overcoat, and my own boots. We fetched out the guns and ax and smashed sign; the weapons went into the gun-locker and the shards of wood and paper went out into the dumpster. Then we hurried back into the Parlor. Kate had taken Judith and Priscilla up to the Infirmary.

Lady Sally went to Diana. "Diana, listen to me carefully, please. In just a minute I am going to send you home in a taxi. But I want you to remember this, always. The next time someone tries to control you, Diana, and every time thereafter, please remember that their reaction to you is as natural as your height and beauty and brains. Forgive them their flaw, as you would have them forgive you yours . . . and you'll find it makes it easier for you to outwit them. Once an opponent angers you, you're his, you know. Will you do that for me?"

Diana nodded her head slowly.

"That's a good girl. Will you do two things for me when you get home tonight? Yes? All right: first, regain the power of speech, and second, forget you've ever been to my House or even heard of it."

Diana nodded again.

"Now please wait there on the couch until I can get you a cab, dear."

Diana did as she was asked.

Lady Sally addressed the room. "Darlings? Lords and Ladies? Attend me please. I am extremely reluctant to do this. I find that a mind is a very poor place to try and bury something ugly for any length of time. Pressure builds and finally blows out a gasket somewhere else. I suspect some of you may, in the fullness of time, end up having some sort of seemingly inexplicable mental turmoil, and most of you will end up in the hands of expensive therapists who won't have a *clue* as to what's really wrong with you. But that can't be helped, I'm afraid. I shall try to be there for you if I can—but to allow this knowledge to remain in your minds would leave a hole in the world too big to mend. Would you all please forget that anything unpleasant or unusual has occurred here tonight?"

"Yes, Lady," came the soft chorus, after which everyone looked vague and slightly disoriented. They found themselves facing her, so they waited, patiently and amiably, to hear what she had to say.

"Would you all," she said clearly, "please consider yourselves now and henceforth, and no matter what anyone else ever asks of you, free to do any damned thing you want that doesn't hurt someone unnecessarily?"

This chorus was more like a rousing cheer. "Yes, Lady!"

"Then let the party resume, my darlings."

As the assembly broke up into laughter and conversation and slightly puzzled good cheer, Lady Sally motioned me to follow her and strolled casually to the fireplace. We stood before the crackling hearth, side by side, silent with our shared knowledge, for several minutes. I had a lot to think about.

Our introspective trance was broken finally by Phillip, who came down the stairs with a puzzled smile on his face. He had taken advantage of Lady Sally's blanket benediction of freedom to dress. "That must have been some incredible client I was just with. Cut me up like a side of beef, and I can't recall a single thing about her— if it was a her—and as far as I remember, it didn't hurt a bit. Who was that naked person?"

"Don't worry about it, lad," Lady Sally told him.

"Okay."

"And see Kate when she's free, get yourself looked after."

"I will," he promised, and wandered off to the bar.

She returned her gaze to the flames.

"I've always liked a fireplace," she said. "My husband, too. Something restful about a bit of domesticated fire caged in stone." She twirled the ring meditatively in her hand. "Handy for throwing things into."

Maybe a professional pitcher could have

thrown that ring harder and maybe not. It shattered into dust on the back wall of the fire-place, and the dust showered down over the flames.

I took off my milk opal earring and watched, mesmerized, what firelight did to it. "You should have waited until I took this off and asked *me* to forget, too," I said.

"For your peace of mind I wanted to," she murmured softly. "But I didn't dare. However unlikely, suppose someone else stumbled across what Diana did? Suppose, for instance, that the KGB somehow did learn what forced Sergei's hand? They're very good, you know. Do you suppose they'd rest until they had a ring of their own? There *has to be* some one moral person alive who knows the secret, is capable of rec-ognizing the signs in news reports that no one else thinks are meaningful, and see that it gets reported to the proper authorities—if, God for-bid, that black day ever comes. And Sherry, I am not a young woman."

I felt more crushed by the weight than pleased by the compliment. But where else could I *put* it? And did I really want memories—even dread-ful ones—removed from my own mind?

"I understand," I said finally.

I turned the earring over in my hand, watch-ing blue fire dance like wit. "A shame to destroy opal like this. Still, opal used to have a reputa-tion in olden times for being an unlucky stone."

"Oh, don't destroy it, darling. It has no

aggressive use: one of the few true purely defensive weapons. There could come a day when we need it. And it would be well to have both. Braces *and* belt, like poor Diana." She smiled, a bone weary smile. "For some reason I'm feeling paranoid."

And you know, I thought then that she was. But now, years later, I'm no longer quite so sure.

How do *you* explain this *glasnost* business, for instance?

BOOK FOUR

DOLLARS TO DONUTS

CHAPTER 8
FUNNY MONEY, HONEY

I'd been raped by three terribly sweet Japanese earlier that evening, and my next scheduled appointment wasn't for hours, so I was in the Parlor nursing an iced tea and enjoying myself when the Professor arrived.

I'm not a rape-simulation specialist, like Brandi or Tim; more of a utility infielder. But the role requires little work or acting skills. And Japanese men, their natural politeness intensified by the current political climate, are a pleasure to work with, before, during, and after. (Every artist in Lady Sally's House knows a code word which will fetch instant help if things get out of hand—and sadly, most of us have had occasion to use it—but to my knowledge none of us has ever used it while with a Japanese.)

191

They had, for instance, taken exquisite pains to leave no marks on me, a courtesy I appreciated since my shift was just beginning.

So I was in a mellow mood as I sipped my drink and bantered with colleagues and customers in the Parlor. I had relieved my clients of two kinds of yen, with minimum exertion, and enjoyed myself in the process. When rape is *not* inevitable, but a matter of free choice—well paid and warmly appreciated—relax and enjoy it, I always say. (Any other time, cripple the bastard.)

And Lady Sally's Parlor is a mellow place to be in any case. It may just be the nicest place on Earth. It is unquestionably the nicest place in Brooklyn.

If you teleported a stranger into that room and told him he was in a whorehouse parlor, he would not believe you. A large, open room, with area rugs and furniture groupings defining smaller conversational areas. Comfortable luxurious furnishings, warm colors, indirect lighting, local pools of greater brightness from table lamps. Half a dozen paintings on the walls, none abstract and only one of them even slightly erotic. (Upstairs Lady Sally maintains a large gallery packed with what I believe to be the finest private collection of pornographic art in the eastern United States, viewing hours by appointment; but the Parlor is not the place for such things.) A ventilation system designed to cope with a lot of smokers and a lot of nonsmokers, aided by a cheerily crackling fireplace. Quiet,

expert piano in the background, sensitive to the
mood of the moment. And in the center of the
room, visually dominating it (without in any sense
overwhelming it) is Lady Sally's trademark: the
magnificent wrought-iron spiral staircase, elabor-
ately filligreed and large enough to allow two
couples to pass each other. It is an intrinsically
beautiful object, its railings forming an immense
DNA double-helix. It winds upward to the second floor, where we artists entertain our clients.
Few indeed are the unhappy feet that have ever
trod its trusty treads in either direction. Especially down.

But while Lady Sally's Parlor may physically
resemble an exclusive men's club, no men's club
ever had such a heterogeneous collection of
members. I don't mean just the obvious fact
that the crowd is co-ed: I mean that the only
things they all seem to have in common are
good manners, good cheer, and a high degree
of tolerance. (You would expect that all of a
whorehouse's customers would have horniness
in common—but you'd be amazed how often
people come to Sal's, have a few drinks and a
few laughs in the Parlor, and then go home.)
I don't know any other place where men and
women of all ages, social classes, and degrees
of pulchritude mingle with such ease and
unselfconsciousness.

From where I sat, for instance, I could see
a stock broker in his seventies earnestly convers-
ing with a twenty-five-year-old bus driver and a

stunning redhead in her forties (a client, not an artist); and an eighteen-year-old second baseman simultaneously carrying on a chess game with Juicy Lucy (his own age and gorgeous) and a tickle fight with Ruth (sixty-one, then, a hundred and seventy pounds, and without question the one who was going to be leading him up the spiral staircase shortly); and in the opposite corner of the room, two Russian attachés in hilarious attempt to converse with an African diplomat and an Irish cop. (There's a decidedly international flavor to Lady Sally's Place, located as it is just across the river from the United Nations.) The Parlor's population that night happened to approximate the ideal fifty-fifty male/female ratio, each of those groups comprising roughly two-thirds clients and one-third artists: a pleasant balance, assuring the artists of work and the clients of minimal waiting.

I was not actively trolling for clients; I'd already banked good tips and had appointments later. But I was still on duty, and a girl can't have too much money. So when a tan, handsome brunette in business dress sat down beside me on the wide low couch, I made room for her and smiled warmly. I didn't recognize her, and I'm good with faces, so I said, "Hello, dear—welcome to Lady Sally's House. My name is Sherry."

"Hello, Sherry," she said in a soft husky contralto. "It's a pleasure to meet you."

Clients need not give even a House name

unless it suits them. "Likewise, love. Have you been a guest here before?"

"No—and I can already see that's been a mistake. My, that's a lovely dress."

"Thanks," I said, pleased; that dress took me weeks to make. Lady Sally insists that artists dress in the Parlor as though they've just come from a party at Gracie Mansion. Once in a while we have. "Can I get you something to drink? Coffee, perhaps, or something stronger?"

"Why, thank you," she said, setting down her purse and crossing her legs. "That's very kind of you. A single malt over a single cube would be lovely."

"Wait here," I said, and got up to head for the bar. Halfway there the penny dropped into the slot; I slowed in mid-step—then continued on my way without looking back. Discretion is something Lady Sally has drilled into us. I built the drink, telling Ginny to put it on my own tab, got another iced tea for myself and brought both back to the couch.

"This one's on me," I said, handing the Scotch over and seating myself again.

"That's sweet of you," the brunette said, and drank half of it in a single swallow. "My, that's delicious. May I ask you something, dear?"

I moved flirtatiously closer on the couch and lowered my voice sharply. "Professor, you can ask me anything . . . as long as you tell me what the hell you're doing in drag. You aren't changing your tastes, are you?"

His control was good, but from up close I could tell I had frightened him. "Oh shit, Mo—" he whispered.

"Don't panic," I murmured. "You did great! I don't think anyone else is going to spot you. I wouldn't have myself: it was that silly single-cube business that gave you away."

"Hell," he whispered, still using a woman's voice. "Are you sure?"

"Professor, maybe a thousand men have come through that door in drag since I took this job . . . and you're the first one that's ever fooled me for one minute. And I know you better than the rest of the staff. So relax. What's the masquerade about?"

He looked somewhat reassured. "Uh . . . Mo, I need to see Lady Sally alone for a few minutes. In complete privacy."

"Privacy we've got plenty of, here. Follow me upstairs—then I'll slip down the back way and send her up to you. Will that do?"

"God bless you, Mo!"

On the way to the staircase I glanced back—and had to admire him. The way he was waggling his hips as he walked made me want to do things to and with him for which he simply was not equipped. That's talent.

The Professor is the best con-man in the five boroughs. He's created some of the most ingenious scams I ever heard of—and worked them so brilliantly that only among his colleagues is he a legend. I *think* he's in his middle thirties, but I've seen him convincingly be both ten years younger and forty years older. I once worked for him briefly, working my way up from bait to player before deciding that my own temperament was happier giving the customers something back for their money. I particularly admired two things about him: his distaste for all forms of violence, and his inability to swindle anyone he did not dislike. "Widows and orphans have nothing to fear from me," he used to say, "nor any honest decent citizen. It's just that there are so few honest decent citizens."

I took him up to my studio, since going one flight higher to my apartment during working hours might have drawn attention to us. (I've heard of houses where the girls are expected to live in the same rooms where they work. Thank heaven Lady Sally has more class than that!) Robin, of course, had long since tidied up after the Japanese, changed the sheets and aired the place out. Robin works harder than anyone else in the House, not excepting Lady Sally herself, and seems to get more pleasure out of his work than most of the clients get from their play. (His only major disappointment in life is that his Mistress Cynthia won't let him wear his maid's costume during shifts: it makes some of the other clients uneasy.) I left the Professor there with a fresh Scotch from the studio bar, and slipped out the other door, the one which leads to the Discreet Wing.

❖   ❖   ❖

I guess I should explain a little of the basic physical layout of Lady Sally's House.

Most customers enter the building through the main door on the south side, are greeted at the reception area, and pass through into the Parlor. A smaller percentage choose either the west or east door, which lead to the female-only and male-only lounges I've mentioned before. All three staircases lead to the artists' studios on the second floor, laid out in three wings like a wide letter U.

But a few customers enter the north door, using a private key. There is a small antechamber inside, but it is unstaffed, and contains only an intercom and a supply of masks for those who wish them. Through this entrance come those clients who must have utter discretion: it's the doorway I was carried through, bleeding profusely, on my first night in Lady Sally's. No lounge or staircase here; an elevator leads upstairs, one-way glass in its door so that clients can be sure the hallway is clear before leaving the elevator. That hallway is sealed off from the other, more public corridors by locked doors at either end. All special-purpose studios (the Casting Couch, the Girls' Locker room, etc.) are in the center of the building, so that they can be entered from either the Public Wings or the Discreet Wing. So are a couple of standard-issue studios, including my own.

So by leaving my studio through the door opposite the one I'd entered, I was able to take a second, staff-only elevator down to Lady Sally's office without being seen by either clients or artists.

Lady Sally answered my knock at once. "Pass right through, darling!" said the familiar husky voice.

She was at her desk, going over accounts. I watched her work, wondering why no one ever seems to hate her. Short, dark, and slender, with permed red hair and a figure I envy, and warmth and style and charm and prodigious energy. Everyone forgives her for it, somehow. She comes across something like a female version of Lord Buckley in his between-raps persona, gloriously high, affecting an upper-class British accent so patently fraudulent that it cannot be taken as pretentious, and treating everyone she meets as though they were fellow members of the Royal Family whose names she cannot quite recall at the moment. I think she is the most unselfconscious person I ever knew. Is that because she never met anyone who did not like her—or is it the other way around? This quality above all others I most envy her.

Her true age is one of the great mysteries. Most of the time she seems like a mother elf . . . but when it suits her I believe she could give a statue an erection. She hardly ever sees clients personally these days—but none of them ever gives up hope. She must have been something when she was younger. She's something now.

There are many things to like about Lady Sally's House. But I think what I like best is what *isn't* there: the kind of clients Sally will not accept. Sniggerers. Ugly drunks. Slobs. Sleazeballs. People of inadequate personal hygiene or deficient manners. Bigots. Those who confuse their personal tastes with morality. People who don't respect us artists, and what we do. You know: shitheads.

Any of the Lady's artists may choose to turn down any client, with no questions asked—but Sally's initial screening is so good that it seldom happens. In the oldest and most demanding of professions, she's a joy to work for.

And a privilege. She is even more fussy about artists than she is about clients, and I don't mean technical skills. Lady Sally is running a permanent party, and she only wants her friends there. I've always been proud to be one of them.

Just seeing her now made me grin, as always. The twinkle in her merry hazel eyes is about the only thing in her House that is contagious. "Got a minute, Your Ladyship?"

"For you, dear girl, always! Take a pew. That was a nice bit of work earlier tonight. You know I don't employ racists, but some of the girls are just a bit reluctant to work with Japanese these days."

"As long as you watch them at the bar, they're fine. I wish all my clients were as clean and polite as Two-san and his friends." The only dismaying thing about the leader of tonight's

Japanese contingent had been his insistence on using the House name "Two-San Arizona." Oh, well, there's no such thing as a perfect rapist, I suppose.

"And as modestly hung. What in the name of Adam's off ox is the Professor doing with those astonishing tits?"

Up on the third floor Big Mary sits in the Snoop Room each night, watching the status board, monitoring the individual studio bugs for sounds of trouble, armed with a panic button and intercom she can use to summon Priscilla the bouncer (and any clients who feel helpful) from downstairs. But as far as I can tell, Lady Sally just reads Mary's mind. She always knows what's going on everywhere in her House.

I shrugged. "Something must have gone very sour for him. He's scared stiff. He wants to talk with you in private. They are impressive, aren't they? And he wears them so well."

She nodded. "Beggar could earn me a fortune . . . if he were willing to work for a living. Always did enjoy making pros out of cons."

I refused to wince. "Shall I try to work up something about a film critic making prose from Cannes?" She'd started it.

She did too. "Dear God, no. As the actress said to the bishop." She closed her account book, stood up and checked her face and dress in the mirror behind her desk. "Well-well-well, let's go see the silly little shit. Must be some way we can extract him from the chowder.

Question is, of course, how badly do we get our fingers burnt?"

"Knowing the Professor, use tongs."

She paused as we reached the door. "Maureen, dear?"

"Yes, Lady?"

"You still care about him, don't you?"

"From you, that's a pretty dumb question. He was my first lover. I've regretted leaving him since the door closed behind me. I still love him, yes, Lady. Tits and all. I just can't live with him."

"That's the way I feel about most men, darling."

He had found the collection of erotica I keep in one of the drawers beneath the bed; we found him leafing through the *Juliette* engravings with an expression of bafflement. Well, some of them baffle me too. He was still in masquerade, but had unbent to the extent of removing the high heels. I noted that he was holding his cigarette the way a woman holds one. The Professor could be a sensation on Broadway—if he didn't insist on writing his own lines and could stand the company of actors.

"This is unbelievable," he greeted us absently, in his female voice.

"No, it isn't," I said.

"No, but I mean this one just isn't physically poss—forgive me!" He sprang from the bed, stood tall in his stockinged feet and bowed deeply from the waist. Somehow it didn't look silly. He spoke at male pitch now. "Your Lady-ship, it is as always an enormous pleasure to greet you. Please pardon my churlishness; I was distracted. Thank you for indulging me with this most discreet meeting." The Professor always comes all over British in Lady Sally's presence, and does it much better than she does. He could steal women from Cary Grant.

"Rubbish," she said, tickled to death. "You silly old horsethief, what have you gotten yourself into this time?" She sat in my armchair and I perched on the hassock.

He sat back down on the bed and recovered his drink. "A steaming tureen of minestrone, I fear. The cry goes round Brooklyn: 'The Profes-sor has the wind up.' My only consolation—and an inadequate one—is the fact that I despise my insurance agent."

"Minestrone? You have come into conflict with the Families?"

"Nothing that simple. Family business can often be negotiated. I'm in much deeper soup than that. Nonetheless, the said soup scores high in tomato, pasta and garlic content. Do you know a man who rejoices in the sobriquet of Tony Donuts?" He gulped the last half of his drink.

"Oh, no!" I exclaimed. I stopped being amused by his predicament and began to get scared for him.

"I certainly do know the son of a bitch," Lady Sally said. "Gorilla with shoes on? Looks like he bites the heads off baby rabbits to floss his teeth?

He was in my Parlor once a few years back. For about three minutes. Bugger had the manners of a hungry weasel. I gave him an invitation to the world." Now I began to be a little afraid for Sally. Big Travis used to get all grey-faced and spitty if he saw Tony Donuts across the street. "One of half a dozen times in living memory that Priscilla required assistance in ejecting a client. He broke a longshoreman's face and two chairs before I arrived with a scattergun. Glad to see the back of that lumbering lump of limburger, though I can't say it was much improvement on the other side."

"He was too drunk to remember where he'd been the next day," the Professor said grimly, "or you'd have seen him again. You've had a narrow escape, Lady. Think of this man as bad news on burnt toast."

"He's not an official wise guy, a made man," I told her. "He's an independent. You know how the world works, Lady. If you're Italian but not with one of the Families, you had better not compete with them. He does. That's how tough he is."

She frowned. "What's his line?"

"Paper products," the Professor said.

"That's scarcely competition," she said. "I know the Families have taken a strong position in that line lately, but counterfeiters don't compete with each other. The capacity of the market for counterfeit money is effectively infinite."

"The same is true of the goods and services

in which you yourself deal, dear lady. Without wishing to be nosy, does it not require considerable effort and diplomacy to retain your own independence?"

"Well . . ." I happen to know the reason that Lady Sally is permitted to remain a free agent. The heads of three Families that do *not* control that particular section of Brooklyn have a better time at her House than they do in any of the sorry joints they own themselves. Pressure was applied; an accommodation was reached. But Family politics are always unstable, aren't they?

"It's a matter of respect, you see. Sicilians kill competitors, even when it profits them nothing, on general principles. It is, they seem to feel, merely what one does. And Signor Donuts offends further in offering a superior product. But him they pretend not to see. He is too dangerous."

She shook her head wonderingly. "Superior product? Hard to imagine a galoot such as you describe being a gifted engraver."

"He didn't need to be. He simply found out who the best paper-cutter on the East Coast was . . . then killed that man and took his plates and paper. A charmingly simple and direct approach is his hallmark. He constructs Tony-Donuts-sized holes between himself and whatever he wants."

She nodded thoughtfully. "That's why I threw him out. It seems I was lucky to make it stick. How did he get that preposterous name?"

"Are you sure you want to know?" I asked.

She considered that. "Yes, I think I do."

"Professor?" I knew the story, but I was curious to see how he would phrase it.

"Ahem. Briefly stated, Your Ladyship, Mr. Donnazio wished to restrict a gentleman's freedom of movement, and the tools at hand included a mallet and two large spikes. Later, when this man's liberty was at least theoretically restored, a policeman was heard to observe that a certain portion of the gentleman's anatomy now resembled a pair of donuts."

"Good God," Lady Sally exclaimed. "How had the fellow offended him?"

"Signor Donnazio was engaged in raping the man's wife at the time, and the man would not stop pestering him."

She shuddered and frowned ferociously. "I begin to see why he gave Priscilla trouble. Nasty piece of work. All right, let's make this march. How and why did you manage to anger Tony Donuts, boy?"

The Professor lit a new cigarette. "Pure rotten luck. In the course of business I developed a need for funny paper in a largish amount. The sting required the best, as the mark knows paper. He'd have spotted Families product in a twinkling. So—"

"You perfect chump," Lady Sally said, "are you telling me you tried to sting this Donuts monster for the bait for your other swindle?"

He drew himself up and thrust out his tits.

"I beg your pardon, Lady! Do I look that stupid?"

Neither of us said a word or moved a muscle.

"I bought his paper fair and square and paid cash, perfectly good cash. The *last* of my cash. Five thousand legit for fifty thousand bogus. We parted company, just as quickly as I could politely arrange it, I assure you, and I passed from his life. Or tried to. But Tony Donuts is like a bad egg. He keeps coming back on one."

"What went wrong?"

"The damned Secret Service. You will naturally understand that the Treasury Department takes a dim view of Tony's present hobby. His plagiarized art is so good that a sizable number of agents have been devoted to tracking him down. Apparently one of them tired of living on his salary. He contacted Tony and sold him a summary of his file. For my five thousand, damn it.

"Follow me carefully, now. The T-men have located Tony's plates. They have tied them to him. What they do *not* have are any samples of currency which can be proven to have been produced *since* the date at which the plates can be proven to have passed into his control. Naturally, mere possession of the plates is a serious criminal offense. But they would prefer to arrest him for a more serious, and more newsworthy, felony. And Tony, though a creature of simple and direct impulses as stated above, is just prudent enough to realize that wholesale massacre of federal agents is simply not cost effective. Are you beginning to see the picture, ladies?"

"Tony Donuts wants his fifty gees back," I said.

"Urgently."

"And you haven't got it anymore."

He bowed sitting down. "Nothing germane remains outside the nutshell."

"Is he willing to return your five thousand?" Lady Sally asked.

The Professor smiled. "You know, I actually asked him. Not bravery; the words just came out of my mouth before I could manage to cut out my tongue. He chortled. Have you ever heard Tony Donuts chortle?"

"As a matter of fact, that's precisely why I threw him out."

"Of course I told him his funny paper was unrecoverable. I also assured him that the nature of the game I was running made it absolutely certain that not a dollar of it would ever get into circulation. He declined to believe me, for the perfectly sensible reason that that is what I would have said whether it was true or not. Moreover, he didn't care. He said that—" He hesitated. "He said that either I could produce his engravings, every last one of them, within two days, or . . ."

"Go on, son."

"Or people would have to start calling him Tony Life Savers."

"It's a damned lie," I told Lady Sally. "They'd be donuts. Big donuts. I *know*."

"So do I, dear," she assured me. "And there are a lot of marks walking around in the certain knowledge that the Professor has large ones. Nonetheless, I imagine he wouldn't want them to become *hammered* brass. You're quite certain the stuff is beyond reach, Professor?"

"Irrevocably. Out of the country. And the sting won't pay off for nearly a month, so I can't simply leave town. The payoff is too tempting."

"Forty-eight hours is your deadline."

"Of which some five are already past. It might as well be forty-eight years. I wish it were. So, since there is no chance of appeasing this man, and I wish to preserve my kegs untapped, I've come to beg for sanctuary. All I need is somewhere to lie doggo until the day comes when his greed outweighs his caution and he runs off another batch. It can't be long in coming. Tony has barely enough brains to keep his ears apart. At worst I'll be gone in a month, when my mark ripens. Uh . . . I'd go so far as to work for my keep."

I stared.

"Not in an artistic capacity, of course. The kitchen, the Snoop Room, clean-up, anywhere out of the public eye."

Lady Sally looked deeply distressed. "Professor, the idea of you doing honest work is like the idea of tearing down Ebbett's Field. No matter what the reasons, it just shouldn't be done. I'd sooner let you run up a tab."

"Bless you, My Lady."

"—but I would much rather get you out of this soup than have you hang around while it simmers away. Freeloaders in a working House are bad for morale."

"I am open to all suggestions. Coming here was, I assure you, a last resort."

"Hmmm. What denominations are involved?" Sally asked him.

"Tens, of course. Who in their right mind would counterfeit anything else? Strike that: we're speaking of Tony Donuts."

"We're talking about five thousand pieces of paper," she corrected. "You could fit it into a largish briefcase."

"I did just that."

"So the question becomes, how do we fill the briefcase?"

"I've told you," he said. "It can't be done. The funny money is out of reach, which leaves me no way to placate Signor Donuts."

"Then we shall simply have to stiff him."

"Eh? I mean, 'Beg pardon?' "

"We'll give him real money."

"Oh."

The Professor got up and began to pace the studio.

"Of course," he said. "We'll just give him fifty thousand dollars of real money. Brilliant. How elegant. How simple. How silly of me to miss it." Then, big: *"How the* hell *am I going to come up with fifty large in two days with no operating capital?"*

"Simplest thing in the world," she said imperturbably. "Rob a bank."

"Rob a bank!" the Professor squeaked. "HOW?"

"I leave that as an exercise for the student," Sally said. "You do call yourself a player, do you not?"

The Professor started to reply, then shut up. And slowly he began to smile. . . .

CHAPTER 9
DOLLARS TO DONUTS

We left him there happy as a clam. Sally told him that if he got bored or when I needed the studio, he could go downstairs and hang out in the women-only Lounge, but he assured her that he would not be bored. The Professor is never so happy as when he has a new scam brewing. He would probably have gotten around to robbing a bank sooner or later; it was the sort of technical challenge that inspired him. If you and he both live long enough, one day you are going to hand him the shirt off your back, and for the rest of your life you'll wonder what ever possessed you.

It worked out that all my appointments that night requested special-purpose studios (one Back Seat, two Casting Couch and a Police

Interrogation), so I didn't see the Professor again until the shift was over at three A.M. When I got to the studio door, still toweling my hair dry, I met Lady Sally, elegant in a silk wrapper and mules, accompanied by her husband and Big Mary. We all exchanged friendly hugs and passed inside.

Lady Sally's husband Mike is a huge red-headed shanty Irishman; he could probably walk normally with her stuffed down one trouser leg. He has a pirate's grin and terrible taste in cigars. He works some job out on the Island that has the same hours as ours, and usually doesn't get in until I'm in bed. I like him a lot, and wish I got to see more of him. He's the kind of man you can hug naked from the shower with his wife watching, if you understand what that means. Big Mary is also Irish, come to think, and in fact could pass for Mike's sister. She wore gaily colored satin pajamas. She ran over two hundred at that time, and was about as far as you can get from the stereotype of the jolly fat lady, having an acerbic wit and no tolerance for fools. Nevertheless there are reasons why she was an *extremely* popular artist until she retired to run the Snoop Room a few years back. I'll hug her naked any chance I get.

Lady Sally introduced them both to the Professor, and he greeted them formally, doffing his wig like a hat as he bowed. Out of deference to his hostess he went British again, appearing to grow a monocle. He had made a pot of tea on the hotplate. Everyone sat and I passed out cups. All three of my friends hit it off at once; neither Mike nor Mary seemed to find the Professor's attire odd. With his permission, Lady Sally brought them into consultation on his predicament. Mary expressed sympathy, and inquired after his progress. It turned out that there was almost none, but the Prof refused to be dismayed. The harder the puzzle, the better he liked it.

"I've done a great deal of basic spadework," he said cheerfully, "chiefly eliminating unprofitable lines of approach. The classical frontal assault is of course out of the question. I have no objection to a spot of violence when necessary, but I have never *planned* to commit violence. Aside from its karmic tendency to boomerang on one, it smacks too much of work. The same objection applies to those silly tunneling gambits beloved by filmmakers, and additionally I have a time problem. For a time I toyed with the notion of representing myself as a vault lock repairman engaged in routine maintenance, and relying on general charm to preclude any check of my *bona fides*. But while I'm confident that I could sustain the role itself after a few hours' research at the library, I am *not* a lock man, and would need more than forty-eight hours' education to become one. Again, too much work. The scheme does not play to my strengths.

"Therefore my course is clear: I must persuade

someone in legitimate authority to take that money from the bank and give it to me."

"Christ, is that all?" Mary said. "I thought you had a problem."

"It *shouldn't* be too difficult, friend Mary," the Professor agreed. "Consider that I will have had few if any predecessors. The worst moments in my profession come when one finds oneself the *second* person to have tried a particular sting on a mark. Your Ladyship, is the House buttoned up for the night?"

"The lodge is tyled," she assured him.

"Ah, so. May I ask you all to forgive me, then? This girdle is *killing* me." All four of us urged him to get comfortable, and he stripped gratefully down to panties and stockings. Mike offered to undress himself; Prof thanked him but assured him that it was unnecessary. "How do you ladies manage to endure these diabolical devices?" he asked us, poking maliciously at his bra and girdle and adding his wig to the pile.

"The same way you men put up with neckties," Mary said.

"I don't," said Mike with some smugness.

"Well, I don't put up with bras," she said. "Except for professional purposes. But they're the flip side of the same thing. A visible symbol to your society of your willingness to endure some small discomfort to please your neighbors. Our culture chooses to bind your neck, bind my belly and breasts; Chinese women bind their feet; some African men scar their faces."

"I just like the way they make my tits stick out," Lady Sally said. "What I've always found silly about men's underwear are those ridiculous openings on the front of jockey shorts."

Mike nodded vigorous agreement. "No man alive knows what the *hell* those things are for," he said. "It is not physically possible to piss with your unit in the shape of a letter Z."

"And the hole isn't big enough to get more than a couple of fingers in," I agreed. "Ladies and gentlemen, haven't we wandered a bit? Professor, have you any idea *whom*, of a bank's personnel, you want to target?"

"Elementary, my dear Nothing's-on," he said, scratching his bra mark. "The manager. Simple economy of effort. Only a bank manager could redirect that much mazuma without the need to involve others. Even a bank president would have to go through the manager for such a sum."

"There are two bank managers presently on my client roster," Lady Sally said, "but damn it, they're both sweethearts. I should hate to see them gaffed. In fact, I don't believe you could work up the necessary dislike, Professor."

"Huh!" Mary said. "Uh, Boss?"

"Yes, dear?"

"I need a temporary suspension of Rule Three."

Rule One at Lady Sally's House is, "Give full value at every performance." Rule Two is, "The customer need not always come first. Enjoy yourself; it's contagious." Rule Three reads: "Thou shalt not gossip about the clients—to each other or to other clients." (And rule Four is, "Thou shalt not recognize clients outside the House unless they acknowledge you first.") Of course Rule Three is impossible for an artist to obey. The stories we have are just too juicy not to share. In practice the rule has been modified to mean that you can tell stories about a client *if* you're careful to phrase it so that nobody can tell which specific client you're discussing.

Any of Lady Sally's Rules can be suspended in an emergency. But she gets to define "emergency."

"Is this client a current account?" she asked Mary.

"Hell, no. He took three strikes in three at-bats."

The third time one of the artists complains to her about a particular customer, Lady Sally gives that client a permanent invitation to the world. The complaint need not be more specific or concrete than, "What a creep." (She sometimes stretches a point for U.N. diplomats, saying that anyone who carries that much weight on their shoulders deserves the benefit of the doubt; as long as there's one artist in House willing to accept their business, and they don't actively annoy the other customers, diplomats can keep coming around.)

"In that case, speak on by all means. We have accepted that the general good presently requires a pigeon."

"Thanks, Boss. We had a bank manager in

here about three months ago. I don't know what his real name was, but his House name was 'Jim Brady.'"

"Winthrop Willoughby, Chemical Corn Exchange," Lady Sally said at once. "You're right, dear, I'd forgotten."

"Why, I filed the second complaint on that greaseball," I exclaimed. "What a creep. I don't mind if a customer needs me to say crude things about his wife . . . but he wanted me to say *creepy* things. I don't think he'd ever been in a House before; I had to lead him by the hand, so to speak. I didn't know he was a bank manager."

"Neither did I," Mary said, "until the third and last time I bugged his boogie-woogie. Brandi it was, and you know how much it takes to make her complain about somebody. The job itself went okay, as those things go . . . but then afterward the goniff started hinting around. Hinting about how much he hated his wife, and how wonderful it would be if she happened to sustain fatal injuries in a manner accidental enough to satisfy his insurance company, and how grateful he'd be to anybody who knew anybody who could bring that day closer."

Lady Sally scowled ferociously, Mike frowned, and the Professor was looking alertly interested.

"Well, naturally Brandi told him to walk north 'til his hat floated. He got nasty and tried to hurt her to make her keep her mouth shut. You know Brandi: she charges top dollar just to *pretend* to get hurt, and he hadn't tipped her for the last one. So she mangled his marbles for him and got the cuffs on him before she hit the panic button. Priscilla happened to be busy downstairs, so I had somebody spell me in the Snoop Room and went down and threw him out myself. Big blubbery windbag with a weasel eye, full of squawk and bluster and 'I have powerful friends in this town.' I'll be surprised if he's got a friend in the world; he must have inherited his job."

"Sounds like an ideal pigeon to me," Mike said.

The Professor sat up straight on my bed. "Excuse me," he said, perhaps to us. His eyes rolled up into his head, and his breathing slowed.

Mike looked at me.

"He's creating," I explained.

"Thought so," he nodded. He finished his tea and poured the dregs from the pot, watching the Professor with some interest. How often does one get to observe genius in action? Much less genius in garter belt and panties?

I was pleased myself. The Professor did not by any means go into such trances every time he planned a caper; not even most of the time. But when he did it was a virtual guarantee that the sting would succeed. It had been a long time since I'd last seen him thus. Too long, perhaps . . .

Besides, I have this peculiar character trait. Watching a man work gets me horny. Even a man I can't live with.

"Can I get a drink without disturbing him?" Mary asked.

"You can fire a cannon, or masturbate, or set his hair on fire," I told her. "He's *away*. Brandy for me."

Brandy suited the other two as well. (Lady Sally, of course, stuck with the tea.) By the time Mary had passed out the fourth glass, the Professor had come back from the Infinite. His eyes unrolled, his shoulders slumped slightly, and he acquired a wistful smile, as of one leaving Paradise to attend a sales convention in Columbus, Ohio.

"Eureka," he said softly, almost sadly.

Mike nodded and passed his own brandy to the Professor. "Funny feeling, isn't it, when you bust a tough one? Triumph, sure. Maybe a little secret relief that you pulled it off. But there's a fine sweet sadness in there, too, because now the golden moment is behind you. For a moment in there you were God . . . and now you're just a guy who used to be God for a minute, and will be again some day."

The Professor regarded him thoughtfully. "You show hidden depths, friend Michael. You are a creative man yourself?"

"In a small way, kinda in my spare time."

"Might one inquire as to your specific field of endeavor?"

"Puns."

The Professor regarded him with new respect. "Capital, my boy, capital!"

Mike looked pleased. "You don't believe, then, that puns are a lower case of humor?"

The Professor winced approvingly. "Not if you put a bold face on it, dear boy."

Mary made a wordless sound of protest and disgust; Lady Sally, perhaps most fittingly for the spouse of a paronomasiac, displayed no reaction at all. Myself, I made a polite grimace—and changed the subject. "Professor, am I right in guessing that you have a plan?"

He smiled at me. "Sherry, dear, you know me so well."

"Is there a part for me?"

Now he beamed. "Darling, an artist of your calibre is a welcome addition to any enterprise." He leered gallantly. "No matter which art is involved. And yet I confess that when I took the liberty of tentatively pencilling you into my new libretto, as indeed I have done, it was as much for the sweet sharp pleasure of your company as for your professional competence. It has always been a pleasure to work with you. Thank you: I am delighted to accept your sword beneath my banner."

My turn to beam.

"Your Ladyship?"

"Yes, Professor," Lady Sally answered.

"May I call upon you for some small assistance?"

"Is any cash outlay required? I ask purely for purposes of information."

"I think not. Spending cash is never a

problem for a resourceful man. Use of your phone, perhaps. Uh . . . would you have a briefcase I could borrow, suitable in size and aspect for the housing of fifty large in sawbucks?"

"Simplest thing in the world. People are always leaving the damned things here; I keep them in the Lost and Found for a year and then sell them. And sometimes the contents, if nonnarcotic." Sally does not permit in her House the use or possession of any drug that goes into the nostrils or the veins. "I can even supply some matched pairs, if that's any help to you."

"Excellent. And do you suppose Phillip could be persuaded to act as a phone shill? I'd be happy to compensate him handsomely . . . in a month's time."

"I'm sure that will present no problem," she assured him.

"Splendid! I am Chinaman to your abacus, Your Ladyship—I can always count on you." Mary kicked the side of the bed sharply, and Mike rolled his eyes. The Professor began gathering up his purse and discarded clothing. "Nothing further can be done until the sun shines again on this corner of Brooklyn, which it will do all too soon. Banner headlines in the *Post:* PROF NODS! Sherry, dear, if I could trouble you for the loan of a housecoat and slippers, perhaps Lady Sally will show me to some cubicle where I can doss for the night with minimal—"

"Professor," I interrupted, "would my apartment suit you?"

He set down his belongings, rose from the bed, and bowed low. "Sweet Sherry," he said, using my House name, "this is good hearing. You are not a sherry but a tawny port in a storm. Any time you offer your honor, I will gladly honor your offer."

" '—and all night long it was on 'er and off 'er,' " Mary said.

The Professor kicked the side of the bed experimentally. "Have I got it right?" he asked her. "It seems a curious sort of applause. Though oddly satisfying now that I've tried it. Well, thank you all very much for your company, as the actress said to the college of bishops, but I fear I'm keeping myself awake. Lovely Mary, friend Michael, it has been a pleasure meeting you, and doubtless will continue to be so. Your Ladyship—"

The three finished their drinks and rose. Goodnight hugs were exchanged. I noted that Mike seemed quite comfortable hugging a new male friend dressed like a female artist with bills due. I am of the school of thought which holds that a hug ought to resemble a number 1 rather than a letter A; so were both of them. Lady Sally, of course, is the one who taught *me* about hugs—and she was fond of the Professor. When it was Mary's turn, she grabbed him by both ears and pulled his face close enough to hers to cross his eyes.

"Prof," she said, "you're going to pop this Willoughby blister, aren't you?"

"The thing is a boat race," he assured her.

She kissed him so thoroughly that when she stepped back, his appreciation was apparent. (Which looked a little strange given the way he was dressed.)

And then we were alone, and *I* was hugging him.

"Maureen, you cuddly little armful," he said in my ear, and in his natural persona, "it's gonna be a pleasure to work with you again."

"Yes, it is," I murmured. His embrace was familiar and pleasant.

"It's only fair to warn you, I plan to make you pregnant."

"*Eh?*"

"But not until the day after tomorrow."

"Oh." There's no use questioning the Professor when he's feeling mysterious. And I had more urgent priorities. "Uh, Prof?"

"Yes, Maureen?"

"Look, I didn't see any reason to bring this up with the others here, but . . . when I offered you my apartment to sleep in—"

"—all you were offering was your apartment to sleep in?"

"Oh, dammit—"

"Maureen, it's all right. I understand."

"I'm not sure I do."

"It's probably for the best. Well, anyway, 'the better.' Thanks for your tact; that was sweet of you."

"Will it bother you to sleep in the same bed

with me?" Necessary if we were going to keep up appearances.

"Not at all, Mo. Not tonight, at any rate; I'm pooped. Besides, I was your friend before I was your lover."

Damn, damn, damn.

It was going to bother *me*. And I'd had more than a dozen men that day, most of them quite satisfactory lovers. . . .

The noon-to-five shift had already started by the time we got down to breakfast in the staff-only basement restaurant. Lady Sally came by as I was finishing my first cup of coffee, and told me that I was out of shift rotation for the duration. The Professor offered to compensate for the lost commissions—and me for my lost income—and we both declined indignantly. But we were both pleased that he offered.

He ate enough for three men. All his appetites are on the same scale. I cursed the scruples which had caused me to spend the previous night sleeping.

At his request I went upstairs after breakfast and dressed in my best drop-dead business outfit, put my hair up in a tight bun, took care with makeup. Back downstairs, I spent some time with Rhonda the phone lady, arranging for the rescheduling of standing appointments. Rhonda looks like Gary Cooper with hennaed hair, and over the phone she sounds like Shirley Temple in heat. She has great tact and an encyclopedic memory, and is a godsend to us artists; I knew I could leave the shuffling to her. I found the Professor in the Parlor picking out Hoagy Carmichael tunes on the piano. He was dressed male today, in a very snappy looking double-breasted from Wardrobe. (He's one of those maddening people who can wear clothes right off the rack . . . and somehow make them look as if a bespoke tailor created them around his personal mannequin.) We praised each other's outfits and left together.

I like to get out of the House once in a while, just to keep my appreciation of it keen. But the world always seems a grey and out of focus place when I first walk out the door. To be fair, it's not one of Brooklyn's better neighborhoods. Warehouses and factories, mostly, at least on the south side of the building. After we'd walked a couple of blocks in companionable silence, the Professor spotted a cab. He seemed to brush a hand across his face and age twenty years. "Play up," he murmured, and stepped out into the street in front of it, raising both hands. One he held palm out, imperiously; the other displayed an open wallet in which something gleamed. The cab shrieked to a halt. He sprinted round and flung open the back door. "Deputy Chief Monahan," he rapped, helping me in. "I'm commandeering yer hack; police emergency!"

"Sure ting, Mac." I didn't know this cabbie.

"Head for the bridge and don't spare the horses! Saints pickle us, what a day. All right, now, daughter, calm down and let's go over this again. Was His Eminence atall purple when you left him?"

I hated to sting a cabbie; they're good for business. But we were too far from the House to be connected with it—and I couldn't very well leave the Professor hanging. "Only in the usual places, Father," I said. "I mean, Daddy. But he was really stiff. In the other places, I mean."

"Park Avenue, you say."

I gave the address of a swanky hotel a few blocks from the Professor's apartment, and he relayed that to the driver. We riffed together all the way over the bridge and across midtown, entertaining the cabbie and—I was mildly dismayed to discover—me. As we pulled up in front of the hotel, the Professor leaned forward and fixed him with a stern glare. "Are you a good Catholic, mister?"

"Lemme put it dis way, chief. I usher at de six forty-five Mass every week."

"I can rely on your discretion then." He lowered his voice. "I want you to drive round to the laundry entrance and wait for me. I may be down shortly with a large rug to go to the Rectory. You take my meaning, laddy?"

The cabbie winked. "I got a big trunk," he assured him.

"Good man. From this day on you can't get a ticket in New York."

We waited in the lobby until the cab was

around the corner and then strolled leisurely to the Professor's place. At my request, he showed me the badge in his wallet. A genuine Junior Birdman badge.

"It's a small calculated risk coming here," he told me on the way up in the elevator. "When Donuts sells you something he means you can have it until he wants it back, and when he says you've got forty-eight hours that means you have until he feels a vagrant impulse to kill you. And this dump is where he'd start looking if the urge struck him. But there's stuff here I need."

"Some dump." The Professor lives well. Frequently; sometimes for months at a time.

"It keeps the rain off."

The elevator came to an imperceptible halt. We stepped out into a sumptuously carpeted hallway. "Yeah, it's handy little lean-to," I said. "When are you going to break down and tell me how we're going to sting Willoughby?"

"Aw, you're no fun."

"Come on, I want my script so I can study my lines. I'm damned if I'm going to go after fifty grand with an improv. I want to know why I have to be pregnant."

"Oh, all right." We reached his door and he put his key into the lock. "But honest, there's nothing to it. You could do it in your sleep, really. It's kind of similar to the job we did together on that diamond merchant back in— oh, hello."

Something large loomed inside the darkened apartment.

"I'm sorry," the Professor said graciously, "Have you two met? Tony, allow me to introduce my cousin Alice. Alice, this is my good friend Tony Donuts."

I gave him my very best smile. "Hello, Tony."

"Nice boobs," he said. "Close de daw."

The Professor was smiling beatifically as he turned back from the door. "Good to see you, Tony." He snapped on a small pole lamp, good for little more than mood lighting. The living room was a wreck. "Thanks for looking after things while I was away; you've done wonders with the place. I always say, what's the good of using first-rate sofa stuffing if nobody can see it? To what do I owe the pleasure—wasn't our appointment for tomorrow?"

I had no contribution to make to the dialogue. I was busy trying to restart my heart.

Trust a whore: there are all kinds of virility. Perhaps as many as there are men. The Professor, for instance, is (in his natural person) extremely slender and slightly built, and generally falls asleep on you after an hour or two. But those two hours are more fun than a whole night with a randy teenager or a muscled performance freak. (And I still regretted denying them to myself the previous night.) There's a little woman in the Professor, enough that he could carry off drag in Sally's Parlor, enough that I can empathize with him. I believe that femaleness and maleness are halves of a spectrum, a curve on which you can graph humanity and get a hell of a lot of overlap in the middle. Some disparage these so-called "in-betweeners," but I believe the true freaks are the few stuck way out at either end of the curve, their sexuality unalloyed by any of its complementary ingredient. Those poor perverts often carve wide paths through the world, driven as they are by untempered engines, inspiring the awe due mighty forces out of control. (I'm not talking here about Colt. His appetites are huge, granted. But they're under control since he came to work at the House. One of the happier men I know.)

The actor Robert Mitchum is about as male as a man can get *without* losing control. That's his appeal. To each man he meets his face says, "I'm so much more man than you that I have no need to prove it, or even rub it in. We're going to get along just fine." To each woman, it says, "We both know I can have you any time I'm ready. So I'll let *you* say when." Brute confidence, resulting in an easy-going disposition. So much strength there can be gentleness.

Graph Robert Mitchum on the female-male curve in your imagination. Now plot a point as far from him in one direction as Liberace is in the other. Label this genetic freak: "Tony Donuts."

The most visibly male thing about him, in that poorly lit apartment, was his instinctively aggressive stance. Then came his size and stature and fitness. He was built like Atlas's gym teacher, yet looked as springy on his feet as a bantam-weight boxer. I believed he could run around the world in a week, packing three oxen for snacks. The next most visibly male thing was what my colleague Tim would call the size of his basket. The lore of my profession to the contrary, there has never been a single medically authenticated case of a man so large that a receptive woman of average dimensions cannot accommodate him. But authentication, it suddenly dawned on me, requires that the woman survive to testify. . . .

But the *most* exaggeratedly male thing about him was the most subtle, and the one I noticed first, even in the dimness. His eyes were as eloquent as Mitchum's, and what they said to the Professor (or any male) was, "I wish you were more man; it would be more fun when I kill you." And what they said to me (or any female) was, "I'm already screwing you; you just don't know it yet. I hope you hate it . . . but you probably won't." I'm very used to men looking at me and wondering what I'll be like in bed, knowing they're going to find out. Tony Donuts already knew, in detail, and he wasn't impressed. What he wondered was how high he could make me scream.

Maybe it wasn't his eyes; the light was bad with the curtains drawn. Maybe it was his smell. It pervaded the torn-up apartment. A girl in my line of work gets a finely calibrated nose for man-smell, and Tony's smell set off alarm bells in my head. I wanted to be back at Lady Sally's, where all I had to do was say the panic word and survive until reinforcements arrived. Failing that, I wanted a large-caliber gun, so that I could shoot myself in the head before he did something worse than that to me. I was like a minnow in the presence of a shark; I could only pray that he had dined recently.

I smiled at him so big my lower lip split in the center, and waited for him to answer the Professor's question. If he had come here specifically to kill the Professor, out of impatience, then I needed to leap bodily through the nearest window in search of a nice merciful sidewalk. If he had some less urgent purpose, I could hold that in reserve. I was curious.

His voice made my lubricant run cold.

"It's like dis here," he said. "I ast youse nice to gimme back my Hamiltons, and ya says to me, 'it can't be done.' Then a little later ya says to me, 'two days.' Later on I get to tinkin', it can't be both. Which time are youse shittin' me? I tink about it, an' I remember when I hoit youse wuz after 'it can't be done' and before 'two days.' So de smart money says da handbills is gone, and dat means youse gotta be lookin' to leave town. So I come over to say g'bye. Maybe help youse move, after ya can't move so good by yaself no maw. I know dis great place in Joizy, a little wet but nice and peaceful."

"Tony—" the Professor began.

"Den I get here an' I see youse ain't packed

nuttin'. All ya stuff is here. So I decide to wait awhile before I go track youse down, see if ya come back fer anyting. Maybe yer out gettin' de posters after all. While I'm waitin', I figure, suppose he *can* get the tickets in two days. Why can't he do it in one? Maybe he's got 'em here right now. So I toss ya place."

The apartment looked as though a large dragon with claws had suffered an episode of epilepsy there. Anything that could have concealed five thousand treasury notes had been torn apart. I could not see any really comfortable places on which to be thrown down and raped to death.

"As I explained to you—" the Professor tried.

"Now you come in wit dis bimbo"—I did *not* look like a bimbo, never did except by specific client request—"an' I gotta figure youse ain't serious about dis. You figure youse got spare time."

"—she's my cousin, Ton—"

"I didn't make it clear, how bad I want de postcards. I gotta make it clear."

He moved forward with a bouncy stride.

The Professor spoke quickly but with confidence. "If you want to lose that dough—worse, leave it in the hands of the kind of clown who doesn't mind talking to grand juries—keep on coming, Tony. I've almost got it back from him for you . . . but this is a square guy I'm dealing with, a solid citizen. If I have so much as a bloody nose when I see him he's gonna get the wind up him and back off. Breaking my arm is

only a momentary pleasure—but beating a bad
paper rap will keep on being fun for three to
fifteen years under present statutes."

Tony Donuts had stopped moving forward.
"Youse almost got it back, huh?"

"It's like money in the bank," the Professor
assured him.

I wanted to kick him.

"So how come ya said youse couldn't do it
foist?"

"When I said it couldn't be done I meant it
couldn't be done without wrecking my own
sting . . . and I was tracking maybe a mil. Once
I realized that wasn't really so important, it
became a simple matter of cooking up a new
sting to get my bait back. It'll leave me broke,
but hey, for a friend . . ."

"A mil, huh?" Tony looked thoughtful. "I could
do sometin' wit' a mil." He frowned, shook his
head like a bull worrying flies. "Nah. I radda
have my fliers back. After tings cool down,
maybe you an' me we go get dis mil togedda.
When do youse get de scrolls back?"

"Like I said, Tony. Tomorrow, Friday."

"Youse can't speed it up?"

"You are my friend and I have a chance to
do you this favor. Can you picture me stalling?"

Tony almost smiled. It was odd to think that
he could be amused by anything other than
inflicting pain. The concept of resistance to his
will must have appealed to his sense of humor.

"No, I guess not. Ya can walk."

He turned to me for the first time since we had entered the apartment, and I stopped breathing. His gaze itched as it traveled up and down me. I was in a strange apartment, strewn with ruin and badly lit; I wanted to look around for hopeless escape routes. But it was more important to watch his eyes. He was about to make a decision on the order of *shall I have another cigarette now, or later?* and I wanted the early returns. I watched closely—

—and saw the danger pass. Even a Tony Donuts cannot rape every woman he encounters; too many women, not enough hours in the day. Perhaps he had a prior appointment to rip someone's ribs out. I watched his eyes, and saw the pupils contract slightly. When they do that, you don't even have to check the crotch; he's lost interest for now.

I decided to start breathing again. The pent-up air came out in a little *peep* sound. I refused myself permission to shudder, and then shuddered.

Before I knew he was going to move, he was right in front of me. I stiffened in terror, thinking I had misread the signs. I wanted to say something quick and confident and distracting, like the Professor had, and I could not remember how to form words. Tony smiled. He reached out with one massive hand and honked my left breast like an old automobile horn. It hurts your throat even more to shriek on the inhale than on the exhale, and takes more effort to stifle it. He released my breast just before I would have started squeaking on the exhale too, and patted me fondly on the head.

"I want youse ta start wearin' special underwear alla time from now on," he told me. "Black lacy stuff. I don't know just when I'll get back to youse, ya know?"

To my horror, I nodded.

And he was gone, out the same window he had come in.

There was a long pause.

When I spoke, my voice was very soft and quite steady. "A million dollars was enough incentive to do business with him?"

"I thought so right up until I met him. And then it was too late."

"Yes," I agreed. I sat down on the carpet.

"As Jethro once said to Homer, I was doing real good right up until gangrene set in. You see why I was willing to actually work in exchange for a hideout?"

"Yes." I said again.

"Well, I guess the next step is to—"

"Willard?" I said, unthinkingly using his real name for the first time in years. "If he ever has me . . . I'll need to die."

He sat down next to me and put his arms around me. "If things get that far," he told me, "I'll be dead already myself. We'll wait for him together in Hell, with the rest of the alumni." He stroked my hair. "But don't worry. To coin a phrase, I have a plan."

"It better work."

"I'll bet it does. Dollars to Donuts."

And suddenly we were both laughing like fools in each other's arms, huddled amid the ruins of the once swanky apartment. It was the kind of laughter that could have turned into tears . . . but it turned into something else instead. Like people in bomb shelters after the bombers have gone for the present, we found ourselves tearing at our clothes, and it turned out that there was a comfortable spot after all. A small one, anyway.

But do you know? the sex actually restored most of the tension the laughter had released.

Oh, it was good sex; we were both ready and we knew each other of old—but I hadn't consciously decided to *have* sex with him again yet. And if we were going to, it should have been a conscious decision. I mean, there we were, doing it, and both of us knew as we were doing it that we were no closer to being lovers again than we had been the night before.

So we settled for what we could get, carped us some diem, and there was comfort in it. But not enough closeness. I don't know that either of us cared a damn about the other's pleasure. We were not making love: we were fucking. Nothing wrong with that; just not enough right with it. When we were finished, we dressed in silence.

And when we did speak, our voices seemed too loud.

CHAPTER 10
FIRST STINGS FIRST

It turned out that the Professor really only needed two things from his apartment; fortunately both had survived the attentions of Mr. Donuts. The first item was a shiny new tape recorder. It was intact, even though it was capable of concealing at least a little money inside it, because Teac builds them solid: even Tony Donuts found it easier to simply unscrew the cover than to tear it off. The second thing Prof needed was access to his own personal printing press. It was a small thing, nothing like the monster that Tony must have used to produce the counterfeit money, and its structure could not have concealed a buffalo nickel. Prof said he used it principally to generate stock certificates and diplomas.

In less than an hour, he had caused it to disgorge something more useful for his immediate purposes: a small stack of business cards, convincingly elegant, identifying him as an agent of a large Hollywood casting agency. The name he used matched other ID which he already had available. (The driver's license and Social Security card were quite authentic, even though no person of that name existed.)

"I've used this agency before," the Professor said. "They're so big everybody's heard of them, but they have no New York branch. It's funny, but even a suspicious millionaire is less likely to check you out if it requires a long-distance call."

"Do I get a card?"

"No, honey. Today you are my loyal secretary, and secs don't get business cards. Your primary function this afternoon will be to make me seem totally harmless and legitimate to a suspicious woman in her home. Take it from me, a male alone can run into a lot of trouble trying to run the casting-agent wheeze. There are so many cynical, suspicious people in the world these days. Even the ugliest woman alive—and I suspect our target will be at least a finalist—believes that a rapist would want her. But a secretary or a fairy assistant usually reassures them."

"A pregnant secretary reassures them?"

"No, no. *Tomorrow* you're eight months pregnant. Today you're a cool, efficient secretary, and I'd be lost without you."

"Play it straight, in other words."

"You've got it."

An hour later we were before the door of a mansion in the ritziest part of Prospect Park South, and the Professor was whanging away with a door-knocker shaped like a horrid cast-iron rose. I wished I could take a picture of it to show Mary, who once worked as a blacksmith; she'd have vomited. The door was opened by a butler I'd have called large and powerful if I had not just met Tony Donuts. He seemed a little young for his job, but he had the gravity and utter impassivity of the best butlers.

"Good afternoon," he said in the totally unaccented voice of a radio weatherman. "How may I help you?"

"How ya doing? Nat Frenkel, Creative Associates, this's my right leg Carol. Here's my card. We'd like to see the lady of the house, Mrs. . . ." He snapped his fingers.

"Willoughby," I said.

"—Willoughby, yeah," the Professor said. "Would that be possible, you think?"

The butler scanned Frenkel's card carefully, then looked us both over. We were both well dressed, and I was carrying an expensive tape recorder.

"Mrs. Willoughby is not expecting you, sir?"

"Friend, she doesn't know us from Adam's off ox. But we only want a few minutes of her time; we gotta be back on the coast by sunrise."

He made his decision. "If you and your companion would care to wait in the parlor, sir, I will find out whether Mrs. Willoughby is at home. In the event that she is, may I inquire as to the nature of your business with her?"

"I'll be honest with you, pal. I won't know until I see her. Just ask her if she's got a minute, okay?"

"Very good, sir."

He led us inside and brought us to the parlor. I set the tape recorder down and looked around. It was a museum of horrors. Never in my experience had so much money been spent to assemble so much ornate ugliness. A huge winding staircase ascended to Paradise, where Mr. and Mrs. Willoughby built their nest. There were actually little cherubs carved into the risers. The butler headed for the staircase. Then he slowed, stopped, turned around and, with some apparent reluctance, came back to rejoin us. "Sir?"

"Yeah?"

"I don't wish to seem impertinent. May I ask you a personal question?"

"Depends how personal, I guess. Shoot."

"Er . . . was there ever a time in your life when some people called you 'The Professor'?"

I tried to unobtrusively step out of my heels. I would run lots faster without them. Take the tape machine? Or leave it?

The Professor never batted an eye. "Which people?"

"Well . . . a man named Slowhand Trudell? He used to work with a man who used the name

Frenkel sometimes, and you resemble the description."

The Professor dropped out of character. "You know Slowhand?"

"He's my old man," the butler said, dropping out of his. "I'm Theo Trudell. It's a great honor to meet you, Professor." He stuck out his hand, and the Professor shook it.

"So you're old Slowhand's boy. He told me you were enormous. How is the grand old fart?"

"Not good. Arthritis in his fingers, he can't work."

"Now that's a damn shame, Theo."

My heart was beginning to return to normal speed. I hate surprises. The Professor introduced me to Theo as his cousin Alice, and we shook hands.

"Listen, Professor—" Theo hesitated. "Look, I put in three months of work already on these diamonds. But now it's different. You're a legend. Maybe I shouldn't be saying this, but it'd be such a privilege to work with you—"

The Professor held up a hand. "Theo," he said. "I wouldn't horn in on Slowhand's boy for the world. The diamonds are yours. I'm running a different game, and I see no conflict."

Theo seemed simultaneously relieved and disappointed. "Well, if you're sure. Maybe another time. Can I help any?"

"Thanks. Just act natural. And give my love to your Pop. Kick him in the ass for me, and tell him he's an ugly old sheeplover."

Theo smiled. "I'll do that. Gee, he'll get a bang out of it."

He left again and disappeared up the staircase to the stars.

"Fame is good for the ego," the Professor said thoughtfully, "but one day soon it could get to be bad for business."

"Nonsense," I told him. "I remember the time you bummed a light from that broker the *day after* you took him for twenty-six thousand, and he never recognized you. That kid didn't know you, he knew the name you were using. Just retire 'Frenkel.'"

He sighed. "A shame. It's always good to carry ID that'll stand up, and it's such a pain in the ass getting it these days. But you're right, of course."

"Do you know I actually didn't get scared? When he asked if you were you, I mean. Alert, sure. But on the day you meet Tony Donuts, nothing else is scary."

Mrs. Willoughby was unquestionably a fool, but even a fool can be shrewd. When a representative of a Hollywood casting agency calls on you, saying that he won't be sure what he wants until he's seen you, certain inferences can be drawn, certain improbable hopes born. She kept us waiting for ten minutes, then made a grand entrance, appearing at the top of the stairs in a dress so expensive that she must have been sure it flattered her, makeup laid on with a trowel. She posed, then descended. My occupation has made me very good at not bursting into laughter every time I see something ridiculous. This strained me. She wasn't even a third of the way down when her perfume hit us. I'm sure she hadn't had a mosquito bite in a long time. She posed again when she reached the bottom of the stairs. She complimented, rather than complemented, the room.

"Mr. Finkle, is it? I'm Constance Willoughby. How may I help you?"

"A minute ago I'd have said one thing. Now I think maybe I'm gonna say another."

"I'm afraid I don't follow you, Mr. Frankel."

"Well, look, you seen my card. I'm casting; I don't do location scouting, that's production's headache. But they find out I gotta come East to see my mother in Queens, they say to me, Nat, keep an eye open, we need a mansion set that'll knock people's eyes out. See, the picture's supposed to take place in Boston, but those goniffs on the Coast think Boston and New York are like next door. But honest, Mrs. Willoughby, your neighborhood here could pass for Nob Hill easy. So I knock on your door to ask would you consider letting Metro make a major film on your premises. But now that I see you I feel my instincts working. Tell me: you've had some acting experience, am I right?"

She emitted what I believe she thought was a tinkling laugh. It would have blown out the candles on a birthday cake. "Hardly any at all," she simpered, "and not for years. Summer stock, mostly. You have sharp eyes, Mr. Funkel."

"I'm gonna lay my cards on the table, Mrs. W. This particular project, the stars are set, actually they're practically set-set, and I got the 'co-starrings' and the 'also starrings.' But I still got a few 'withs' to cast. There's a part for a banker's wife."

"I *am* a banker's wife," Mrs. Willoughby managed to say.

"There you go. Kismet. I got a picture in my mind of what I want—and wham, here you are. I cast a lot of real people. I find most of the people walking around on the street can act circles around the so-called professionals, and they give you less aggravation. It's not a real large part. You probably wouldn't be on screen for more than ten, fifteen minutes altogether. You get kidnapped by Robert Mitchum and Kirk Douglas. Is it worth talking about this?"

It took Mrs. Willoughby a few seconds to get her mouth working. Finally she said, "Well, I am quite busy with my charity work . . . but I suppose it couldn't hurt to discuss it. Would you and your lovely assistant care for anything to drink?"

Within minutes we had her seated on a low couch with the tape recorder in front of her. "There's three reasons for this machine," he told her. "My instincts tell me that you are a natural talent, it's all there in the way you carry yourself. But I see the doubt in your eyes, the natural modesty of a beginner. So in ten minutes I'm gonna use this tape to prove to you that you're as good as I think you are. Then tomorrow morning when I get off the plane I'm gonna use it to prove it to the shmucks in production, excuse my French, when they tell me I'm crazy to cast somebody with no track record in the industry. Then the third thing, I'm gonna keep the tape in my files, to refer to whenever something comes up that might be right for you."

"Well, all right," she said. "What do you want me to do?"

"Well, naturally I don't carry a script around with me when I scout locations, so we're just going to have to improvise a little bit. You're kidnapped, see? Douglas and Mitchum have a knife at your throat, and they're talking to your husband—Burt Lancaster, by the way—on the phone about the ransom. You're totally terrified, and they put you on the phone so Burt knows you're still alive, get it? Carol, baby, do me something? You be Douglas: take this pen and hold it on Constance like it's a knife, okay? Can I call you Constance? All right, let's try it." He prepared the tape recorder, took up tension on the reels. "This machine will only record your voice, but try to play it like there was a camera on you: it'll come across on the tape. Remember now, these guys have scared the living crap out of you, excuse my French, and so you tell your husband you think they're really gonna cut your throat, just for the fun of it. Scream and carry on a lot. Use your real husband's name, whatever it is; it'll sound natural."

"I understand," she said. I took the pen and stood next to her. "Let me see," she said. "My hands would be tied, wouldn't they?" She put them behind her.

The Professor shook his head admiringly. "What did I tell you? A natural. Carol will feed you your cues; just remember, she's Kirk Douglas."

"Just give me a moment," she said. She closed her eyes, began to breath faster, more agitatedly. "I'm ready!"

He started the recorder. "Rolling. Action!"

"All right, Mrs. Brentwood," I snarled, doing Douglas. "See if you can't convince your husband here we mean business!" I held the pen to her throat, and put an imaginary phone to her ear with my other hand. And she started to act.

And I started to hate this. And myself.

Because she wasn't bad at all.

Somehow that made the whole thing sad and crumby. I know that's not logical. A great deal depended on her performance being convincing. I should have been happy to find that, beneath her ridiculous exterior, this pampered rich woman actually harbored the imagination, insight, empathy and expressive skills to convincingly portray a terrified victim. But as I listened to Constance Willoughby screaming, I knew I was hearing a lonely, unloved woman, who wanted desperately to earn a small measure of fame, a morsel of recognition, by winning a bit part in a movie with Mitchum and Douglas. On the strength of her audition, she deserved to get it.

And what was she *going* to get? A kick in her neglected butt, that's what. A brief moment in the sun as a national laughingstock, once the Professor had worked his scam and the truth came out. Plus whatever retribution it suited Mr. Willoughby to visit on her once the dust had settled.

Followed, in a matter of days or weeks, by the theft of her jewelry—of the only tangible thing she had gotten in return for her lifelong loyalty to that venal toad.

But we *had* to con her this way, we had no choice. If we didn't, shortly the Professor and I were going to have to deal with an annoyed Tony Donuts. . . .

"Winthrop, for God's sake help me!" she cried. "Please, I think they're really going to kill me, Winthrop! Whatever it is they want, do it—*don't let them kill me!*" My hand twitched and the pen dug into her throat; she must have interpreted that as a cue, for she shrieked and began to babble brokenly. "Please, darling, I love you so, *don't let them take me from you—*"

That did it for me. I released her and stepped back. I met the Professor's eyes over her head, saw a mix of expressions on his face. I shook my head. "I can't," I said. "I know it's our ass . . . but I can't."

She must have been puzzled, but she struggled gamely on . . . until the Professor sighed and shut off the tape machine.

"Thank you, Mrs. Willoughby."

She trailed off. "Was I that bad?" she asked. Her voice was steady, but her lower lip trembled.

I sat down beside her at once and put an arm around her. "You were *wonderful*," I told her. "That's the problem."

"I . . . I'm afraid I don't quite—"

"Professor?"

He looked sad. "You know how it goes against my grain to tell the truth. But I'm afraid I agree with you. I can't sustain the necessary contempt. Go ahead."

She stared at him, and then back at me.

I dropped my eyes and took my arm back. Then I forced myself to meet her eyes again, and took her hand in mine. "Constance, I'm very sorry. We've been lying to you ever since we met you."

Her hand tensed in mine and her eyes widened.

"This man is a liar, and I'm a whore. I don't mean we're from Hollywood: he's a professional confidence man and I'm a prostitute. We came here to bamboozle you into making this tape for us."

I saw her start to get angry, waited for her to yank her hand from mine and spring up from the couch. She nearly did. But it was character that made her a good little actress. She controlled herself, relaxed her hand in mine, and looked from me to the Professor and back again. "Why?" she asked. "And what made you pick *me*?" she added before either of us could reply.

I swallowed. The die was cast. "Constance, I work in a house, here in Brooklyn. Your husband came there a few times." She stiffened, but did not remove her hand. There was no way to soften this. I plunged on. "The owner finally kicked him out. He had the idea that since prostitutes are criminals, we're evil. He kept asking the girls if . . . if they knew anyone who would be willing to murder you for a fee."

I'd never seen someone actually shudder on receiving bad news before. It started as a violent headshake, then spread to her shoulders and down, her whole body saying what her mouth cried: *"No!"* Her fingers crushed my hand. She looked up to the high ceiling, then down at our hands. She began to cry.

So did I.

We sat there like that for a time. I'm sure the Professor felt just as lousy as I did. And then she did a splendid thing. She chopped off in mid-snuffle, held her head quizzically to one side for a moment, and then looked up at me.

And said, clearly and firmly, "That rotten son of a *bitch*."

I looked into her eyes and came as close as I will ever come in this life to feeling sorry for Winthrop Willoughby.

"You've got that right, Mrs. Willoughby," the Professor said quietly.

She turned away from me and closed her eyes for a while. I am proud that she did not release my hand. When she opened her eyes again and spoke, it was to the Professor.

"Am I to understand that you and your friend are moralists? You go about punishing the wicked?"

"Good Christ, no," the Professor exclaimed. "Nothing so admirable. We're *thieves*. I'm here because I suddenly developed an urgent need for a lot of money. It is my affectation that I'll only swindle people I dislike, and your husband fit the bill; that's all. Unfortunately, you don't. You're quite talented. You did just now what only real actors can do: you made the audience sympathize with you. I might have bulled on through sheer momentum—but my associate couldn't stomach it. For which I salute her. Thank you, baby. God knows this town has no shortage of pigeons; we'll simply—"

"Excuse me," Constance Willoughby said.

"—find a—beg pardon?"

"I want to be certain I understand this. You needed the recording we were making for your scheme?"

"Badly."

"This . . . scheme: it would inconvenience Winthrop?"

He blinked. "Drastically," he said slowly.

She thought about that. "You know," she

murmured, "I think Winthrop would actually rather be tortured and killed than lose a really *large* amount of his precious bank's money. . . ."

Now the Professor looked thoughtful, a momentary echo of the trance he'd undergone in my studio last night. "What would you say," he asked in a faraway voice, "if, in addition to being robbed, Winthrop were to do hard time in Sing Sing?"

She frowned. "You could arrange that?"

His eyes refocused and locked on hers. "With your help."

"How much time?"

"Let me see." He performed mental addition. "I think I could guarantee fifteen years, Mrs. Willoughby."

She smiled.

"Constance," she said. "Shall we try another take?"

I squeezed her hand and kissed her cheek.

He grinned at her. "Atta girl, Connie! Uh . . . since you offer, sure, let's do a backup. But we won't need it: that first one was just terrific."

She turned and stared at me questioningly.

"That's what made me confess," I agreed. "I had reason to know that your marriage couldn't, forgive me, be much of a love feast for you— so all that love in your voice had to be great acting." Which had made me realize how badly she must yearn to have a marriage that really *was* that good.

"But you've got all you need? That was it? I mean to say: you could have just thanked me and left with it and gone ahead with your plans?"

The Professor grimaced. "If we could have, ma'am, I assure you we would have."

She gave me a quick peck on the cheek, got up quickly and kissed the Professor's forehead.

"Didn't you say there was some other way I could help you?" she asked.

The Professor smiled. "Two. First, spend all of tomorrow morning here, on the phone with someone. Second, forget that we met. If the police should ask, forget that any of this ever took place."

"That what ever took place? Heavens, what am I doing talking to myself like this? I really shouldn't woolgather this way; so much to do . . ." She wandered to the stairway, ascended with stately grace. I watched her until she was halfway up, feeling oddly like saluting. Then I packed up the tape recorder and the Professor and I left.

The moment the door closed behind us, I set the machine down and kissed him emphatically.

A cab took us to the bank. As we settled back into the seat cushions I whispered, "Professor? Why didn't we just play it like that from the beginning?"

"Too risky," he murmured. "Who knew she'd have stuff? Besides, crookedness is a reflex with me."

"Uh . . . it's still risky, isn't it? She's an amateur, and stupid."

"But she's talented. And motivated." He sighed. "Yes, Mo, it's still risky."

"I'm sorry," I said bleakly. "I had no right to decide for you back there."

"It turned out for the best, I guess. I'll sleep well tonight, thanks to you."

I started to tell him that he didn't know the half of it, but something made me hold my tongue.

And within a matter of only a few blocks, I understood what it was.

The cabbie was willing to accept an expensive men's watch for the ride, so the Professor gave him something that looked just like one. He would never forget what minute that deal took place: the watch would never show another time unless he changed it himself. It was the third cabdriver we'd burned that day, the Professor having also stung the one who'd taken us to Chez Willoughby. For the third time, I let it go by, because we were busy, but we were going to talk about this. And we were not going to make love tonight.

We stood before the Chemical Corn Exchange Bank and stared at it. It looked like the part of the Parthenon that got maintenance, massive and ugly and solid. It looked like a very tough place from which to take fifty thousand dollars.

The Professor was ignoring the building, scanning the passing pedestrians as he took off and pocketed his tie. He selected a very tough-looking guy in a brown imitation leather bomber's jacket and sunglasses, and accosted him. "I'll give you this sport coat for your jacket and specs," he offered. The man examined the sport coat suspiciously, but it was excellent, in impeccable condition and worth three of his jackets; he went for it. As the Professor donned the jacket and shades, he *became* the former owner (who failed to notice and walked on). He was now a small-to-medium-time hood, a tough customer whose slacks and shoes showed social pretensions.

I had altered my own appearance subtly in the cab, at his direction. I still wore the same clothes, my hair was almost unchanged—but now I *looked* like a hooker trying to look respectable.

"Prof," I said, "wouldn't it be smarter to catch him on his way out the door? People are going to notice us in there."

"You're right. But I want a look at the physical layout. And the characters we're playing would be that careless."

"If he thinks we're clever he might get the wind up him?"

"Right. You want me to give you your lines?" he asked.

I shook my head. "I think I know where you're going. Let's set the hook."

We took our stage.

Prof went through a swinging gate and headed for a desk. Behind it sat a thin woman in a tweed suit and glasses with a hair-bun like the one I'd started with and a no-nonsense expression. She sized me up in about half a second, then devoted three times as long to a thoughtful study of the Professor. "How may I help you?" she asked dubiously.

"Which one of these offices belongs to Willoughby?" he asked.

"Have you an appointment?"

He gave her a Jimmy Cagney grin. "Look, sis, why don't you just tell him Sally's niece Sherry is here? See what he says."

She hesitated for a long time. He kept grinning. She studied us both. Finally she said, "Sally's niece Sherry," in a well-*this*-will-probably-be-entertaining sort of voice, and rose from her desk. She had great legs under the tweed. "Why don't you both have a seat for a moment?"

I could *feel* him look at me from his office doorway. Miss Tweed returned. "Will you step this way, please?" She looked like she would be smiling if she knew how. She clearly believed we were here to try and blackmail her boss for his erotic indiscretions, and I sensed that she approved of the idea.

We went through a doorway and down a short corridor. Past the door at which we stopped, I could see the vault face, behind massive bars, its mighty door ajar and two clerks working inside. An armed guard stood on our side of the bars watching them. I looked around for exits and saw none. Miss Tweed knocked and ushered us into Willoughby's sanctum, closing the door behind us.

The office was huge and overfurnished, heavy with the scent of very good cigars and very bad digestion. He sat behind a small altar, a grim look on his face. I saw him recognize me. I smiled pleasantly. He glared.

He was a long, lean man with a small pot belly which, I was in a position to know, got bigger when he undressed. *Why* does a man try to comb hair over a bald spot? Is he afraid you'll fail to notice he's a jerk? Seeing his pursed lips reminded me of his teeth, which reminded me of his breath. Don't ever think my profession is not hard work sometimes.

He waited for us to open the conversation. We sat in uncomfortable chairs at the foot of the altar. Prof sprawled back lazily in his. "Before we go any further," he said, "let me start by sayin' we didn't come here to work no cheap blackmail angle, OK?"

Willoughby did not lose his sour look. He sat back on his throne and hooked his thumbs in his vest. "You'd better not have, by God," he rumbled. "What the hell do you think you *are* doing here then?"

Prof let me take it. "I waited and waited for you to come back, Mr. Brady," I said, deliberately using his House pseudonym, "but you never did. I see a lot of guys, and you kinda . . ." I lowered my eyes, ". . . stuck in my mind, you know?" I looked at him through lowered lashes and smiled.

Take it from me. *Any* man is willing to believe that he was the best you've ever had. He knew it all the time.

He wanted to smile, but frowning came more naturally. "I, ah, had no complaints myself, my dear. But that does not give you the right to—"

"And I remembered how you told me what a drip your wife was—"

One eyebrow rose. "Yes?"

"And I thought maybe if you din't have her bein' a gallstone around your neck, maybe you'd have more time on your hands, you know? One of the other girls said you were talking about that. And my friend Slick here, he fixes little problems like that sometimes."

He turned to stare at the Professor. His frown was nearly gone now. "And exactly how do you fix such problems?"

The Professor stared up at the ceiling. "I saw this movie once. This guy's wife got taken dead. And the way it happened, he came out a tragic hero, completely above suspicion. And it didn't take a cent outa his own pocket. What would you say to a deal like that, bud?"

He actually glanced around his own office, as though to surprise some careless policeman. "I would probably be skeptical," he said at last. "In such a hypothetical case, I should probably ask something like, what is in it for you?"

"All right," Prof said, "I'll tell you a sad story. There was this guy, ran a bank, see? And one

day a coupla people come into his office, and
they stuck him up."

"Preposterous. A teller could give you more
money than I . . . than a bank manager could. No
one would be permitted to accompany him into
the vault, and once out from under your guns,
he would naturally have to call for help."

"Ah, but these guys in my story was real
brained up. They give this guy a good reason to
cooperate. They had him call home. And his wife
answered the phone and said, darling, bad men
are here and they'll croak me if you don't do like
they want. So what choice did the poor guy have?
He drifts into the vault and comes out with fifty
grand, and he gives it to them and they blow. And
he's so concerned for his poor wife that he lets
like half an hour go by before he calls the bulls."

There was a silence.

"And then?"

"Well, like I said, it's a sad story. How it
went was, the dirty bastards that stuck him up,
they were so rotten they croaked his wife
anyhow, just for laughs. He was real broken up
about it. Everybody felt sorry for him. And
thanks to the Banking Act, the bank got its
money back from Washington, so at least his
job didn't suffer."

"I see."

Willoughby got out a cigar and made a
lengthy ritual of lighting it. By the time he
had it going to his satisfaction, he had made
his decision.

"Would you care for a cigar, Mr. . . . uh, Slick? Cigarette, Sherry? Coffee for either of you?"

As we were leaving, we passed by Miss Tweed's desk. She got up and caught my arm. "Excuse me, Miss?"

The Professor continued on. "Yes?"

She hesitated, then took the plunge. "I hate that jerk in there. Forgive me, I know this is a rude question, but . . . does it really pay as well as they say? I mean . . . do you enjoy your work?"

I had a split second to make a decision. It was all I needed. I let my eyelids flutter and my mouth tremble. "I'd kill myself if they'd let me," I whispered.

Her eyes widened in shock and she stared at the Professor. He was waiting for me by the door, and met her gaze with the expressionlessness that only sunglasses can achieve. A look of fascinated queasy horror came over her face. I turned on my heel and half ran to join him.

It was an easy decision. There were no openings at Lady Sally's House, and nowhere else in the five boroughs will you find a happy hooker.

Except for the ones that have just fixed.

CHAPTER 11

WILLOUGHBY, WEEP FOR ME

The afternoon shift had ended and the evening shift wouldn't begin for a while yet. We were the only ones in the Parlor except for Mary, taking a break from the Snoop Room, and Robin, cleaning the place up under the stern eye of Mistress Cynthia, happy as a pig in Congress. (Since there were no other clients in-House now, he was allowed to dress as he preferred, and I could see that he was welting up nicely.) Mary smiled when she saw me, gave me the eyebrow lift that means, *Okay if I join you two?*, and I gave her back the wink that says, *Sure*. As she was freshening her own coffee, I said hi to Cindy and politely insulted

Robin, who preened. Then the Professor and I hugged Mary hello.

"How goes the hunt?" she asked when the three of us were seated.

"The quarry has taken the bait," the Professor said. "It's just a matter of time now before it turns into a ten-pound hairball on him."

I gave her a quick summary of the day's events. "Prof played it brilliantly," I concluded. "Willoughby thinks we're bright enough to pull off the job, but he also thinks he's smarter than we are."

"The fact that those two statements are incompatible escapes him," the Professor put in. "He thinks *he* can put one over on *us*. You could see it in his eyes when he asked how I wanted the money."

I nodded, smiling at the memory. "Prof just said, 'tens,' and then there was this pause."

"You could hear the wheels turning in his head. 'This jerk is so dumb he didn't even ask for used bills, with no serial-number sequences. So I will give the jerk brand new bills in numerical sequence, and in a matter of days he'll be in custody. What can he do then? Implicate me in murder? It'll be my word against his.' The man has all the cunning of . . . well, of a bank manager."

"—and new bills in sequence is exactly what you need," Mary said, seeing the joke and grinning.

"Well, we'd have trouble persuading Tony

Donuts that Prof's pigeon personally fondled each of five thousand bills," I said.

"Oh, I don't know," he mused. "Tony is easily that dumb."

"Really?" Mary said. "That could be a problem."

He looked puzzled. "You lost me."

"Well, look, I'm only familiar with your work by reputation—but on that basis alone I'm prepared to bet you don't often sting morons. No challenge in taking candy from babies, right?"

"I admit I do appreciate the battle of wits even more than the money that comes from winning," he admitted. "I have an emotional conviction that evil is inherently stupid, and I enjoy proving it to myself. And so the greatest enjoyment comes from outwitting a clever opponent." He grimaced. "In the case of Tony Donuts, of course, the minimal mental exertion required is compensated for by the risk factor. Even against the cleverest mark, all you risk is ten to life, with an excellent chance of sneaking out of prison. With Tony Donuts, you risk a horrid and degrading death. It balances out."

"But you're at a disadvantage in conning someone as stupid as him. Don't you see? From force of habit, you'll keep expecting him to react intelligently—and he won't always oblige."

The Professor frowned ferociously. "Oof! Buddha's bloody boody-butt, I never . . ." He broke off and extended his hand to Mary. "My sincere thanks, you rotten bitch."

Now it was her turn to look puzzled.

"You may have just saved my life and Maureen's . . . by forcing me to spend this evening re-examining every rivet on a scam I was sure was airtight. It is relatively foolproof—but you're right, I forgot to make it moronproof. And I was looking forward to an evening of recreational debauchery upstairs. Oh, well—can't be helped. Really, thanks, Mary; I'll be more careful from now on. I owe you one."

"Thinking like a moron shouldn't be much trouble for you," I said pleasantly.

Mary raised an eyebrow.

"On the way home, he tried to stiff a cabbie," I said. "After giving him this address."

Mary glared at him.

"Dammit, Mo, I *said* I was sorry!"

"Half a second's thought would have told you that Lady Sally would value the good will of cabdrivers, for God's sake—"

"Were we supposed to *walk* here from the—"

"—I took care of it, didn't I—"

"—it's not my habit to let my dates pay for my cabs—"

"—it's not my habit to let my dates screw up Lady Sally—"

"*—I-said-I-was-sorry, I said—*"

"WHOA!" Mary said with enough volume to override us. Robin and Cynthia were pointedly not staring at us. "You know the rules. No fighting below the third floor. And especially not in a place of eating. But before you go . . . Maureen, you did pay off the hack?"

"After a fashion," the Professor said sourly.

"I just did the same thing *he'd* been doing to cabbies all day," I told her. "Only literally."

"And who donated the handkerchief?" he demanded.

"As long as he was happy," Mary said. "All right, beat it, the both of you."

Rules are rules. We kept silent until we reached my apartment, and then resumed the argument.

"Dammit," I said finally, laying back on the bed, "this is exactly why I left you."

He winced, and slumped in his chair. "You left me because you outgrew me," he said.

"And I've been waiting ever since for *you* to outgrow you. Instead you've been regressing."

"What the hell is that supposed to mean?"

"This thing you used to have about only shafting people who deserve it—"

"—what do you mean, 'used to have'?—"

"Used to have. Or can you explain what makes all cabdrivers fair game?"

He snorted. "Have you ever ridden in a cab?"

"Have you ever driven one?"

"Eh?"

"I sure haven't. I'd rather walk the streets. In two years on the street, I only got knifed once. If you know a lonelier, more dangerous, more frustrating job in New York City, tell me what it is."

"Mo . . . dammit, conning people is what I *do*."

"And you've always been so proud of conning

only people you dislike. The trouble is, I've never been comfortable with your criteria for dislike—and I see they've gotten looser since I left."

He squirmed uncomfortably in his chair. "Okay, look, I'll concede that you may have a point about cabbies; I'll have to rethink my position on that. But when *else* have you ever known me to burn anyone who didn't have it coming?"

"How about the last guy we took together?"

"Flanders? My God, the man was a pimple—"

"He was ugly and dull and tasteless and he had more money than he deserved. None of those things was his fault. There was no evil in him anywhere; he wasn't imaginative enough. And you didn't just take his money, Prof, you took his dignity too."

"But—"

"I could understand distaste for him . . . but he hadn't earned dislike. When I first joined up with you, I thought we were going to be Patricia Holm and Simon Templar, outlaws who preyed on criminals, punishers of the ungodly. And all too often, it seemed we were punishing the unfortunate—those unlucky enough to have been born displeasing to you. That's why I walked out on you. Stinging Flanders was like laughing at a fat girl."

That wounded him. "Hey—did I back you up today with Mrs. Willoughby, or not?"

I softened slightly. "Yes, you did. And that earns you points, even though I forced your

hand. But you're still at least two cabdrivers and
a Flanders in the hole."

He opened his mouth and then closed it again
and frowned.

I stood up, skinned out of my clothes quickly,
got back into bed and turned my back to him.
After ten or fifteen minutes, he got up, undressed
himself and lay down beside me on the bed, keeping carefully to his side. Three or four hours of
pretending to sleep tired us both out so much that
we fell genuinely asleep sometime after ten—I
did anyway.

I woke exhausted, sweaty, stiff, thirsty, and
depressed. And, dammit, horny. The latter two,
at least, are rare in Lady Sally's House. I eased
out of bed and peered dolefully out my window at a disgustingly sunny day. He did not
wake while I showered; I slipped into a robe
and slippers, and went downstairs to the dining room.

People awake at eight in the morning are rare
in the House, too; I had the place to myself. I
made a pot of coffee, drank a solitary cup with
a corn muffin while listening to the radio play
Bach. I thought about pleasuring myself, but
decided against it. In the day to come, edginess
could be an asset. I poured more coffee into one
of the insulated cups Lady Sally stocks, put it
and an orange and a selection of muffins and
pastries into the dumbwaiter on a tray, and sent
the lot up to the third floor. Then I cleaned up

after myself and went back upstairs, stopping at
Wardrobe for a maternity outfit.

He was still asleep as I let myself back into
the room. He'd kicked the covers nearly off
himself. I stood there in the doorway with the
tray in my hands and my clothes under one
arm, watching the sunlight roll like mercury
around his snoring chest, for a long time. Oh,
it couldn't have been long, the smell of coffee must have woken him in less than a minute.
A long time for me. Why is the sight of a
sleeping loved one so tender? I wished—not for
the first time in my life!—that I had not been
cursed with scruples.

"Oog."

"Good morning. I know you like to work on
an empty stomach, but you should have a little
breakfast."

"Thanks." He sat up and pulled the sheet over
his morning rampancy. I set the tray down on
it with some care and went into the john to dress
and do my face and hair.

When I emerged he was nearly dressed himself, just affixing a false mustache so enormous
and ugly that no one who saw him today would
remember anything else about him. "Excellent,"
he said, looking me over carefully. "Let's complete the illusion." He selected the fattest of my
feather pillows. "Come here."

I let him position it under my maternity
clothes. Halfway through the job he froze. I
sighed.

"Maureen—"

"Professor—"

"You don't have to do that—"

"Look, I debated a long time before I put the stuff on, okay? Hopefully this is all going to go smoothly, you'll give Tony his money, he'll let you walk away, and neither of us will ever see him again. But if it goes sour somehow, and he gets his hands on me . . . well, maybe if I'm wearing what he told me to, he'll be pleased enough to kill me *quickly*."

He frowned fiercely, but couldn't argue with my logic. I almost wished he had. Most black lace underwear is uncomfortable to wear for any length of time, worse under street clothes, and the damned pillow didn't help any. But it was the prudent course.

He let me pay for the cab to the Chemical Corn Exchange Bank. With money. The cabbie looked at me so oddly as I paid him that I wondered if somehow he sensed how lucky he was.

Willoughby's secretary the Tweed Lady smiled politely at us, but failed to recognize us from the day before. Not surprising; we now resembled Ozzie and Harriet more than Bonnie and Clyde. We killed a few minutes asking her about transferring our bank account from out of state. Then it was the appointed time, and I went into labor.

Willoughby was alert; at my first yell he came bustling out to take charge. He had the old fat security guard help me back to his office, then dismissed him, retaining Miss Tweed as a witness. The guard would have made a good additional witness, but Willoughby had warned us yesterday that the man was just the type to try and play hero, and one witness was sufficient. As soon as the door had closed behind the guard, the Professor pulled his toy gun.

We sketched out the tale for the benefit of the secretary. Willoughby registered, in turn, shock, outrage, quick acceptance of the new state of affairs, manly courage, and a heroic concern for Miss Tweed's welfare: she bought everything but the last two. The Professor picked up the phone, got an outside line, and dialed a number, announcing loudly that it was Willoughby's home number. Only I knew he was lying. He handed the phone to Willoughby. On the other end, I knew, was my dear friend Phillip, doing his George Raft impression. Willoughby went through a convincing charade with him. Who the devil are you? You monster, if you've harmed my wife I'll— Let me speak to her.

The rest of us could then clearly hear the sound of his wife's high distant voice pleading, and then screaming. The secretary went pale, and stared at the Professor and me.

We listened with Willoughby until the tape chopped off at Mrs. Willoughby's shriek. Willoughby kept listening intently. In addition to his George Raft, Phillip does sound effects well; I'm sure his imitation of a silenced gun firing, following closely after the shriek, was perfect. The secretary, of course, could not have heard it. I saw Willoughby buy it; his face strained with the effort of not smiling. "All right," he said gruffly, "don't do anything hasty, I'll cooperate. Damn you."

He hung up. As far as he knew, the job was done, his wife murdered. Now it was just a matter of stiffing the hirelings with traceable money, and his morning's work would be through. "They have my wife hostage," he told Miss Tweed. "I have to get fifty thousand dollars from the vault for them. For God's sake don't do anything rash while I'm gone—they're desperate characters."

"Fifty thousand?" Miss Tweed said. "Why not the whole damn vault full?"

He glared at her, then looked hastily at the Professor, afraid he would approve of the revision.

"Shut up," the Professor explained.

Willoughby took an attaché case from a closet, and left to get the money from the vault. While he was gone an idea came to me. I gestured the Professor near, and whispered in his ear while he held the toy gun on Miss Tweed. After a minute he smiled broadly, and nodded. "You're right," he murmured, "that's even better."

"Lady," I said to her, in the bimbo-voice I'd used the day before, "do you *really* hate that bag of shaving cream?"

Her eyes widened as she recognized me. But

she was quick on the uptake. "Want to see the pinchmarks on my butt?" she replied sourly. She frowned . . . then smiled. "Why? Can I help you two out some way?"

"Can you act?"

"Try me."

"When he comes back with the cash, we'll leave, and tell you both not to stir from this office for fifteen minutes. Once the time is up, you just go back out to your desk and go back to work. And when the cops arrive, play dumb. You don't know what the hell Willoughby is talking about. Robbers? What robbers? The pregnant lady had a glass of water and a short rest and left with her husband fifteen minutes or so ago."

She looked thoughtful. "But won't the wife back him up?"

"His home phone hasn't rung all day. Phone records will support that."

She smiled broadly. "I don't know how you managed that . . . but I like it. Sure, I'm in. I can't wait to see his face."

"Thanks. You've improved a good day." I hesitated, weighing debt against risk. "Look . . . if you were really serious, yesterday . . . I'll call you in about six months."

"It's not like you said? You really like the life?"

"The place where I work is great. The boss-lady doesn't tolerate sleaze. I lied yesterday because there are no openings right now, and all the other houses in town *are* awful. But in a year, one of my friends is leaving on her honeymoon, and six months is long enough to train you as a sub. Just don't do any free-lance experimenting in the meantime, or you'll have a lot to unlearn. Besides, it's dangerous."

She chewed on her lip—then scribbled down her home phone number and gave it to me. "Thanks. I'll think about it."

"Good plan. Wups—places!"

Willoughby came back in with the briefcase. The Professor examined the contents. Fifty thousand dollars in crisp new tens, serial sequence, still in the wrappers. "Fine," he said, and Willoughby again hurt his face not smiling. He riffed a few lines for Miss Tweed's benefit about exacting a terrible vengeance if we had harmed his wife; we riffed a few lines for his benefit about not budging until we'd been gone for fifteen minutes. During all this boilerplate I busied myself replacing pillow feathers with fifty thousand dollars—leaving just enough feathers to round off corners—and tucking the resulting bundle back under my maternity clothes. The leftover feathers rolled in a scarf were malleable enough to tuck up between my thighs, helping me to walk like a pregnant lady. It was a shame to break up such a happy group: all of us were pleased, and two of us were ecstatic. But the two who were merely pleased had a pressing engagement with Tony Donuts. . . .

Two steps out into the corridor the Professor

stopped, spun on his heels and went back in. Mildly alarmed, I followed. What had he overlooked?

Willoughby too was surprised. "What is it now?"

The Professor took his gun back out. "Empty your pockets."

Willoughby flushed and stalled, but he had no choice. He was carrying a little over a hundred cash. We left again.

On the way out through the lobby, Prof thanked the guard so effusively for his assistance, with hugs and double-handed handshakes, that the man was sure to recall later that the pregnant lady's husband hadn't been carrying anything in his hands. I gave him a peck on the cheek myself, so he could feel my bulging "belly." Then we hit the street.

"*This* time," the Professor said, flinging up his arm, "*I* am paying for the God damned cab."

A hack idling just up the street roared into life and screeched up before us. It was tricky getting my pregnancy cantilevered into the cab without spraying feathers on the sidewalk, but we managed with some care. Sitting on that roll of feathers was uncomfortable. As the Professor was sliding in beside me, the cab jerked away from the curb, slamming the door.

"—and not tipping much, either," he grumbled. "Hey, cap, can't you see the lady's in a delicate condition? I haven't even told you where we're going!"

"You don't know yet," the driver said. He stood up on the brakes for a red light, turned and grinned over the seat at us.

Suddenly I had acute morning sickness.

"That's one of the things I've always liked about you," the Professor said. "You never just drop in; you always phone ahead first. Alice, you remember my friend Tony."

Now I noticed that the rear door- and window-handles were missing. The roll of feathers was no longer a nuisance; very absorbent, feathers. My heart was pounding so loud in my ears that it drowned out even his resonant baritone. I read his lips:

"Dat my leaflets unda ya dress, Alice?"

I nodded, twelve times.

"An' youse got some udda stuff unda dere I'm gonna like too, like I tol' ya, huh?"

I was one of those little toy birds perched over a glass of water, who can't stop bobbing her beak up and down.

"Good goil." He dismissed me. "So ya mark is a bank guy, huh, Professa? Pretty neat: who could move funny paper bedda dan a bank guy? I shoulda figged when ya said he wuz good fer a mil."

Honking horns announced the green light; he faced forward again and accelerated like a carrier pilot.

"Where *are* we going, Tony?" the Professor called over the clashing of gears.

"A ways out onny Island. I know dis

mout'piece out dere, he's got his own beach onna Nawt Shaw, wid a boat parked on it. He sez I can use it any time I want, as long as I don't make no donuts out of him. I figger I deep-six de play-dough, it's too hot taday ta boin it."

"Sensible. You know, I've got to hand it to you, Tony. I kept a careful watch for tails all day after we left you, and I never saw you once. I never imagined a man your size could be stealthy."

"Nah. I didn't bodda tailin' youse; too much agg'avation. I watched what kinda cab ya took, and later on I went down ta da cab comp'ny an' ast guys until I knew where ya been."

The Professor winced. "Oh Mary, you tried to warn me," he murmured.

Even in my paralysis I felt a pang of guilt. The Professor had intended to re-examine his plans last night, to check them for overlooked flaws in dealing with a simple, direct moron like Tony Donuts. But I had decided to pick a fight over his moral shortcomings. . . .

"And damned nice of you to go to the trouble, Tony. I thought we were going to have to go all the way to Manhattan to post a note at my place telling you where to meet us."

"I hate goin' ova da bridge. Da foist two guys tell me right away. Da toid guy, funny, he gives me a hod time for some reason, an' by de time he's ready to talk I can't unnastan' him so good. But dat's okay—once I get him quiet again he don't need his cab no maw, so I take it an' wait for youse at de bank today, an' I get lucky."

"He was repaying a favor. Alice gave him a hand, once."

One of the things I've always admired about the Professor is his calm in a crisis. My father told me once that that single quality has won more battles than any other factor. I like to think I'm not bad at it myself—but here was a master at work. I was too terrified to think, much less speak, and he was making puns.

More: it was a pun that only I would get. He was talking to me, right under the nose of Tony Donuts, telling me to have courage.

I agreed with him in principle. Courage was a fine quality intrinsically, and certainly could prove useful here. But I couldn't seem to find any, rummage as I might. This exchange (the money for the Professor's life), even if it went smoothly, was going to take place in much too secluded a spot. Tony would want to celebrate. . . .

It might, I thought, actually be better if he figured out that we were trying to stiff him with real money, and killed us promptly. He probably intended to kill the Professor anyway. . . .

No, I simply did not have whatever kind of fiber it takes to deliberately anger Tony Donuts. Even if that *was* the better option, of which I was by no means sure. I was a rabbit in the presence of a tiger: incapable of action, of forming plans, incapable of anything but animal terror and a mindless eagerness to oblige.

It shames me to recall it, but a small part of my mind was desperately glad that I had dressed as he had told me to.

CHAPTER 12
SWITCH AND BAIT

As the cab crunched over gravel I realized I was repeating a short syllable over and over again. It was the Panic Word, the innocent-sounding code word that will, if whispered any-where in Lady Sally's House, bring Mary and Priscilla on the run with weapons. Quite useless here, of course; just a reflex.

We were somewhere in Nassau County, on Long Island's North Shore. A secluded private beach, with a boathouse, a dock, and a cabin cruiser. On the overlooking bluff, a single large house could just be seen through the trees. We'd driven past it on our way down here. Tony's law-yer acquaintance and his family were not home today; there had been no cars or other signs of life. The sun was high in the sky, and the only humans visible were at least two miles offshore in a sailboat. Could I scream that far? If by some miracle they heard me, would they radio for help—or come ashore and get on line?

The Professor took my hand and squeezed it firmly as the cab came to a halt. "Break a leg, kid," he whispered.

"Beat him to it, you mean?" I whispered back as Tony Donuts got out of the cab.

He grinned approvingly. "That's my girl. Keep smiling."

I tried to smile, but I was disposing of the soggy roll of feathers, and it spoiled the effect. They hit the floor of the cab with a splat.

Tony opened the door on my side, picked me up and set me down standing. He seemed to leave handprints on my shoulder blade and thighs. The Professor got out after me. "Charming spot, Tony! Simply lovely. Yonder boathouse seems a suitable place to conclude our business." And the only potential source of weapons around.

"What wrong wit right here?"

"Tony, Tony—suppose that sailboat out there were full of Feds with telephoto lenses?"

Even granting the Feds godlike powers, they could not possibly have guessed where Tony was going to take us. But Tony was a moron. "Yah, ya got sometin dere. Ah'right, let's go t'da boathouse."

It was the size of a two-car garage and stank of mildew and fish. It was utterly empty of what I'd been hoping for, cans of gasoline that could be poured over Tony Donuts and set afire. It contained a wide selection of utensils, but nothing I could imagine Tony considering a threat. A garage-type door at one end opened onto the sea, but it was closed and locked. I wondered how long it would be before my body was discovered, and what the lawyer would do with it. Tony was not the kind to bother cleaning up after himself. . . .

"Ah' right, sugar, whip it out."

I lifted up the front of the maternity smock, worked the pillowcase out from under the skirt, and handed it over. My hands shook.

He grinned as he took the sack, grinned broader as the maternity skirt, no longer held up by the bulk of the load, fell around my ankles. He lifted up the smock with one finger, nodded his head. "Good cherce," he said approvingly. "My sista useta have a pair just like dat." He let the smock fall again. "Wait a minute whilst I check da handbills, okay?"

I nodded. Take your time. Don't hurry on my account.

"Count them if you like, Tony," the Professor said. "Not one bill is missing."

I almost managed to be amused at the notion of Tony Donuts counting to five thousand.

He tore the pillowcase apart in his hands, spilling the stacks of bills all over the damp floor. I guess he figured he'd have my clothes to wrap them back up in when he left. He nudged at the heap of money with his toe, grunted happily. "I quit countin' dough years ago. Nobody ever tries ta stiff me. Looks like fifty gees ta me."

"That it is. Well, I'm certainly glad I was able to do this favor for you, Tony, and this has certainly been an exhilarating morning, but Alice and I have to go now. Don't worry about driving us back to Brooklyn, we love to hitchhike. What I was thinking was, just in case those *are* Feds out there, perhaps it would be best if Alice and I left first and went east, and then ten minutes later you left and went west; that should fool—"

"Hang on a minute." Tony Donuts was squatting, poking at the stacks of bills with fingers like bratwurst. He went rigid.

Was it possible he had noticed the serial numbers were wrong? Was Tony Donuts capable of retaining a ten-digit number?

He took a crisp bill from his own wallet, glanced at it. He stood slowly . . . and suddenly he was holding the Professor clear off the floor by the collar with one enormous hand.

"I'm gonna rip ya head off an' drink outa da hole," he said.

"Iv fumfing w'ong, To'y?" the Professor choked out.

Tony set him down again. "Dese ain't my posters."

Oh God.

"What on *earth* gives you that idea?" the Professor tried. But even his voice was trembling now.

"Dey all got diff'rent numbers on 'em."

The Professor gaped, so astonished he almost forgot to be scared. "You printed all five thousand bills with the *same serial number*?"

"I couldn't figger out da part dat changes de numbers ev'y time. So I figga, what'sa difference? I give a guy a sawbuck, he takes it." He held up the bill he'd taken from his wallet. "See? Here's da number I used—an' yaws is all differnt. None o' dis is my paper." He tucked the genuine bogus note into his shirt pocket.

The Professor closed his eyes. "I never even thought to look. Oh, Mary, you called it again. . . ."

"Bye bye," Tony Donuts said, and reached forward—

"The bank guy wasn't the mark!" the Professor shrieked.

Tony stopped moving. "Huh?"

"I clipped him for fifty large this morning, yes, but he's not the mark who has *your* money. Once you kill us, you'll never find it."

"Huh." I watched rage and greed battle in his tiny mind. He set the Professor down to conserve energy for the struggle of thinking.

"Let Alice go get it," the Professor suggested. "She knows where it is. Keep me as a hostage until she gets back."

He was lying to save my life, sacrificing himself to get me clear. I opened my mouth to say that I did not know where the funny money was . . . and could not utter a syllable. I did try.

Tony thought about it. "Easier ta beat it outa youse."

"The mark carries heat, Tony. Being shot five or six times would be a nuisance for you, wouldn't it? And he'll give the money to her, he knows her."

Tony looked at me thoughtfully. "Youse fond o' yer cousin here?"

"He's not really my cousin," I heard myself say. "I love him."

"Huh," he said again. "Okay. I buy it. How long does it take youse, sugar?"

"Uh . . ." I thought frantically. How long could I stretch it? How many hours of life could I negotiate for my love? Was it any favor to him to drag it out? "I don't know, three or four hours, maybe more."

"Take da cab. I give youse tree hours. Den I break his back a couple times an' come lookin' fa youse."

My mind was racing. Afternoon shift would just be starting at the House by the time I got there. Suppose I could round up a posse and beat it back here in three hours: how the hell could a posse sneak up on this damned boat-house?

The Professor caught my eye and smiled a sickly, heroic smile. "Drive carefully, Alice. Tony and I will be fine. I'll teach him the baritone part to 'Lida Rose' and we'll all have a singa-long when you get back." He stepped up and gave me a goodbye hug, kissed me quickly and stepped back before I could cling to him like a drowner.

"Prof?"

"Yes, dear?"

"I'm sorry I was mad at you last night."

"Don't worry about it. You were right."

"I know—but I'm sorry."

"Quit yappin' an' go get my leaflets," Tony Donuts said. "An' rememba: when youse come back, if youse carry true dough, youse'll be dunes-buried."

The Professor and I looked at each other. "God," he breathed, "a pun that awful is almost worth all of this."

"No. It isn't," I murmured back.

"Well, perhaps not."

"Bring back some lunch," Tony Donuts said. "And tree-faw six-packs."

I nodded, pulled up my maternity skirt and left, stifling a sob.

And of course the cab blew a tire the moment I hit the parkway; and of course there was no spare in the trunk; and even though several helpful Samaritans pulled over when they saw me waving in my maternity clothes and weeping, of course the first half dozen had the wrong wheel size; and once that was taken care of, of course I ran out of gas in Queens. By the time I burst through the front doors of Lady Sally's House, crying and raving incoherently at the startled crowd in the Parlor, two hours and thirty-seven minutes had elapsed.

CHAPTER 13

LADY AND THE TRUMP

It was Robin, of all people, who slapped me across the chops to steady me down, and then got me downstairs to Lady Sally's office, chattering unnecessary apologies every step of the way. He stood by forgotten while I sobbed out the bare bones of my story to her, and then he truly surprised me.

"Perhaps I could be of some help, Miss Maureen," he said.

I stared at him, *"How!"* I got a mental image of him mincing up to Tony Donuts, in his maid's outfit and bondage harness, and slapping Tony to death.

"I'd be happy to give you fifty thousand dollars, if it would help you and the Professor. I only wish I'd known earlier."

I just looked at him.

"He can certainly afford it," Lady Sally said. "Heavens, Robin is one of the ten wealthiest men in America—I thought you knew that, Maureen?"

And he paid for the privilege of living here and doing scutwork under the stern eye and merciless riding-crop of Madame Cynthia. I remembered that Lady Sally pegged clients' membership fees to what they could afford to pay, guesstimated what Robin could afford to pay, and understood for the first time how this opulent House managed to show a profit.

And put it out of my mind. Just then I would not have been much interested if someone told me that the pilot light had just gone out on the Sun. "Never came up, I guess. Thanks, Robin, but it wouldn't help. Even if it was possible to get back in time, it can't be just any fifty thousand dollars. It has to be genuine fakes." I glanced down, saw something in my breast pocket, took it out by a corner and showed it to him. "Like this," I said. "Huh! Now how the hell did I get that?" It was a single counterfeit ten.

There was only one possible way. Con-man and cannon are distinctly different occupations . . . but so are con-man and bank-robber: the Professor was versatile. He had to have dipped this ten-spot from the shirt pocket of Tony Donuts—as Tony was in the midst of strangling him—and slipped it into mine when he hugged me goodbye. Why?

Of course: evidence. He intended for me to avenge his murder by giving this bogus bill, with Tony's fingerprints on it, to the Feds. I began to cry softly again.

Oh, Willard, I'm sorry! I'll get him for you, I swear—

"May I see that, dear?" Lady Sally asked.

"Just don't touch it," I said. "Somewhere on it is the fingerprint that is going to put Tony Donuts in the electric chair." I set it down on her desk. I had never felt so bleak and helpless in my life; even cold rage was no comfort at all.

She picked it up with a tweezer and examined both sides carefully. "Robin, would you leave us, please?"

"Oh, but I want to *help*. There must be *some*thing I—"

"Thank you, dear, that's terribly sweet of you . . . but if you leave this *instant*, I'll personally give you the caning of your life later."

The sound of the door clicking shut behind him came between the last two words.

"Darling, don't give up hope," Lady Sally said instantly, *"there's a chance."*

I checked my watch. "No, there isn't," I said forlornly. "A guided missile couldn't get me back there in time, even if I happened to have Tony's money. And if I did and it did, he'd kill us anyway."

She reached across the desk and took my hands. Her eyes caught mine and held them. "Maureen . . . do you trust me?"

"Yes," I said at once. Not even "Yes, but—"
Just "Yes."

"Do you have faith in me?"

"Yes, Lady."

"I tell you truly: there is a chance."

My heart did not wait for proof; it swelled
with relief at once, until I thought it would
burst in my chest. And almost immediately it
began to hammer rapidly. Terror leaves you
when you despair; once you let yourself hope
again it returns redoubled. *What do we do?*

"Come with me."

She rose from her chair, still holding the sawbuck with the tweezers, crossed the room to one
of the two floor-to-ceiling bookcases, and pressed
hard on the spine of a thousand-page hardcover
textbook titled *The Ruffed Grouse*. Like many
others in the House, I had browsed Lady Sally's
bookshelves often; it had never occurred to me
to touch that volume. The entire bookshelf slid
smoothly and quietly down into the floor, leaving a bare wall.

"Used to have a hinged sort of affair," she said,
"but you couldn't *open* the damned thing without moving all the furniture out into the hall.
Come along, child."

She walked through the wall.

I got up and followed her.

Even when my nose was an inch away from
it, it looked like a solid wall; I could make out
paintbrush marks and even a dirty fingerprint or

two. But I did *not* bang my nose on it an instant later.

There was no tingling sensation involved in stepping through it, no perceptible sensation at all. I just walked through it as though it were a hologram image at Disneyland—

—and was *elsewhere*.

I don't think I can describe what it was like on the other side of that wall. I didn't see *anything* familiar. It was enclosed, there, but there were no walls or ceiling as such, not even the one I'd just stepped through . . . I know that doesn't tell you anything; it's the best I can do. There were things of various kinds around, some of them seemingly suspended in mid-air, others resting decently on the . . . whatever was under our feet . . . but some of those looked like they ought to be toppling over, and I couldn't identify a single item. Some didn't seem to have any fixed shape; others were sometimes there and sometimes not. I think one of those latter was alive. A pet? There was a fragrance unlike anything I'd ever smelled, pleasant but elusive.

One and only one thing was familiar enough for me to grasp; somewhere, with a clarity attainable by no sound equipment I knew, Hoagy Carmichael was singing "The Old Music Master." He was just up to the line where the 1890's composer asks the little colored boy how he can be sure that his prophecies of new musical phenomena call "jazz," "boogie-woogie," and "swing" are accurate, and the boy explains that he *knows* . . . because he was born a hundred years from now.

I made a major effort and got control of my breathing. Shortly I began to calm down. *Priorities, Maureen. Willard needs you.* My eyes found and clung to the only thing they understood: Lady Sally.

"You can relax now, darling," she said. "We're no longer in a hurry."

I nodded. "Uh huh."

She was just letting go of the phony ten-dollar bill—which remained suspended in the air, parallel to the floor, trembling very slightly. She made some manual adjustments to . . . something nearby, and a rectangle of cool green light appeared in the air next to the ten. It moved from left to right so that the bill threaded it like a needle, then it flipped, did the same thing vertically, and vanished. The thing nearby grew a tray, which began to fill quietly with neatly stacked ten dollar bills. As a stack reached the top of the tray, a new stack began beside it. Within less than twenty seconds, it was filled to the brim by five stacks of tens. Somehow I knew there were five thousand of them. I leaned closer and looked at the ones on top. They all had the same serial number.

I looked up at Lady Sally. "Double-sided color Xerox?" I asked.

"No, dear."

"Uh huh. Tell me about it."

"We've left my House, dear. This is my Home."

I nodded. "Uh huh. What planet are we on?"

"We call it Harmony."

I nodded. "Uh huh. What year are we in?"

"We don't use Gregorian, so I'm not certain. I could look it up."

I nodded. "Uh huh. To quote James Taylor, 'Is that the way you look?'"

"This is my true appearance, yes, dear. I've used cosmetics to make me look older than I would naturally, of course—I'm only three hundred and fifty-something. But this is me, all right."

I nodded. "Uh huh."

She smiled. "You boys and girls have always tried so hard, and so ingeniously, to trick me into talking about my past before I opened the House. Now you see why none of you ever succeeded. I have over three centuries of past— but none of it took place *before* I opened the House."

"A *lot* of things are just beginning to make sense for the first time," I said. "Some day I must ask you what made you go to all the trouble."

"Some day I'll tell you. But we have more immediate priorities."

What I thought of as reality came back with a rush. "Oh, God, the Professor!" I glanced at my watch.

"Maureen, listen to me!" she said sharply, taking me by the shoulders. *"The clock is not ticking!* It stopped the moment we left the House. All that watch is measuring right now is your own consciousness. When we go back through the membrane we can emerge into the instant we left, or any space-time we like—as long as it is one we do not already exist in. What we must do now together is decide which one would be most useful."

My adrenal glands sent word that they were on strike until I for Crissake made up my mind. "You mean we could both pop out of the air in front of Tony Donuts?"

"Yes—but I don't know if it would be the best idea. Suppose he had his hands around the Professor's throat at the time?"

I shuddered. "Right. Tony would react badly to surprises. And he's too stupid to be startled by the impossible." I looked around the . . . place. "Would you have anything like a wallet-sized laser cannon around the joint?"

"Yes, dear. And I certainly would have no deep-seated objection to seeing it used on Tony Donuts. But are you absolutely sure you wish to be that kind to the son of a bitch?"

I thought about it. "You have a better idea? One that's safe? I don't want to spend the rest of my life looking over my shoulder."

"I believe so, yes."

I smiled for the first time in a thousand years. "My Lady, tell me all about it."

Just then her husband Mike walked into the room. Don't ask me from where. He had a soiled apron around his waist, and the scent of his cigar clashed horribly with the fragrance in the room. "Hi, Mo," he boomed cheerily. "Here you go, Sal." He gave her what, at first, I thought just might be a wallet-size laser cannon. When I realized it was technology of my own space-time, and recognized it, my smile got even bigger. . . .

It took me awhile to get the knack of finding the membrane again: from that side, its location was not so much a *place* as an *attitude*, if that makes any sense. But with Lady Sally's help I figured it out.

I emerged bang on target. I was standing on the gravel road that led down to the shore, just around a corner from sightline of the boathouse. In a briefcase which was less than two minutes old, I was carrying the fifty thousand dollars of counterfeit-counterfeit money. (Would that be "feit money"?) Lady Sally had reset my watch to correct local time for me. I found that I had four minutes' grace. I started walking.

I could feel Tony's eyes on me from the moment I was first visible from the boathouse. I gave some attention to my face. I felt alert and cautious, but it took an odd effort to remember how it felt to be utterly terrified of Tony Donuts, and let that terror show in my expression. Thespian challenge.

On the other hand, Tony was not a subtle observer. He was smiling as he opened the door for me. "Hiya, sugar-pie. Youse cut it pretty close."

"I had to go a long way. Is the Professor okay?"

"Just fine, babe," his sweet voice came from within. "Did you say hi to Rube for me?"

I drew the first totally painless breath in a long time—how long I could not even guess. *Thank you, God!* I hadn't been absolutely sure Tony Donuts could tell time. "That I did. He said to tell you everything is copacetic."

"I'm relieved to hear that."

Tony cleared his throat, a disgusting sound. "How bout it?"

"You have the right to remain silent," I told him.

He stared at me for a moment, and roared with laughter.

"If you give up that right," I said while he guffawed, "anything you say can and will be used against you in a court of law. You have the right to counsel; if you cannot afford an attorney one will be provided for you. Do you understand these rights?"

He laughed a long time. Finally he said, "Funny. I didn't *see* no balls on youse when I looked before."

"It's called graveyard humor," I said dully.

Tony stood aside for me. "Maybe I'll hafta take anudda look fer 'em. Come on in and jern de potty, honey-pants. Dat my present youse got dere?"

"Yes." I brushed my tits against him as I stepped into the boathouse, and handed him the briefcase. He liked both actions. He leaned out, scanned the horizon carefully in all directions, and followed me in, closing the door behind him.

The Professor was looking a little pale but otherwise fine. I could see him trying to understand what I had up my sleeve, and failing. I winked to reassure him. At once he looked happier. Flattering.

Tony was squatting over the briefcase, popping it open. His smile became a broad grin as he saw all the money. He reached into his breast pocket, and took out the single bill I had put back there while he was paying attention to my nipples a moment ago. He compared numbers—laboriously, moving his lips—and grunted joyously. "Dat's maw like it," he boomed.

"It's okay?"

"You got it, dollface."

"You're satisfied that's the same fifty thousand dollars of counterfeit money you ran off yourself?"

He grin shrank a bit; the question made him suspicious. He picked a couple of tens from the briefcase, squinted at the numbers again, held the bills up to the light and fingered them carefully. The grin broadened again. "Yah, dese is de ones I made, aright."

"They're very good," I said. "How did you ever get such good plates? Prof never said."

"I never have much trouble wit stuff like dat," he said smugly. "Once I decided ta get inta da paper business, I just ast aroun' 'till I found out who de best cutter was, an' looked him up. Finkelstein, his name wuz. Kind of a shame. I wuz gonna keep him around, so he could help me wit stuff like changin' da serious numbers an' stuff. But dese old Jews, youse just put ya hands on 'em an dey comes apart like a stewed chicken."

I'm happy to say I had and have no idea what a stewed chicken is like, but the image was self-explanatory. "You killed Finkelstein."

"T'urrily," he agreed.

"Well, now that I've brought you your counterfeit tens, will you let us go like you said?"

"Nah."

I did my best to look shocked, then angry, then terrified. "You promised! What *are* you going to do with us?"

"Well, dis mug," he said, indicating the Professor, "tried ta stiff me, an' I don't like dat. So I t'ought of a funny joke. Like yous wit dat right ta remain silent gag, kinda. I found out once accidental dat if youse break a guy's arms in just da right place, youse can tie 'em in a knot. So I t'ought maybe I'll do dat, an' toss him off de dock, and see how long can he float." He looked suddenly thoughtful. "Maybe it's even funnier if I break his ankles too." He nodded judiciously. "Yah, dat's good. After I stop laughin' I t'ought I'd look over dat lawnjaree I had youse put on, an' maybe we c'ud have some laughs." He smiled again. "Youse c'ud have de right to remain silent . . . but I don't tink youse will."

"You're going to kill him and rape me?" I quavered.

"Youse got it," he said happily.

Lady Sally tapped him on the shoulder from behind. "I'm delighted to disappoint you," she said. She seemed to brush his hair with her fingers as he turned.

If I'd expected him to jump a foot in the air, I'd have been disappointed myself. But I hadn't, I knew he was too stupid to be fazed by the impossible. The question of how she could have managed to sneak up on this isolated place in total silence and enter it undetected was so complex that he ignored it. And it wasn't as if a red-and-grey haired old lady could represent a serious threat. . . .

"I know you," he said in a tone of mild complaint. "Where do I know youse from?"

She held up a small rectangular object. "Do you know what this is?" He gaped at it in incomprehension. "It is a Nagra. One of the best hand-held pocket-sized stereo tape recorders in the world."

"Smile, Tony," I suggested. "You're on candid tape-deck."

He stared at the thing for several seconds. Then his face showed the exasperation of a small boy whose kid sister has just taken his favorite toy. "Give me dat," he said indignantly.

"Come and get it," Lady Sally said.

She did not move a muscle as his big hands reached for her. But somehow they missed her

by inches. He roared with astonishment and outrage, made another grab—and missed again. The
third and most violent attempt was the least
successful of all; he overbalanced and fell to one
knee.

"You may rise," she told him.

He gaped at her. An expression came to his
face which I'm sure was utterly new to it: wonder. "I know you," he said slowly. "Youse run
dat crib joint in Brooklyn. Wit de muscle
broad."

"I have never in my life run a 'crib joint,'"
Lady Sally said with great dignity, "although I
grant you my establishment does resemble a day-
care center in certain respects—but yes, I am
the woman who had Priscilla throw you out of
my House. I'd do it again."

He shook his head like a horse besieged by
flies. "I'm gonna tear youse in pieces an' piss on
de pieces," he said.

"You're welcome to try, but I really think
you're wrong."

He stood, planted his feet, and cocked a
punch that would have punctured a safe—

—if it had connected. It whistled harmlessly
past Lady Sally's ear. Even he knew, this time,
that she had not moved an inch.

"It's a relatively trivial adjustment to your
brain," she explained. "Even a neuroanatomist
armed with a C.A.T. scanner might fail to find
it. But I'm afraid it's permanent and non-
correctable. From now on, every time you

attempt to perform an aggressive action of any sort, your coordination will fail."

He bellowed with rage and launched another titanic blow. It didn't even come close.

"You are helpless, Tony Donuts," she said quietly, "and will be for the rest of your days. Watch:" She slapped him across the face. *Crack!* He stiffened, thunderstruck. "That was for Solomon Finkelstein." She backhanded him hard enough to cross his eyes. *Crack!* "And that was for Priscilla's sprained back. The next one will be for me . . ." He tried to grab her wrist, and missed. *Crack!* "Professor," she said, "I believe you have next claim?"

He looked at me, profoundly puzzled but certainly not displeased. "After you, my love. Your privilege."

I blew him a kiss. "Thank you, darling. My pleasure."

And I walked right up to Tony Donuts, unzipped my skirt and stepped out of it to gain maximum freedom of movement, took two running steps and kicked his donuts up into his abdominal cavity.

He fell to his knees, grabbed uselessly at my legs, then gave up and let his hands drop to his sides. "Back to you, darling," I said.

The Professor applauded me. "Nice *shot*, Maureen!" he said enthusiastically. He sauntered over, stood over Tony Donuts, and waited. After a while Tony started breathing again, and began to emit an astounding high-pitched *peep* sound. His eyes were very round and his lower lip protruded even more than his forehead. He touched his crotch experimentally, then let his hands fall again.

The Professor's voice was as cold and stern as interstellar space. "By rights, Anthony Donnazio, I ought to wait for your eggs to descend again—however long that might take—and then pick up that mallet and marlinspikes over there and turn you into Tony Cheerios. I confess I am sorely tempted. But I have tried all my adult life to avoid physical violence, and I'm damned if I'll break that tradition for the likes of you. So I will content myself with pointing out something that may not have occurred to you yet. I'm going to enjoy watching you think about it during your trial. Can you hear me?"

Still *peep*ing, Tony Donuts nodded.

"You are too stupid to unlearn a lifetime of behavior patterns, no matter how hard you try. You'll continue to act and conduct yourself like a tough guy. But you can no longer back it up.

"You may be able to bluff for a long time. Days, even. But they have animals in Leavenworth just as ferocious as you are. Sooner or later one of them will try you. And then another. The word will spread. Leavenworth also has its share of weak, skinny, defenseless guys—they call them 'punks'—and you simply can't *imagine* how overjoyed *they*'ll be to meet you. You'll be exactly what they've been fantasizing about for a long time. You're going to be a very popular fellow."

Rocking on his knees, hands at his sides, Tony Donuts began to weep.

"Look on the bright side," the Professor suggested. "You've still got your figure. Maybe if you start looking right away you can find a protector to marry you. Then you'll only have to deal with him, and a few of his closest personal friends."

"Say 'please' and 'thank you' a lot," I advised him. "It's always worked for me with nasty old macho types."

"I'd be happy to give you a few tips on makeup," Lady Sally said generously. "And there's some of Mary's old lingerie around the House that might fit you with only a little alteration. You'll pick up sewing in no time. Why, you could end up a model prisoner. . . ."

Tony sobbed.

The Professor gathered up the satchel of double-counterfeit money, I used my maternity skirt to wrap up the fifty thousand dollars of real money, Lady Sally patted Tony Donuts on the head, and we took our leave.

"Lady?" I said as we trudged across the sand, listening to the high keening wail of the scariest man I had ever known behind us.

"Yes, darling."

"The Professor is going to have to know too."

"Yes, I know, dear. And he'll keep his mouth shut just as you will."

"I certainly will," he said firmly. "Whatever it is."

"And you're going to have to tell us *why*," I insisted. "What you and Mike are really doing here."

"Yes, it seems I must." She sighed. "It's not the first time, you know. A few other members of the House know."

"Why would you blow a secret that big?"

She stared at me in astonishment. "There was no other way to save your lives, dear child."

"But how could the lives of two Stone Age ancestors be worth risking whatever your mission is here?"

"For one thing there are practical considerations. Now that you know, I can use your help, both of you. I need all the help I can get, and I'm reluctant to recruit anyone I do not have to. Perhaps that is why I keep on having to.

"But that is mere serendipity. You know the real reason why I broke cover for you, Maureen."

"I do?"

"I love you, darling. Both of you."

I stopped walking and looked at her. My eyes filled with sudden tears, and I bit my lip. "Hell," I said weakly, "I knew that."

The Professor seemed to have an arm around me. "We love you too, Lady," he said. "What is your secret, and what is it you want us to do? And what is that damned noise?" In the distance, ten terrified falsetto Valkyries seemed to sing "hiyoto" octaves.

"Oh, that's just the T-men coming for Tony," she said comfortably, fiddling with her Nagra.

"I had my husband call them from farther out on the Island, to muddy the trail. I know your shy, retiring nature, Willard—perhaps you and Maureen would care to disappear for a few minutes? Oh, and would you mind terribly being officially dead? I have the distinct impression I saw Tony murder you both. What with counterfeiting and *three* murders, it might actually be ten years or more before he's eligible for parole."

The Professor smiled. "I'm sure his new boyfriend, whoever that might be, will appreciate your thoughtfulness. And while I can't speak for Maureen, I for one have not officially existed for years." He turned to me. "Will you come into the woods with me, little girl?"

"Actually, I was just on the way to my grandmother's Home, Mr. Wolf. Let's go there, instead."

So we did.

CHAPTER 14

AN IMMODEST PROPOSAL

Some hours later:

"Maureen?"

"In a minute, okay? I'm still coming."

"Sorry."

"S'okay."

Timeless time later: "Maureen?"

"Yes, Professor?"

"Do you suppose that if we were to give Theo Trudell that fifty thousand—the realies, I mean—he might be persuaded to give Mrs. Willoughby's diamonds a pass? She'll need them, now that her husband's going to prison."

I blinked lazily up at him, and the smile on my face got bigger. "You chump. You're not supposed to say things like that *after* we make love. How am I supposed to reward you now?"

He cleared his throat softly. "Well, you could always marry me."

My eyes opened all the way. "Hmmm. Yes, I suppose I could always do that."

Was he asking me to *quit my job?* If so, would I?

"Before you make up your mind, I have relevant information to offer: I'm thinking of changing careers."

Three major surprises in three sentences. "What sort of grift did you have in mind?"

"Well, actually, I was sort of thinking of trying honest work."

Four for four. I thrust him off me and sat up. "You have just exceeded my gullibility threshold," I said stiffly.

He lay back and sighed. "I know, I know, I can scarcely believe it myself. But I swear to God, I'm dead serious."

I softened, and bit my lip. "Okay, I believe you. But I'm not at all sure I like this. What kind of work were you thinking of?"

He looked mildly embarrassed. "Uh . . . my love, perhaps you knew . . . or possibly suspected . . . that once upon a time, Lady Sally and I were on rather . . . er . . . intimate terms?"

"Then you're a lucky man. What's your point?"

"Well, darling, it's like this. I've been thinking for years about what you said the day you left me. About how you and I both screw people for a living, but yours are grateful. And Lady Sally says that in her opinion I have enough potential to be worth training. And that husband-and-wife teams are good box-office. So I thought—"

I shut him up by kissing him. "I'll supervise your training myself," I said. "For openers, let me show you a little something I call Emergency Overdrive. . . ."

You know what? When Willard and I hold hands nowadays, and our wedding rings touch, they always look to me just like a little pair of solid gold, very tony donuts.